THE BABYSITTER

GEMMA ROGERS

B
Boldwood

First published in Great Britain in 2021 by Boldwood Books Ltd.

Copyright © Gemma Rogers, 2021

Cover Photography: Shutterstock

The moral right of Gemma Rogers to be identified as the author of this work has been asserted in accordance with the Copyright, Designs and Patents Act 1988.

All rights reserved. No part of this book may be reproduced in any form or by any electronic or mechanical means, including information storage and retrieval systems, without written permission from the author, except for the use of brief quotations in a book review.

This book is a work of fiction and, except in the case of historical fact, any resemblance to actual persons, living or dead, is purely coincidental.

Every effort has been made to obtain the necessary permissions with reference to copyright material, both illustrative and quoted. We apologise for any omissions in this respect and will be pleased to make the appropriate acknowledgements in any future edition.

A CIP catalogue record for this book is available from the British Library.

Paperback ISBN 978-1-80048-682-9

Large Print ISBN 978-1-80048-678-2

Hardback ISBN 978-1-80280-870-4

Ebook ISBN 978-1-80048-676-8

Kindle ISBN 978-1-80048-677-5

Audio CD ISBN 978-1-80048-683-6

MP3 CD ISBN 978-1-80048-680-5

Digital audio download ISBN 978-1-80048-675-1

Boldwood Books Ltd
23 Bowerdean Street
London SW6 3TN
www.boldwoodbooks.com

For Dad, who never got to see me published.

AUTHOR'S NOTE

This story takes place over three days in October 2020 and is told from the perspective of three of the main characters:

Brooke Simmons is twenty-six years old and desperate to move out of her overbearing mum's home in Redhill. She works part-time and looks after her friend Ali's daughter, Eden, twice a week. Brooke met Ali when they used to work together at an online magazine. Jimmy is her ex.

Ali Tolfrey is thirty-three years old and a freelance writer. Married to GP Christopher for almost two years, they have a daughter, Eden, who has just turned one. They reside in a town house in affluent Reigate. Brooke is one of Ali's closest friends.

Jimmy Pearson is twenty-eight years old and lives on his own in a flat in Redhill. Currently taking a sabbatical from his work in maintenance at Gatwick Airport, he's a self-proclaimed ladies' man. His father recently passed away and his younger brother moved to Australia four years ago. He is Brooke's ex-partner.

DAY ONE
THURSDAY 29TH OCTOBER 2020

11AM – 1PM

1

BROOKE SIMMONS

My head screamed in pain as I forced heavy eyelids apart and tried to focus on the gloomy sky above.

Where am I?

Terracotta leaves squelched beneath me as I struggled to sit up, one hand reflexively reaching up to the back of my head, trying to staunch the pounding in my skull. A small amount of sticky liquid from my hair transferred to my trembling fingertips.

What's that?

Bringing my hand back, I recognised blood smeared on my skin.

I'm bleeding?

The throbbing was so intense it muddled my thoughts as I struggled to get my bearings.

Panicked eyes darted everywhere, searching for her.

Where's Eden?

A sensation of dread swelled in my stomach, culminating in an immense scream, its release stuck in my throat.

Where is she?

I let out a strangled moan as my nails dug into the mud

beneath me, trying to cling onto something real as my world turned on its axis.

No, no, no!

She was gone.

There was no buggy, no change bag, no sign of her at all.

I blinked rapidly, vision swimming.

This isn't happening.

A spark of something, buried deep in my subconscious niggled at me, but I was too confused to make sense of it.

'Are you hurt?' A woman crouched beside me, knees on the sodden grass, staring at the blood on my hands.

I shivered; teeth chattering. Damp jeans clung to my skin. Thoughts came in short bursts as I tried to remember what happened, how I came to wake up on the grass.

What did I know? It was Thursday. I was at the park. A trip to the swings. Who were we meeting?

Oh God, where is she?

Terror wrapped itself around me as I scanned the park for her.

Where's Eden?

Airways shrinking, I began to hyperventilate as it became real. Eden was nowhere to be seen. She'd disappeared. Palpations ricocheted in my chest and I could hear my pulse in my ears. Thud, thud, thud, faster and faster. Someone had taken her from me, stolen her.

The woman crouched down next to me was talking but I couldn't hear what she was saying, the only sound was a ringing in my ears as spots danced in front of my eyes.

'Where's Eden?' I croaked, throat like sandpaper.

'Who's Eden?' the woman asked as I clambered to my feet, wobbling on shaky legs.

I lurched forward and she grabbed me, holding me upright,

her handbag falling from her shoulder to the crook of her arm. Her mouth hung open, aghast.

'Eden. The baby. Where's the baby?' I screamed, head spinning.

'I'm going to ring the police,' she said, alarm evident in her voice as I shrugged out of her grip, stumbling onto the path, and howling like a woman possessed. Someone had Eden, snatched her from me. She was only a baby, a defenceless baby.

Overwhelming nausea hit me with each movement as I turned left and right, scanning the park, shouting her name.

A couple in the distance walking their dog looked over, the noise drawing their attention.

I could see a family in the play area, their children on the swings but too far away to make out.

Fuck, where's Eden?

I doubled over, fearing I may be sick, sucking in air as I vaguely registered the woman on the phone to the operator, requesting the police and an ambulance.

The police? Did I want the police? Something told me it was a bad idea.

My head began to clear, the niggling thought from earlier returning. All the while, I listened to the lady tell the operator we were at Bushy Park, Reigate. I dropped to my knees, eyes level with a full bag of shopping from Sainsbury's which been discarded at her feet.

Did I have a bag? Only the change bag and it was gone.

Checking the pockets of my jacket, my fingers wrapped around a phone. I pulled it out and unlocked the screen with clumsy fingers, hovering above Ali's mobile number but unable to find the words. What could I tell her? That I might be responsible for her daughter being abducted?

'They're on their way, come and sit down, love. Tell me what happened?' the woman encouraged; her voice as soft as silk.

'I've been attacked,' I stammered as she helped me up and led me to the wooden bench, and I sank onto it.

She took off her red woollen coat and draped it around my shaking frame. I wanted to protest, drizzle hung in the air, and she was older, around fifty, but she wrapped her arm around me and held it firm. All the time, white-hot pokers were being inserted into the back of my head and I reached up again tentatively to check they weren't really there.

'Did you have a baby with you?' she asked.

'Yes. She's gone,' I whined, unable to stop myself shivering.

'Good Lord, your daughter?' The woman's voice was shrill, the sound tormented my ears.

'Eden. No, no, she's not my daughter. I'm the babysitter.'

I put my head in my hands and sobbed. The woman's hand caressed my back, soothing strokes as sirens wailed in the distance.

2

JIMMY PEARSON

'There you go, it's okay, here's your dummy,' I said, keeping my gravelly voice steady as I hurriedly tried to clip the grisly child into the car seat. Fingers fumbling with straps I wasn't used to. 'We're just going on a little drive.'

Eden wriggled in protest, trying to break free, flexing her body to prevent being constrained.

'Come on,' I said through gritted teeth, more to myself than to her, the vein in my forehead pulsating. We had to get on the road and fast.

Eventually I wrestled her in, the fasteners snapping shut, catching the skin of my finger.

'Fuck!' I growled.

In defiance, she spat her dummy out and screamed, the noise jarring instantly. My eye twitched, blood pressure soaring. Clenching my jaw, I picked the dummy up from her lap and put it back in her mouth before adjusting the seat belt to make sure she was secure. The toy bar I clipped to each side of the seat grabbed her attention immediately and the dummy remained in place.

Closing the door, I collapsed the buggy as quickly as I could, initially struggling to find the clips. I contemplated leaving it behind, but then it gave and flopped to the ground. I threw it in the boot and hurried around to the driver's side, keeping my head low as I ducked into the seat. I took a second to straighten the navy Three Lions baseball cap I'd retrieved from the holdall in the rear footwell, pulling it as far down as I could whilst still being able to see.

The engine started straight away, windscreen wipers springing to life, but I was too heavy on the accelerator, tyres flicking mud into the air from the grass verge as the wheels spun. My heart thrashed like it was going to burst out of my chest, and I looked through the rain-speckled windows to see if anyone was around to witness my revving.

Luckily there was only one lady and her dog, around fifty metres away, and she seemed absorbed in her mobile phone. The sky was grey, and it continued to drizzle. We'd been hit with a week's worth of rain in the past few days, but this morning it had been dry, up until half an hour ago anyway. That's why I'd suggested a trip to the park, some fresh air, knowing Brooke would agree. She thought she'd be getting paid, so it was an added incentive to come. I had the money with me, more than the five hundred pounds she'd asked for this time, but I had no intention of paying her ever again.

I'd left the car right by an underpass, using a cut-through of woodland to get into Bushy Park to meet Brooke. I'd checked and there were no cameras nearby, the closest house was fifty metres away. It wasn't the obvious route into the park and hadn't been forgiving when attempting to wheel the buggy back the way I'd come, hastily dragging it through pine cones, rotting conkers and twigs. I'd had to carry it most of the way, sweating from the effort of trying to jog with it, desperate to get Eden into the car and out of sight.

Blood rushed into my ears as my heart continued to race, sweat pooling at my lower back from the exertion. I was adding to the musty smell of the car, but I didn't dare lower the windows. Instead I turned on the hot air, hoping to disperse the condensation building up on the windscreen. Outside was cold, the clocks had gone back the week before, autumn was in full swing and the days had become grey and uninviting. Enough to stop you wanting to get out of bed, although that morning I had a reason – Eden.

Despite the adrenaline coursing through my veins like lightning, I had to keep calm, remember to drive slowly, safely. I was carrying precious cargo and didn't want to draw unnecessary attention. We'd made it back to the car quickly and, more importantly, unseen. Everything had gone to plan. I had my beautiful daughter, and now we had to get as far away as possible.

I'd left my car at home, opting to use my dad's old burgundy Mondeo, which was still registered in his name. He'd bought it new in the late nineties and it only had fifty thousand miles on the clock, having spent much of the past few years in his garage. Taxed and MOT'd every year but not often driven since we'd grown up. As kids, we were in it all the time. I remembered sitting in the back with my brother off to footy training, the new-car smell making us feel sick as Dad tortured us with Capital Gold on the radio.

Driving it felt alien in comparison to my Audi and I shifted in my seat, trying to get comfortable. Glancing in the rear-view mirror, I could see plump rosy cheeks working away on the dummy as Eden spun the plastic dolphins on the toy bar in front of her, chestnut brown eyes still watery with tears. Hopefully she would go to sleep soon. It was dark in the back as both rear side windows had black fabric sunscreens stretched over them. They were a spontaneous purchase yesterday while I shopped for baby clothes, on sale at the till. I fitted them before I left this morning, figuring with them attached to the windows at the back either side, no one would be able to see in if they pulled alongside us. I'd take the risk of someone thinking it was strange being late October and summer a distant memory.

Behind me, a spinning mirror rattled as it rotated, causing Eden to kick her legs excitedly. It was distracting and I scratched my stubble, skin catching on a torn nail. I'd find it easier to concentrate on the road if I pretended she wasn't there.

As I followed signs for the M25, I tallied everything I'd packed: food, formula, nappies, wipes and clothes. Hoping I hadn't forgotten anything.

My eyes darted to the mirror again, careful to keep them returning to the road every few seconds. Eden's eyelids were already heavy. The motion of the car lulling her to sleep. I put the radio on low, for background noise.

Another hour and we'd reach the M1.

One more hour and we'd disappear for good.

3

BROOKE SIMMONS

The police arrived within minutes of the phone call, blue lights still flashing outside the park gate as two officers in reflective jackets hurried towards us on foot. Helen, the Good Samaritan, who'd introduced herself as we'd waited, flagged them down. She'd tried to keep me talking, to calm my hysteria as the relentless drizzle turned into fat droplets of rain, but nothing could ease my racing thoughts.

Part of the bench was sheltered by an oak tree and she'd shuffled me down to try and keep dry. I couldn't stop shaking, my body moving of its own accord. Brain pulsing, like it was about to burst out of my skull. The sharp stabbing pains made me nauseous and I struggled to concentrate. I just wanted Eden back – where was she?

I knew I needed to call Ali, but I couldn't bring myself to do it. How could I tell her, her worst fear – *every* mother's worst fear – had come true? Her beautiful daughter had been taken and I had no idea where she was. How could I look her in the eye when it had happened whilst she was in my care? Not when I thought I knew who'd done it.

As the officers approached, I handed Helen back her coat and lurched towards them, the tarmac slapping beneath my trainers. I came up short, the swift movement sent me reeling and I doubled over.

'Help, please. They've taken my friend's daughter,' I yelled as they came closer.

One of the officers immediately radioed for reinforcements, rushing forwards to assist, worried I might topple. The other, tall and gangly, came to a stop in front of me, a notebook already in his hand and, underneath today's date, noted the time as twenty-five past eleven, and our location, Bushy Park, Reigate.

'I'm PC Barrow and this is PC Kempton. The paramedics are on their way. What's your name?' he asked.

'Brooke Simmons,' I replied shakily, standing to full height. I shouldn't have moved so quickly, my vision blurred.

PC Kempton took a step forward, watching me closely, ready to catch me if I fell.

'Brooke, I understand you've been attacked?' PC Barrow asked.

'Yes, I was hit around the back of the head, but it's stopped bleeding now.' I was getting impatient, I'd be okay, but they needed to search for Eden.

'And you say a child's been taken? What's the name of the child?' he continued; his pen poised.

'Eden Tolfrey, I babysit her.' I tucked my unruly hair behind my ears to stop it flapping in the wind.

'How old is Eden?'

I shuddered at the question.

Helen appeared at my side, her arm around my middle as my knees weakened.

'She's just a year old.' Tears streamed from my eyes. She was so small, so little. What had I done?

'Can you tell me what she looks like, what she is wearing?'

'Um, she's blonde, short hair, brown eyes. Wearing grey leggings, a pink striped top, cardigan and coat. The buggy has gone too, it's a yellow Bugaboo and there was also a change bag on the back.'

PC Kempton soaked it up, happy to let Barrow do the talking. He was a stocky Asian man, much shorter than Barrow; the pair couldn't have been more opposite. He scanned the park, as I had, before speaking into his receiver again. Reiterating Eden's name, age and description.

'So, what happened this morning? What time did you arrive at the park?' PC Barrow asked, his tone matter of fact.

'I got here about ten thirty, taking Eden to the swings.' I sniffed, wiping my tears away.

'Did you see who attacked you?' He jumped in, stare expectant.

I shook my head, wishing I hadn't as the park spun. It was the truth; I hadn't seen who'd attacked me. I told him we were heading back because of the rain just before eleven when I was hit around the back of the head. The next thing I knew, I'd woken up on the grass and Eden was gone.

I wrung my hands as I spoke, the words didn't feel real, like I was reciting something I'd seen on television, not what had just happened to me. It made my stomach churn.

'Can you tell me where Eden lives and her parents' details.' PC Barrow's manner was authoritative, like that of a teacher scolding a schoolgirl. It put me on edge.

I gave the address, retrieving my phone so I could supply Ali's mobile number too. PC Kempton radioed it in.

'Where exactly did the attack happen?' PC Barrow asked, creases etched into his forehead.

'I'll go get some tape,' PC Kempton chipped in instinctively, before jogging back to the car.

'Over here,' I said, leaving Helen on the path and leading the officer towards the flattened grass where I came to. I must have only been out for a few minutes. I shuddered, spotting tiny specks of my blood on the path.

'Okay, we'll tape this off now.'

PC Kempton returned a minute later with bright yellow tape and quickly secured an area of around ten metres, wrapping it around two trees, a lamp post and bin. The tape billowed in the wind, marking the location of the crime. It was something I'd seen on television, advertising a grisly scene on a police drama, but never in real life. It was surreal.

'November Papa to Whiskey Mike four eight, paramedics now on scene, waiting at entrance to the park, opposite the church, over,' the radio on his chest blurted, making me jump.

PC Kempton spoke into the radio, acknowledging the message received.

'Are you okay to walk?' Barrow asked.

I nodded and let him take my upper arm to lead me out of the park.

'The paramedics are out here. We need to get you seen to.'

'You've got to find her, she'll be frightened,' I pleaded, eyes filling again.

'We've put an alert out; all available officers in the area will be searching. In the meantime, let's get the paramedics to take a look at your injury.' He arched back slightly, grimacing at the back of my head as we walked.

PC Kempton was a few feet behind, in step with Helen, who was telling him how she found me unconscious on the grass. He wrote everything in an identical notebook, and I heard him take her contact details.

'What about Ali, she'll be frantic when I don't return with Eden,' I worried.

'We'll visit Mr and Mrs Tolfrey shortly,' PC Barrow said, his voice strangely soothing.

I felt crushed when I thought about how much pain she'd be in; how frantic she'd be when the police arrived at her door. Cowardly, I was relieved I wouldn't have to tell her what I'd done. She knew me so well; she'd see I knew more than I was telling.

With legs like jelly, I let PC Barrow pull me along. It was like an out-of-body experience as my eyes drifted in and out of focus, but I wasn't sure if it was due to shock or the whack around the head.

We neared the gates, the park now empty. The rain grew steadily heavier and I was soaked through, shivering in my bomber jacket, jeans saturated. A bright yellow ambulance was parked at the entrance and another police car arrived as we exited.

PC Kempton thanked Helen and left her at the exit of the park, heading for the patrol car and PC Barrow led me towards the rear of the ambulance, doors already wide open. He helped me climb inside and physically handed me over to the petite blonde paramedic. She manoeuvred me onto the bed, lifting my legs as I pivoted. All my strength had evaporated.

Thoughts melted away and I tried to listen to the officer explain to the paramedic what had happened to me. A foil blanket first, then a red woollen one was draped over me and something clipped to my finger. I started to drift, succumbing to the rhythmic throbbing in my head, lulling me to sleep. Exhausted from the trauma.

'Brooke, stay with us, okay. I know you're cold, we're going to try and raise your temperature. I'm going to look at your head, but I'll try not to touch it too much.'

My teeth chattered loudly as she parted my hair, fingertips gently probing.

'It's stopped bleeding, but I think we're going to have to take you to hospital to get you properly checked out. It may need a couple of stitches.' The paramedic tapped my shoulder comfortingly. She had a friendly bedside manner and I found it calming. 'She's going to need her wound looked at, may well have a concussion. We'll take her to East Surrey,' I heard her say in a quieter voice to the officer.

'Okay, do you mind if my colleague PC Kempton rides with you. We'll need to get as much information from her as possible.'

The paramedic nodded and Barrow smiled, before turning to me. My eyes glazed over and I struggled to keep them open.

'Brooke, can you hear me? PC Kempton is going to stay with you. I'm going to head over to the Tolfreys,' he said, slipping out of the ambulance.

PC Kempton replaced him a second later, sitting down opposite me.

'Did you see a car or where Eden was taken?' He spoke in a voice most people reserved for the elderly, softer than PC Barrow.

I gave the slightest shake of the head and wished I hadn't straight away.

'I'm going to be sick,' I said, already aware of the bile rushing up from my stomach.

The paramedic whisked a cardboard bowl out and put it in front of me as I sat forward and heaved. Splashes of vomit landed on the blanket. Once finished, she handed me a tissue to wipe my mouth.

'Let me take that, sweetheart,' she said, removing the bowl.

I sank back with a groan, resting my head on the cool bed and listening to rain patter on the roof.

'Do you know of anyone who would want to take Eden, to harm her, or the Tolfreys?' PC Kempton asked, his dark brows knitted together as he leaned towards me.

'No,' I replied, swallowing hard, the lie stuck in my throat, refusing to go down.

4

ALI TOLFREY

I'd just finished composing an email to my accountant, a Spotify playlist on in the background, when the doorbell rang. I assumed it was my friend, Brooke, returning with Eden, I'd heard the drumming of rain on the skylight in the office moments before. I'd said it was a bit damp for a trip to the swings, but Brooke had convinced me fresh air would be good for Eden. Babies needed fresh air, and Eden was only a year old.

The weather had been utterly awful all week, and we hadn't been able to get out at all the past few days, other than a coffee at the local garden centre with the NCT girls. They had a soft play corner for babies, and I made sure we met up regularly. Socialisation with other children was vital for an only child and I wanted to make sure Eden developed properly. I'd read it promoted confidence and prevented separation anxiety, which I hoped wouldn't be an issue when I upped my working hours.

Returning to work as a freelance writer, I'd had to push to get my foot in the door with the features editor at *Your Beauty* magazine with an in-depth article on a new foundation. The foundation had gained popularity because of its ability to perfectly match customers' skin tones from an online quiz. I'd seen it on Instagram, recommended by a twenty-something influencer and given it a go myself. It wasn't bad and pretty impressive that you didn't even have to leave your house to get a match. I loved buying make-up, unable to resist a new product to the market, and wrote a lot of articles about new trends, looks and must-haves.

Since Eden had been born last September, I'd been a bit lax in producing features, preferring to concentrate on her, but now I was in a place where I could juggle both and was keen to get back to working more hours.

I missed being creative, the flow of words and the buzz of getting a feature just right, knowing I'd hit the mark. Getting commissions from editors was the best thing and it gave me something other than Eden to focus on. I'd never intended to be a full-time mother, although with Christopher's salary I didn't need to work. However, it was nice to earn my own money and feel independent, not the 'little wife at home' receiving a weekly allowance.

I'd finished the foundation article that morning and was waiting for feedback, so I moved on to research moisturisers in preparation for a winter skin feature. Taking advantage of the time I had whilst Eden was out.

I'd met Brooke around four years ago when we both worked for a small online lifestyle magazine, she was a junior accounts assistant and her exuberant personality drew me in. We'd chat over coffee and eat lunch together when I had the time. She was as sharp as a tack and never failed to make me laugh. We'd clicked; she brought me out of myself. A tiny little firecracker with wild mahogany hair, always with black eyeliner framing her steely eyes.

Two years later, the magazine folded and all of us were made redundant. We were gutted but Brooke and I still met regularly and our friendship blossomed outside of work. When her fiancé, Karl, cheated on her, she was inconsolable and had to move back in with her mum. I would invite her round for girlie chats, involving bottles of Prosecco, with dinner thrown in to try and lift her spirits.

I barely noticed the seven-year age difference between us. Christopher teased me that Brooke was my pet project, but I genuinely worried about her. One day I'd had enough of her moping about Karl's infidelity and her lack of career, and sat her down to talk about the future. I convinced her to enrol in a bookkeeping course at the local college, to continue along the accounting path, telling her she could open her own business once she was fully qualified. Then she could quit the night shifts at Tesco she'd taken on to tide her over.

I told her I'd happily be her first client and had plenty of freelance contacts who'd be glad to hand their tax returns over to someone else. With a little convincing, she enrolled and was now in her second year of the part-time course, beginning to see light at the end of the tunnel.

Brooke was thrilled when I accidentally became pregnant with Eden shortly before Christopher and I were due to tie the knot. We'd had a long engagement, having been together for eight years, but a wedding had been put off until Christopher completed his foundation and became a qualified GP.

It was a small registry-office affair, neither of us wanted any fuss, it was more a natural progression. We'd already bought the town house and were living together, it seemed like the obvious next step. The surprise pregnancy was the icing on the cake. However, it was a tough time for Brooke. She'd started going on a few dates, although she was still bitter about Karl. I knew she'd wanted them to settle down and have a baby, but that had been snatched away from her. She worried she was being left behind.

Brooke was a lifesaver during the early months when Christopher went back to work. I was frazzled and she took Eden off my hands for a couple of hours here and there, initially so I could get some sleep. It was wonderful to have her for support and it brought us closer still. My mother wasn't the most maternal and never offered to help, even when I dropped some hints. I wasn't surprised, I'd been raised by the nanny and Mary Poppins she was not. Growing up, my father worked abroad and only came home a few times a year. It was no surprise their marriage had imploded by the time I was a teenager.

As the months went by, the routine became fixed. Every Tuesday and Thursday mornings, Brooke came around to spend time with Eden, allowing me to get some work done. Later on, I'd make us lunch and we'd catch up with a gossip in the afternoon when Eden would nap.

The arrangement seemed to suit everyone, and I made sure to pay Brooke for the hours she was here, knowing she was desperately saving to get her own place. She refused at first, we were friends and she loved Eden, but eventually she gave in. Brooke was always squirrelling money away, she was careful with what she spent, knowing every penny put aside meant she'd be out of her overbearing mum's house quicker.

At twenty-six, she hated living at home again and desperately missed having her own place. A few shifts a week at Tesco whilst studying meant the saving was slow-going. It was another reason I wanted to pay her for her time. I knew no one else would look after my daughter as well and I trusted her implicitly.

However, I was apprehensive about Brooke taking Eden out in the damp air this morning. She'd had a bit of a runny nose, which I didn't want to develop into a full-blown cold.

Last time she wouldn't sleep, and no amount of cuddling or Calpol would appease her. She'd been a monster for a few days, refusing to eat and I was beside myself with worry. I'd ordered all sorts of natural remedies and a humidifier for her room. Of course, Christopher thought I was overreacting and assured me she was fine. As he was a GP, I could hardly argue. He checked her over thoroughly, told me it was a combination of a cold on top of teething and it would pass. Typically, the next morning she'd been right as rain and back to her usual smiley self.

I could tell Christopher was trying not to gloat when my homeopathic order arrived and was no longer needed, but I told him next time she had a cold I'd be well prepared. He championed fresh air and plenty of fluids which was why I relented and let Brooke take Eden to the park, despite it being damp.

Positive it was them coming home, I left the Mac and headed downstairs to answer the door. Surprised to find no one outside, just a small parcel left on the doorstep. An Amazon delivery for Christopher – we had one almost every day. He needed to add impulse buying to his CV. I dreaded to think of the credit card bill. Probably why I never saw it.

Sighing, I picked up the package and looked across the street at the row of town houses, mirroring our own. No one was around, it was that lull between morning rush hour and lunchtime, where most people were working – which was what I was supposed to be doing.

The doorbell rang a second time as I'd returned to the Mac to refresh my inbox. I'd submitted the edited foundation article around an hour ago and was eagerly awaiting a response, disappointed it hadn't materialised yet. With a sigh, I pushed myself out of the leather chair and came back down the stairs, this time seeing a blurry figure through the patterned glass.

'Oh hello,' I said with surprise as I pulled open the front door, expecting to see a soggy Brooke on the step. Instead, in her place stood a wiry police officer, his pale face wearing a grave expression. Another officer stood slightly behind him, blocked from view. The hair on the back of my neck stood to attention and I fingered my diamond earring, a habit when apprehensive.

'Mrs Alison Tolfrey?' he enquired.

'Yes,' I said, my voice an octave higher than usual.

'My name is PC Barrow,' he said as he held up his warrant card, photo on display.

My bottom lip quivered but I couldn't make myself speak, mind whirring with endless horrific possibilities at why the police were at my door. Where was Eden? Had Christopher been in an accident? What had happened?

'May we come in?' he said, unperturbed by my mute state.

I glanced over his shoulder to see if any curtains were twitching, grateful that our street was still quiet, before moving aside quickly.

He stepped past me into the hallway, his baby-faced colleague following.

Heart already sinking, I closed the door. Whatever they were here for, it wasn't good.

5

JIMMY PEARSON

I pulled into Toddington Services as Eden stirred, her eyes blinking rapidly as if trying to work out where she was. We'd made good time; in just over an hour, we'd already reached the M1. All the way, I kept expecting to hear the wail of sirens behind me, a stream of police cars with flashing lights, signalling for me to pull over.

My knuckles were white on the wheel and although I told myself to relax, fear wrapped itself around me, settling on my skin in a blanket of perspiration. On the journey, I'd passed a couple of police cars, cruising the M25, but I told myself no one would be looking for the car. I doubted they were even looking for me yet. It depended on how long it took for Brooke to raise the alarm.

At the least, we'd had a good head start. Lunchtime was fast approaching and although my stomach was too knotted to consider eating, I knew Eden would be getting hungry. She always ate at midday on the dot and woe betide you if you weren't on time, she'd ball her hands into fists and scream at the top of her lungs until she was fed.

Parking in the furthest corner from the entrance to the services, I rummaged in the change bag, but the only food it contained were puffed carrot crisps. Brooke had been intending to take Eden home for lunch and had only brought snacks to the park with her. I had food in the holdall, but no way to heat it. No matter, it would have to do. I wanted to avoid going into the services if I could, knowing there would be cameras everywhere.

The first jar I pulled out was rice pudding, I found a spoon and got out of the car, moving around to the back so I could climb in next to Eden, shutting the door behind me. She was rubbing her eyes, awarding me with a toothy grin, her arms outstretched assuming she was about to be let out of her car seat. Instead I opened the jar and I spooned some into her mouth as she flexed her fingers excitedly. I made the aeroplane noises she was used to, and she gobbled it up. She was a good girl for her daddy, never a problem when I fed her.

It wasn't the best parenting, pudding for lunch, but I just needed to get her fed and changed so we could be on our way again. We had another hour-and-a-half drive ahead of us and I didn't want to have to stop again.

Eden managed half a jar and almost an entire pack of the carrot crisps, which turned her hands and face an illuminous orange. She fed herself, squishing the carrot into mush, oozing it through her fingers, while I checked the news app on my phone.

I'd bought a new handset and pay-as-you-go SIM card for the trip, having left my contracted smartphone in the glovebox of my car at home. The news didn't bring up anything of interest. There were no reports of a missing child, not yet anyway, but I knew it wouldn't be long.

I didn't have to worry about my disappearance. No one would miss me. Only my best mate, Dave, but I'd message him every now and again. My boss at Gatwick Airport had agreed to a six-month sabbatical, knowing my dad had recently passed away and I had a lot to sort out.

Eric, my younger brother, had emigrated to Australia when he was twenty-one and Mum had died when we were both teenagers. I had no family left in the country now Dad had gone, other than Eden.

It had hit me hard when I lost Dad; we were close and his deterioration after a diagnosis of stage four pancreatic cancer was rapid. He'd lived for only another six months and three of those were spent in a hospice. I was still grieving but trying to keep it together. I had to; I was a father myself now.

Dad had been a property developer. The flat in Redhill he'd signed over to me in my early twenties to get on the ladder. Back then, he bought houses, often at auction, refurbished them and sold them on, making a profit each time. He'd cashed in on the property market boom in early 2000.

Eric and I never paid much attention and it wasn't until his will was read that we realised he owned property all over the country. Most had tenants and were being managed by letting agents. That's where his income came from.

Eric returned to Australia soon after the funeral, where his girlfriend and job were waiting, leaving me the task of consolidating the properties, giving notice to those renting and putting them on the market.

It was partly why I'd asked for the sabbatical; there was so much to do, and I wouldn't need the money from my airport job. The sale of Dad's bungalow a few miles away had been pushed through quickly to a cash buyer when he was alive, to pay for his stay in hospice. Even with inheritance tax, the hospice bill of fifteen thousand pounds and half the remainder wired to Eric, I had plenty to keep me going. My job didn't seem so important any more. With Dad gone, I realised how precious time was, time I could be spending with Eden.

Looking around at the other cars in the services, people were coming and going, moving about their business seemingly uninterested in us. Although I held my breath when a police patrol car drove around, doing a circuit. Instinctively I lowered my head, realising afterwards they wouldn't have been able to see me with the shades on the windows. They appeared not to pay any attention to the car, but after they'd gone, I quickly wiped Eden down and laid her on the back seat to change her nappy. It wouldn't be good to stay any longer than necessary.

'I'll be quick, I promise,' I said as she struggled, handing her a teething ring which she launched into the front seat. I held out my keys which she snatched out of my hand.

Undressing her, aware the door was open, and it was cold, I put on a clean nappy as quickly as I could and pulled out the new mustard dungarees and grey long-sleeved T-shirt from the holdall. Ripping the tags off with my teeth.

When I sat back, strapping her in again while she was distracted chewing my car key, I marvelled how the change of clothes made her look instantly like a boy. Eden's hair was blonde, short and wispy, Brooke said she'd been practically bald for the first six months of her life. She had big brown eyes and long eyelashes, but there were no distinguishable girlish features. If anyone saw us, we'd be father and son, out for the day.

I checked the time, wanting to get back on the road and put more miles between us and Brooke. Guilt scratched at my skin, knowing how distraught she'd be, but she gave me little choice. I wasn't about to lose the best thing I'd ever had.

Eden babbled in her seat, trying to find the dummy at the end of the chain wedged by her thigh.

'Right, honey, we're all set and ready to go again... And we've got a brand-new name for you, sweetheart. Daddy's going to call you Eddie.'

6

ALI TOLFREY

'What's this about?' I asked, taking them through the hallway into the kitchen, my tone a little brusque, trying to mask the fear engulfing all my senses.

'Mrs Tolfrey, can you tell me where can I find Mr Tolfrey? Is he at work?'

'Yes, he's a doctor at Hillcrest Surgery, he'll be with patients.'

PC Barrow nodded towards his colleague, who looked like he was barely out of school.

Without a word, he cocked his head and spoke into his radio positioned on his chest. 'Zulu Mike 274 to November Papa, over.'

'November Papa to Zulu Mike 274, go ahead, over.'

'November Papa from 274, this is urgent. Mr Tolfrey is a GP at Hillcrest Surgery; please can we arrange to have him collected and brought back to 64 Beacon Rise ASAP? Over.'

'November Papa received, dispatching now, over,' came the immediate response. All the tiny hairs on my arms bristled.

'I'm sorry, but can you please tell me what's going on.' My voice had become shrill, and I folded my arms across my chest.

'Mrs Tolfrey, please take a seat.'

I remained standing belligerently. But sensing I wasn't going to be graced with any further information until I'd followed his instructions, I pulled out a stool from under the breakfast bar.

'I'm afraid there's been an incident this morning. We received a call to say a woman had been attacked in the park and a child in her care has been taken.' He pressed his lips together, exaggerating his sharp cheekbones.

'God! Brooke! Is she okay?' I spluttered, gasping as the words slotted into place, my brain slow to make sense of the relevance. 'Hang on, taken? What do you mean taken? Abducted? Eden? Someone has got Eden?' I could hear myself getting hysterical as the questions exploded out of my mouth like rapid fire.

'I'm afraid it would appear she's been abducted, yes, although we're still gathering information. We have Miss Simmons en route to the hospital; she has suffered a head trauma but is reported to be stable.'

The colour drained from my face and I shrieked. 'Oh God, not Eden. No!' I jumped up, a sob bursting from my chest as I caught sight of a photo of Eden attached to the fridge.

'No, no. You have it wrong. Eden is with Brooke. I'm sure she's fine. I'll call her,' I cried, looking around for my phone.

'Mrs Tolfrey, I'm so very sorry to be the bearer of such news. A car is being sent to collect your husband now. He'll be driven straight here.' PC Barrow put a hand on my arm, trying to calm my hysteria, but I shrugged him off.

'It can't be her, it can't be,' I whimpered, still pacing as tears streamed down my face. I felt sick to the stomach, fear consuming every part of my body. It wasn't real, it was a nightmare. Someone would wake me up, tell me it wasn't true.

'A detective will be assigned to your case. They will be here shortly, along with a family liaison officer.'

PC Barrow's eyes were small and deep set, I searched them for the answers to the horror I'd been plunged into but came up empty-handed.

'I understand this is a massive shock, Mrs Tolfrey. Time is of the essence and I have a few questions I must ask. Firstly, do you know of anybody who would want to take Eden? Anyone that would want to harm you or your family in any way?'

I shook my head, eyes glazed. 'I can't imagine anyone who would do this. Oh God, Eden!' I sobbed, sinking back onto the stool.

'Eden is your only child, yes? I have here that she's one year old, her date of birth is thirtieth September 2019, is that correct?'

'Yes,' I managed.

'Miss Simmons is your babysitter?'

'She's a family friend who looks after Eden for me.'

PC Barrow nodded.

'I'm sorry to ask you this, but under the circumstances, I hope you understand. How's your marriage, Mrs Tolfrey? Any issues there? Is this a happy home?'

'Of course it is,' I snapped my head up, dark cocoa hair whipping my face.

The officer pursed his lips; cheeks ruddy.

I glanced at the clock on the oven; it was almost half past twelve. I hadn't realised it was so late, Eden would be hungry. Terror clawed at my skin, but I couldn't let myself think of the reasons it was happening to us. Had she been stolen to order? The scenarios filling my head were unbearable, the images tortured me. How was this happening to us? I had to ring Brooke – no, Christopher first. Where was my phone?

I hadn't even noticed that PC Barrow had moved, but the kettle was on and the box of tissues usually on the island were in front of me. I plucked one out, wiping my eyes, black mascara coming off in smudges. For once I didn't care how I looked.

'Where did this happen?' I asked.

'At Bushy Park, we believe the abduction was at around eleven this morning.'

'That's over an hour ago!' I cried, my frustration building. I knew she shouldn't have gone out this morning, it was too damp for a trip to the swings. I should have kept her home, kept her safe.

'The alarm was raised at around quarter past eleven. It appears that Miss Simmons was knocked unconscious for a short time.'

I shuddered.

'So, Eden could still be at the park, we have to go and look for her.' I jumped up.

'Mrs Tolfrey, I assure you the park has been cordoned off and a thorough search is taking place as we speak.' PC Barrow placed a cup of steaming hot tea on the breakfast bar; the sugary smell made me queasy. I sucked in air like a fish out of water, waiting for the nausea to pass. I knew I should be worried about Brooke; she'd been the victim of a horrendous attack, but instead animalistic rage consumed me. How could she let my child be taken from her?

'You have to bring her home to me,' I wailed through a haze of tears.

The doorbell chimed and I rushed towards it, blocked by Barrow holding out his hand to ward me off.

'I'll go,' he said calmly.

I gritted my teeth; this was my bloody house, damn it. I had no control, was helpless and I wanted to scream into the abyss. My child, my beautiful baby girl was gone.

Muffled voices flowed from the hallway and PC Barrow

returned flanked by a man and a woman both wearing navy blue suits.

'Hello, Mrs Tolfrey, I'm Detective Chief Inspector Marianne Greene and this is Detective Constable Adam Benson, he'll be your family liaison officer for the duration.'

I wiped my eyes and shook hands weakly with them both, turning away as I heard the front door open once more and Christopher entered. He looked panic-stricken, his face ghostly in contrast to his copper hair. Ignoring the police, I raced into his arms and wept. He stroked my head, the tremble in his hand obvious.

'It'll be okay,' he whispered, his voice as shaky as his hands. My hair caught in the prickle of emerging stubble as he lifted his head to look at the strangers in our kitchen.

'We'll head over to the park, mam,' PC Barrow said to DCI Greene as he loitered in the doorway, head almost brushing the top of the frame, his colleague already at the door.

'Yes, please do. The site's been cordoned off. SOCO are on scene and there's a fingertip search of the area going ahead imminently, if you can coordinate and update the DC who'll be with you shortly. We need to get going on house-to-house.'

PC Barrow nodded and left the four of us alone.

The atmosphere was electric, a current pulsating around the room. I didn't dare breathe.

DCI Greene turned to address Christopher and I, still clinging to each other for support. 'I'm sorry about that,' she said as the front door closed, brushing a lifeless fringe out of her eyes. 'As I was saying, my name is DCI Marianne Greene and I'm the senior investigating officer appointed to find your daughter. I want you to know, finding Eden has my full attention. The safety of your daughter is my priority, but I will need your help.' DCI

Greene looked at each of us in turn, the weight of her words hanging heavy in the air.

'Whatever you need,' Christopher said, pulling himself up to full height, shoulders rolled back. He gestured towards the kitchen and she followed us in.

'I understand you've already been asked some questions, some of which we'll need to go over again. Please bear with us, we need to gather all the facts as quickly as possible. Can you please supply me with some recent photos of Eden? Also, I'll need her hairbrush or toothbrush to take with me.' She pulled a clear bag from her pocket and laid it on the breakfast bar.

I moved away from Christopher to pull the photo from the fridge; it had only been up a few days, taken at the park on the last warm day before autumn truly hit. We'd been feeding the ducks on a Sunday morning. I had many more recent ones on my phone, but I hadn't got around to printing them out yet.

Fear lodging in my throat, I ran upstairs to fetch Eden's hairbrush from the nursery. I knew what it was for. DNA. To identify our little girl if necessary. A thought I wouldn't entertain. She didn't have a lot of hair; it had only started to grow in the last six months. Blonde strands remained in the soft bristles and I stroked them, feeling a visceral tugging in my chest as I returned downstairs.

'What's your relationship to Brooke?' DCI Greene asked as I entered the kitchen.

'She's our babysitter,' Christopher jumped in.

'And friend,' I added.

DCI Greene nodded, noting the information down.

'Can you give me an account of your morning please; from the moment you both woke up,' DCI Greene asked.

I gave her my full attention, as she pulled out a stool and sat, notebook open in front of her. She must have been in her early fifties, no make-up adorned her face, no effort made to hide the lines around her eyes. Light brown hair hung limply, tucked behind her ears. She looked tired and it briefly crossed my mind whether she was up to the job of bringing my daughter home to me.

7

JIMMY PEARSON

My head pounded, a stress headache from running on high alert all morning. The culmination of the plan that had been rolling around my mind for a week. Adrenaline pumped through my system, heightening every sense, every thought, but what went up always came down. Now my body was running on empty. I needed caffeine, should have bloody brought that energy drink from the fridge this morning, but I was too worried about packing the baby stuff. There were snacks in the holdall, but it was in the back and I couldn't reach the bag whilst I was driving. I opened the window, the rush of air taking me back to the park, the swoosh of the cosh in my ears.

I hadn't meant to hit Brooke hard, only enough to daze her. The run up from behind must have magnified my swing. She had no idea it was me; she thought I'd gone in the other direction when we'd said goodbye at the swings. One tiny whack with the cosh and she was sparked out on the ground. Luckily, she'd staggered to the left of the path, hitting the deck underneath a tree, I didn't have to move her. Once I knew she wasn't getting up, I'd grabbed the buggy and made a dash for it before anyone came along. I didn't hang about. My heart was hammering so hard it was all I could hear in my ears.

The cosh had been gathering dust by my bedside and seemed like a good idea to bring at the time. I'd had it for years, mainly for when Dave and I went down The Den, and we knew a good row with the West Ham firm would be on the cards. Millwall never backed down.

That was my old life, when I was young and stupid, but the rage inside remained, although now I channelled it elsewhere. The cosh was hidden under my seat, I hadn't had a chance to clean it, but I would. I hoped I hadn't left anything of myself behind at the scene. I'd get rid of it all anyway, everything I was wearing. Maybe I was being paranoid, but you could never be too careful.

Despite my football days, I'd never been arrested, so there was no record of me on any database. Although I knew as soon as Brooke gave them my name, they'd visit the flat, seize my car and phone. Then the manhunt would begin.

My employers wouldn't know anything, of course, but I guessed they'd contact neighbours, friends too, but not even Dave knew where I was going. Only that I'd be off grid for a while.

I was going to lay low in a property owned by my dad's company in Bingham, on the outskirts of Nottingham. I'd have a few days before moving on. Sure it would take time for the police to trace any locations where I might be hiding. I just needed to figure out where Eden and I were going to go.

We'd be okay, I didn't have a lot of experience with kids before her, and this was our first time together on our own, but we'd muddle through. I wasn't going to let Brooke stop me seeing my own daughter. Shit! Son! I'd have to get used to calling him son for a while if my plan was to work.

I glanced in the rear-view mirror, checked the cars behind us.

We'd reached Northampton and still no sirens. The traffic was on my side, even the M25 had been unusually kind. We might make it in less than an hour. The Mondeo was behaving, and I'd got used to the seat. Dad had always said it was an excellent runner.

If he was still here, he would have supported what I was doing, even if he'd believed it reckless. I wanted to be a dad to Eden, like he'd been to me. Someone to look up to, who would provide for me and never let me down. Brooke wasn't going to deny me that. I'd only been in Eden's life for six months as it was, before I hadn't even known she'd existed.

'Dadadadadada,' Eden called from the back, waving the slimy teething ring in her hand. She'd perked up since lunch; she was a real food monster.

I grinned at her. 'That's right! Dada's here. Just me and you now, kiddo, like two peas in a pod.' I beamed, heart swelling.

Despite the risk, the nerves, the headache and stress, I knew I'd done the right thing. Brooke couldn't stop me seeing Eden, she was my daughter and I had a right. I couldn't be prosecuted if I didn't leave the country, could I? I'd read about it; parental abduction usually referred to when children were taken abroad by separated parents, which didn't apply to my situation.

I hoped Brooke would see sense. She was so bloody secretive, wouldn't tell me where she lived, what nursery Eden went to. Kept her cards close to her chest. I knew she didn't trust me, and I wanted to show her I'd changed. She had all the control and would only get in touch right at the last minute for me to see Eden. Usually on the same days every week. I arranged my shifts at the airport around it, working the weekends so I could see her during the week. The meetings were always on her terms and only when it suited her.

She'd come to me or we'd go to the park, nowhere too far. I'd play with Eden, overjoyed when Brooke taught her to call me

Dada. I'd get excited, knowing I was going to see her that day, then would sit like a twat, by the phone, waiting for her to call or text to let me know she was on her way. I'd even suggested getting back together, trying to make a go of it for Eden's sake, but Brooke wasn't convinced, although she let me have a go while Eden napped the second time she came to the flat.

She'd said back then I hadn't treated her right, but we were only together for about six weeks before I ghosted her in favour of Dave's cousin, Yasmin. She was too good to pass up, legs right up to her armpits. All tits and teeth, although everyone had had a ride. At least I hadn't cheated on Brooke.

Yasmin turned out to be a nutcase as well. What was it with these clingy women, didn't anyone want a bit of fun any more? Before you knew it, they'd turn up at your flat, slowly moving their stuff in. I was too young for all that, not even thirty yet. Plenty of shagging around to be done before I settled down. Still, I gave Brooke the option to get back together. I would have been faithful too. I'd have done anything to make sure I saw Eden every day; I fell in love the moment I laid eyes on her.

Her blonde wispy hair, big chestnut eyes, I knew straight away she was mine. When I bumped into Brooke on that gloomy March morning, both of us sheltering from the downpour outside the library, it changed my life. Eden was so tiny; she barely filled the buggy. I couldn't stop staring at her, she was the most beautiful thing I'd ever seen.

I'd never been broody, but I felt an instant connection. Brooke didn't even have to say anything, although I could see she was desperate to get away. Face flushed and stuttering, embarrassed she'd been caught out. Brooke told me the baby's name was Eden and she was six months old. Realisation hit as I counted back the months in my head, the last time I'd seen Brooke, the last time we'd been together. Words tumbled out of my mouth; it wasn't even a question. Eden even looked like me as a kid.

'She's mine,' I'd mumbled, unable to tear my eyes away as Eden had gurgled and played with her shoes. Brooke didn't deny it.

I'd kept my cool, knowing it wouldn't do me any good to blow my top. Not if I wanted to see my daughter again. I was in a state of shock anyway, the knowledge that I was a father still sinking in. I remembered saying I wanted to be involved, to see my child, offering her money. I wanted to make sure my little girl had everything.

Brooke seemed as shell-shocked as I was, completely unprepared to see me and for the secret she'd been hiding to come out. Why hadn't she got in touch? But how could she? I'd blocked her number, as I did with all my exes. Same on social media, it was easier that way. Surely, she could have found me somehow. Perhaps she didn't want me in Eden's life?

That wasn't going to be an option for me. I gave Brooke my number and made her promise to call, so we could meet up again, so I could see Eden. She'd said she would, and when they left, I'd wandered around in the rain, reeling at the monumental development that was going to turn my neat little life upside down.

I knew one thing from that moment. From the second I saw Eden, when the realisation she was my flesh and blood slammed into me, I vowed to be the best father I could be. No one was ever going to take her away from me.

8

BROOKE SIMMONS

The bubbly paramedic told me her name was Mel and tried to keep me talking as her colleague, Peter, drove the ambulance to East Surrey Hospital. There were no sirens or flashing lights reflecting off the window as we drove along, so I didn't believe I was in any imminent danger. The throbbing in my head had dulled slightly, or I'd tuned it out. I was numb in every sense.

I didn't want to talk, and I could feel PC Kempton's eager eyes burning into me, assessing, trying to work out what I knew. Maybe I was being paranoid?

To calm my jitters, I concentrated on the rhythmic beeping of equipment, the pressure of the gauge on my finger and the weight of the blankets on top of me, slowly bringing my temperature back to normal. Things I knew were real.

My brain was struggling to compute what had just happened.

Jesus, Eden! Where was she? My little cherub snatched away in a second, when I should have been taking care of her. Protecting her. Ali must be going out of her mind, I had to talk to her, to comfort her. I wanted to tell her everything was going to be all right. I imagined I could hear her screams at home, hammering her fists on the walls, demanding her daughter be returned to her. It shattered my heart, but there was no way I could tell her about Jimmy; I couldn't tell her what I'd done.

It had to be him, who else could it have been? Fuck, I should have seen it coming. I was so stupid, what else did I think would happen? I had to call him as soon as I could, tell him to drop Eden off somewhere; anywhere public where she'd be found quickly. No one would have to know. He'd get away and I'd be in the clear.

Shit, I couldn't believe he'd taken her. It was my fault; I'd pushed him to it, telling him we were moving away. He must have thought there was no other choice.

'Brooke, we're almost there, try not to go to sleep. It's likely you have a concussion and we need you to stay awake,' Mel said, checking my readings.

I wasn't even aware I'd closed my eyes. I wanted to shut everything and everyone out. Pretend it was all some awful nightmare I'd been caught up in. Soon I'd wake up, in my own bed, a normal day ahead of me.

What I wanted more than anything was to go back to when it all started. A split-second decision made on the spur of the moment which had spiralled out of control. A decision which now had the potential to ruin all our lives. I chewed my lip, tears prickled behind my lids. I had to act, before Jimmy wrecked everything, but I was stuck with no way out. Not for a while anyway.

The ambulance came to a halt and seconds later the rear doors swung open, cold air forcing its way inside. The gurney jolted as Mel unlocked the brake and I shivered as they wheeled me off towards the Accident and Emergency entrance.

Blinded by the lights on the ceiling, I squeezed my eyes shut, the illuminous strips seared onto my retinas. One of the wheels of the gurney squeaked as it was pushed along, the motion making me nauseous.

We came to an abrupt halt, but I didn't open my eyes, vaguely hearing the paramedics hand me over to the nurse, listing the treatment I'd received. Cold hands immediately touched me, pulling away the blanket and tugging at my clothes. I flinched away, eyes snapping open despite the stinging.

'Brooke, we're going to leave you now, take care, lovely. You're in good hands,' Mel said, smiling, flashing me a row of perfect white teeth.

I gave her a weak smile and she patted my leg before she left.

'Vitals look good, temperature steadily rising. Let's take a look at her head.' A young doctor with his sleeves rolled up and glasses on the end of his nose loomed above me.

There was no sign of PC Kempton, he must be in the waiting area. Miffed he wasn't allowed inside the curtained space. I was hardly a dangerous criminal about to flee, why did he need to accompany me at all?

'Definitely going to need intervention here, the wound is small so glue will be sufficient,' the doctor said to a nurse, jolting me from my thoughts. 'Brooke, can you tell me where you are?' He had tiny lines etched into his forehead, a warning of the crevices that would grow there as the years passed.

'Hospital,' I mumbled after a couple of seconds.

'Okay and what day is it today?'

'Umm, Thursday.'

He paused to shine a light into my eyes, asking me to follow his finger, which I did, although the brightness made me want to clamp my lids shut.

'Great, and who is the prime minister?'

'Boris,' I replied.

'Excellent, now, other than your head wound which needs

some attention, we don't have too much cause for concern. However, because you lost consciousness for a short period, and you were sick in the ambulance, I want to send you for a CT scan so we can check there's no swelling or further injury.'

I licked my lips, mouth suddenly dry. Those things were like coffins, weren't they, long tunnels where you couldn't move or get up. My pulse quickened, but I didn't respond. I could hardly say no, and I didn't want them to see me aggravated in case they sedated me.

Stars danced around the doctor's head because of the light shone in my eyes, so I shut them again, despite the nurse trying to make me open them. I had to resist the urge to tell her to fuck off. Didn't she realise the brightness hurt?

'Can you call and book her in for a CT, we need to rule out any haematomas.' The doctor spoke brusquely, as the nurse put a fresh gauze over my wound. She agreed. 'Oh, and the police need her jacket and jeans, can you give her a gown?'

He disappeared behind the curtain, returning with two clear bags.

The nurse looked at me apologetically as I removed my bomber jacket, emptied my pocket of my iPhone which I tossed onto the bed, and dropped the coat inside the bag she held open.

I paused after I undid the buttons of my jeans, glancing at the nurse, who smiled her understanding and turned around to give me some privacy. The old Nokia phone I used only for Jimmy was in the front pocket and I slipped it under my sweatshirt and into the cup of my bra before I began removing my jeans. They were still cold and damp as I peeled them off, desperate to warm up. It was freezing and I was covered in goosebumps. The prickling on my legs made me itch.

Hearing my teeth chattering, the nurse turned around and helped me on with the gown, tying the back before draping the blanket back over me. My fingers curled around my iPhone as I settled back on the bed, closing my eyes to block out the overhead lights.

I almost wished I was still unconscious or too out of it to have any idea what was going on. Unfortunately, I was all too lucid and pinched the outside of my thigh under the blanket, hard, until it gave me something else to focus on other than the crushing guilt.

Ali must be hysterical. It weighed on my chest like a boulder, squeezing the air out of my lungs so I couldn't catch my breath. I'd seen her cry only twice in the four years I'd known her. The first time was when she'd reversed her new car into a skip, denting the bodywork, and the second was the day after her hen do. On both occasions she'd had a raging hangover and was simply unable to function.

She'd be in bits now. What could be more terrifying than your child going missing? Thank God she had Christopher; without him, she'd crumble, but he'd be good in a crisis. I wanted to tell them how sorry I was. How I hadn't meant for any of it to happen. That I was sure Eden was safe, somewhere. Things would go back to normal as soon as I could get out of the hospital. I just had to talk to Jimmy. I had no idea what I'd say, but I'd make him see sense.

It wasn't as if Eden was in danger, I took comfort from that. After all, Jimmy wouldn't hurt her – would he?

9

ALI TOLFREY

DC Benson put the kettle on, making us a cup of tea. The one made by PC Barrow had gone cold, untouched.

Christopher and I remained frozen at the breakfast bar, sitting across from each other in silence. Both shell-shocked and unable to comprehend our beautiful daughter was missing and Brooke was in hospital. I cried quietly, dabbing my face with a tissue, whilst Christopher stared out of the bifold doors onto the expanse of artificial grass. He'd not even taken his blazer off since coming in, even though the heating was on.

The wind was getting up and I watched the spirals of our topiary trees wobbling precariously on the patio. At least Eden had her new bouclé coat to keep her warm. I'd given it to Brooke to put on her before they'd left. Had I mentioned the coat to DCI Greene? I couldn't remember.

She'd taken details of our movements that morning, scribbling reams of information down. Then the questions came, everything from who our friends were and how well we knew Brooke to whether we'd had any altercations recently. It was a barrage and we answered in quick-fire succession.

Was Eden in nursery? Did Christopher have any problem patients or issues at work? Did we know anyone who could have a grudge against us? She delved into our lives, probing our marriage, our relationship with Brooke and how things were at home. Leaving no stone unturned, she raked through it all. Absorbing every single word, with DC Benson looking on. We told her everything we knew, anything that could help, although it wasn't much. I had no idea who would do this to us. Who would be so cruel as to torture us this way?

Once DCI Greene had gathered everything, she'd stood to leave.

'The first twenty-four hours are critical in any investigation, and we need to move fast,' she'd advised before telling us she was heading to the incident room. I'd had to stop Christopher, who got up to go with her. She'd awarded him a sympathetic smile. 'We need you both to stay at home, I'll be in touch with DC Benson with news as soon as I have any updates. He'll be your direct link to the investigation, if you have any questions. We're going to look at any CCTV surrounding the park to see if we can pick up Eden leaving or being put into a car. We'll be knocking on doors of the homeowners that live on the perimeter and contacting everyone on this list.' She'd gestured to the list of family and friends I'd given her.

I'd looked away; it would be a dead end. No one I knew would have done this to us. Who would have thought that our completely normal morning would have turned out like this?

'Please know, every available officer will be working on bringing Eden home to you,' she'd said, eyes imploring.

Alive; I wanted her to say alive, but she didn't.

The only reason someone would have taken Eden was because they wanted a child of their own and didn't have one, or because of some other disgusting, depraved motivation. No, it couldn't be. I couldn't think about that. My throat tightened.

'Can I get you anything to eat?' DC Benson broke the silence.

I shook my head; I couldn't eat a thing. It felt too normal to eat; I wouldn't until Eden was back with us.

'No, thank you,' Christopher replied.

DC Benson joined us at the breakfast bar, gliding onto the stool and momentarily scratching his blond beard. His fingernails were short and clean; it was obvious he cared about his appearance. The beard wasn't straggly, it was trimmed close to the skin, speckled with auburn if you looked hard enough. 'Do you have any questions you'd like me to answer? Can I call anyone for you, your parents perhaps?'

I snorted, my mother was little use in a crisis and would be no comfort. Christopher's parents lived in the Cotswolds and by the time they would arrive, surely Eden would be home.

'No, we have each other, we're fine.' Christopher reached over and held my hand, mirroring my thoughts. He looked like he'd aged ten years in the past hour, the stress etched all over his face.

'Is there any news on Brooke? Is she okay?' I asked stiffly, knowing my anger was misplaced. It wasn't her fault; she would have protected Eden as best she could.

'She's being treated for the head wound she received. To my knowledge, she's yet to be discharged. We have an officer with her.' DC Benson interlocked his fingers on the worktop.

I glimpsed a frown upon Christopher's face which quickly disappeared.

'I don't understand why?' I said, my voice sounding whiny.

'Could the motive be money?' interjected Christopher and it was my turn to frown.

'Ransom?' he said to me, looking almost hopeful. I guessed the other alternatives weren't comprehensible.

'It's a possibility, one DCI Greene and her team will be considering,' DC Benson agreed.

Christopher rested his head in his hands, fingers knotted through copper hair.

The idea was ridiculous. Yes, we were comfortable, well off even, but to think Eden had been taken for money seemed too far-fetched.

I glanced at the clock; it was almost one in the afternoon, which meant Eden had been gone two hours. I got up and paced around the kitchen. It was wrong to be sitting, doing nothing, we could be out looking for her. Helping the police search the park – something. Anything. I scrunched my fingers into my palms, pushing nails into flesh, frustration threatening to boil over.

After a few minutes, I found solace upstairs, not bothering to excuse myself, and sat on the floor of Eden's nursery, holding one of her blankies to my face. It smelt of her, our sweet, beautiful daughter, so defenceless. The pain was unbearable. If anything happened to her, I wouldn't survive it – we wouldn't survive it. It already felt that I'd had my heart ripped from my chest.

Tears stung my eyes, which had become red and swollen. I didn't have any more left to give, but they came anyway. Laying down, I curled my legs up to my chest and sobbed. *Please God, please bring my daughter back to me safely.*

1PM – 4PM

10

JIMMY PEARSON

The satnav directed me onto Chapel Close, where I found my father's orange-bricked new-build. I'd visited once before, a few weeks ago, intrigued because it was the only property Dad owned that wasn't being rented out, other than the bungalow he lived in. There was no management company associated with the address when going through his paperwork. So, I'd decided to take a drive the weekend after the funeral to see what secrets the property held.

I wasn't sure what I was expecting, but 49 Chapel Close was a three-bedroom detached property built in 2005. I'd envisaged a flat, or maisonette, like the other properties he owned, so was surprised to see a family home when the satnav had declared I'd reached my destination. Inside was clean and fully furnished, with some household items scattered around – toilet paper, washing-up liquid under the sink, but nothing personal of his.

I didn't remember Dad ever having lived there, but perhaps he'd intended to or was going to rent it out like the other properties. I assumed whatever his plans were, he hadn't got around to fulfilling them before he became ill. He'd never mentioned it, although all we talked about was Eden as soon as he found out he was a granddad.

I hadn't told him straight away, not sure what he'd make of it, that suddenly I had a kid that was already six months old, but when I did, his face lit up. Soon after he'd had to move to the hospice. I'd hoped to take Eden to visit him but never had the chance, he'd deteriorated so quickly. It was a regret I'd carry with me.

He'd given us a gift with Chapel Close, which was the perfect spot for Eden and me to lay low for a few days. If I'd had the choice, I would have opted for somewhere more remote, but at almost three hours' drive away from home, it would do.

I reversed up to the garage, noticing Eden had fallen asleep again. At least I'd be able to unpack the car without trying to juggle her. The garage door was automatic, and I pressed the fob to raise the door. It would be too tight to reverse in and unload, but there was a door at the rear of the garage which opened into the back garden. The less time I spent out front, the better.

I pulled the keys from the ignition, checking the ones I'd added yesterday, making sure I had the one for the back door. It would be good to get out of sight of the street as quickly as possible. Opening the boot, I took out the buggy, and retrieved the holdall from the rear footwell. Eden stirred as I opened the door, eyelids fluttering before closing again.

The rear door from the garage to the garden was wooden and stiff to open with my hands full. Eventually it freed itself from the frame and opened onto a small patio. The rest of the back garden was mostly grass, with six-foot fences either side. A bit of privacy wasn't a bad thing. Dumping everything in my hands by the back door to the house, I unlocked it, pushing it open. It didn't matter about the cold for a minute or two, I'd have the heating on shortly to warm us up.

When I returned to the car, Eden had woken up and was grisly as I pulled her out of her car seat. By the smell of her, I had a present waiting for me in her nappy.

'Well hello there,' came a droll voice which made me jump and I nearly knocked Eden's head on the roof of the car as I lifted her out.

I scowled, so much for not being noticed. I hadn't had a chance to check the news. Had my face been plastered all over the television already? My stomach clenched automatically.

'Hello,' I said, pulling my mouth into a smile over gritted teeth, hauling Eden up to my chest as I straightened up and shut the car door. My heart galloped as the stranger eyed me curiously and I rubbed at my stubble with my free hand. I had to change my appearance, shave off the carefully cultivated growth, if nothing else.

'Moving in?' she asked. The woman was young, blonde and reasonably attractive, although her nose was a little too large for her face. She had a full face of make-up and her hair was tied up in a high ponytail. Tight leggings stretched over her pert behind. She obviously did a lot of squats.

'Yes, renting,' I said, looking past her shoulder to see a curtain opposite twitching; someone was watching our exchange. Shit, I knew this street was a bad idea. No doubt everyone knew each other's business here.

'Oh.' She smiled, a devilish look in her eyes. 'I'm Georgina; we're neighbours,' she said, pointing across the street.

I raised my eyebrows; smile stretched tightly. Eden squirmed.

'And who's this cheeky chappy?' she asked, waving at Eden.

I cleared my throat, remembering my manners.

'Sorry, I'm James and this is my son, Eddie.'

She cooed, appraising his outfit. Changing him had been the right thing to do. At least the police were looking for a girl.

'Well, I'm off for a run, welcome to the neighbourhood, James,' her voice chimed, and she sashayed away.

I watched her go, enjoying the Lycra jiggle. I'd tap that given half a chance.

Eden wiped a drool-covered hand across my cheek, and I stared at her.

'Yes, I know, I'm changing my ways, I remember,' I whispered, kissing her forehead and locking the car before carrying her through the empty garage and using the key fob to lower the door.

I'd never had any trouble attracting women; they loved my dark unsettling eyes and olive skin that tanned as soon as the sun came out. I'd been told I looked a little Italian, especially in the summer months, and women loved Mediterranean men. I found it relatively easy to get what I wanted by using my face and my charm. I didn't even have to work at it, there was barely any chase any more. Women were too easy.

However, I was a changed man, or so I kept telling myself. A father, I had to be respectable, I wanted Eden to avoid men like me when she grew up. Ones that would break her heart.

Inside the house, I put her down on the kitchen floor and immediately she made a beeline on her hands and knees for the dining room. I brought the bags in quickly, leaving the buggy outside.

The house was cold, and I turned the thermostat up, hearing the gas central heating burst into life. Behind me, there was a thud and a scream from the dining room. I rushed through to see Eden on her back, legs in the air, wailing, with one of the oak chairs on its side. Shit. I raced to pick her up, checking her head for any cuts, she must have pulled herself up on the chair and it toppled over. Thank goodness it hadn't landed on top of her. I rocked her in my arms as she tried to catch her breath, the wailing reduced to tiny sobs.

I had to buy a playpen or something. How on earth did Brooke do anything with Eden roaming around, getting into mischief? She was at a funny age, not yet able to walk properly but could pull herself up and shuffle along. Cruising, wasn't it? Although cruising to me was an entirely different term altogether. I had so much to learn.

In the kitchen, I grabbed the change bag which had been on the back of the buggy when I took Eden and brought it into the lounge. We sat on the carpet, the bag open, and she helped me empty the contents. Toys, rattles and Sophie the giraffe teether were discarded for the baby wipes, which she began pulling out. She got five before I managed to stop her, pulling them from the pack like handkerchiefs from a magician's sleeve.

As soon as they were taken away, her bottom lip quivered, and the screams rang out. I laid her on the unfolded change mat retrieved from the bag and popped her dummy into her mouth. She tried to wriggle, but as soon as I shouted at her, she put her hands over her face, blocking me out. Guilt washed over me, and I changed her foul nappy as quickly as I could, switching on the TV to check the news. I had to be better, I couldn't afford to lose my temper around Eden.

11

BROOKE SIMMONS

I waited a while to be taken for the CT scan, trying to distract myself by scrolling through my phone. It was pointless, I couldn't concentrate, even as I searched the news and social media for word of Eden's disappearance. There was nothing but the usual rubbish on my feed. As much as I tried not to think about the scan, by the time the porter arrived and wheeled me away, I'd worked myself up into an anxious sweaty mess.

I hated enclosed spaces and the palpitations came thick and fast as we moved through the brightly lit corridors. One of the nurses, who could see my agitation before I'd even left resus, asked if she could contact anyone for me. Perhaps she thought I needed a bit of morale support, but I couldn't call my mum. She would be a nightmare, fussing around, acting like I was made of glass. She was so overbearing; I couldn't handle her right now. I wanted to get discharged as soon as possible so I could ring Jimmy. He could be anywhere with Eden by now.

As we left, PC Kempton popped his head around to ask if I was all right, checking the porter wasn't breaking me out of the hospital. What was his problem? I wasn't a criminal. Maybe he was bored of pacing the family room. He'd said he needed to ask me some more questions, but the doctor had told him he'd have to wait until the results of the CT scan were in.

I'd had a short reprieve. However, he'd sent in a forensic investigator called Brian, tasked with collecting my DNA, so I could be ruled out of any crime scene analysis. The words 'crime scene' had sent shockwaves through me, doing little for the squirming in my stomach. I was going to be in so much trouble if the truth came out. I'd never be able to explain it away, but if Eden was returned safely, I had a chance.

When Brian came in and introduced himself, he'd pulled out the swab and unwrapped it. I'd opened my mouth obligingly, then let him scrape my nails. The sensation made me shudder and tiny deposits were placed in a tube whisked away along with the bags containing my jacket and jeans. Would any of my clothes have Jimmy's DNA on them? Was he on the national database? I had no idea if he'd ever been in trouble with the police before.

At the park, I didn't believe we'd touched; brushed shoulders at most as we pushed Eden on the swing up until the point he'd hit me of course. Even then I didn't think he'd used his fist, something else had made the connection with the back of my head as I left the park.

We'd met inside the playground, which was empty because of the recent rainfall. I'd had to dry off the baby swing with Eden's muslin. The atmosphere between us had been frosty. We hadn't been there long, maybe half an hour or so, before the rain began. As expected, Jimmy was in a foul mood after I'd dropped the bombshell last week. I'd told him we were moving down to the coast and he wouldn't see Eden as regularly.

He'd taken it badly, but after a week of sleepless nights, it was all I could come up with. A little like shutting the gate after the horse had bolted, but what else could I do? It wouldn't be long before she could talk properly and then the game would be up. What if I brought her home one day and she told Ali she'd been to see Daddy? The thought gave me nightmares, but I didn't think Jimmy would react so badly. I never thought he'd hit me and take Eden. When I said it, I'd hoped he accept it; thought maybe I could still send him pictures and updates and he'd keep sending money.

I needed that money; it was my lifeline. I'd been back at Mum's for too long and I was desperate to move out. I couldn't breathe there, she followed me everywhere, always wanting to know what I was up to, where I was going, what time I'd be home. I'd been doing as much overtime as I could, saving every penny for a deposit for my own place. My friends had moved out, bought places, got married, some even had kids, and I was stuck living like a teenager with a curfew.

I hated it, but with Jimmy's money there'd been light at the end of the tunnel. It was partly the reason I'd met up with him again, how the plan all came about. It struck me now how short-sighted I'd been because I hadn't seen this coming.

On arrival at the CT scan, I relaxed; it wasn't the tunnel one, but the doughnut-shaped scanner. They asked for my jewellery and I took the opportunity to discreetly remove the Nokia from inside my bra and place it in the tray offered. I'd get it back afterwards. No one asked why I had two phones and I was glad PC Kempton wasn't around to notice.

The machine hummed as the scan began.

'Try to slow your breathing, Brooke,' came a voice through the speakers. Easy for him to say.

I sang Big Mountain's 'Baby I Love Your Way' in my head. It was one of my favourites growing up, my mum said I used to sing it all the time.

'Okay, all done,' the nurse reassured before the bed slid out a few minutes later and I was free again.

My body seemed to uncoil; I hadn't realised I was so tense. They handed back my jewellery and the Nokia, which I hid away again.

The porter, who could possibly have been the happiest man I'd ever encountered, hummed as he wheeled me back to resus.

I'd been back in bed for a little over twenty minutes before the doctor with the glasses returned.

'Your scan showed a perfectly healthy brain with no signs of swelling or bleeding so I'll get Janette here to glue your wound and we can discharge you.'

I nodded gratefully.

'Can I get you some painkillers, paracetamol?' Janette asked; she was the one he'd barked at when I'd arrived.

'Yes please,' I replied. Although the throbbing had dulled to a constant ache, I'd take all the drugs I could get.

Janette disappeared for a minute and returned with a plastic cup of water and two tablets, as well as a tray bearing the equipment for my head. I winced; I'd never had a wound that needed anything more than a plaster before.

'It might sting just while I glue and pinch it together, but it won't take long, I promise.' She raised the back of the bed and plumped up my pillow.

I took the pills and shifted until I was comfortable while she bustled behind me.

Less than a couple of minutes later, she told me it was all done.

'Thank you. I need to use the toilet, can I go?' I asked, already swinging my legs over the edge of the bed and removing the clip from my finger.

'Absolutely, are you okay to walk?'

'Yes,' I replied as I stood gingerly. I had pins and needles in my legs and wiggled my toes in my trainers.

'Okay, it's just down there to the right,' she said, frowning as she watched me go.

Thankfully the toilets were empty. I pulled out the old Nokia which I'd put back in my bra after the scan. Jimmy hadn't called or text. I selected his contact, the only number on the phone, and clicked to call him. It rang a few times and went through to voicemail. I gripped the basin and glared into the mirror. What the fuck was he playing at?

Dialling again, after a few rings, the generic voicemail message played out.

I ran my tongue over my teeth as I absorbed my hollowed reflection. I looked like I needed a bath; my skin was grubby, a mixture of dirt and sweat. A streak of dried blood adorned my forehead and I rubbed it with my fingers as I dialled for the third time. What was I going to do if I couldn't get hold of Jimmy? I'd have to go to his flat, start banging on his door, but I couldn't believe he'd be so stupid to take Eden there. How could I make this nightmare stop if he wouldn't talk to me?

12

ALI TOLFREY

I lay on the floor of the nursery for what seemed like an hour, comforted by the plush carpet surrounded by Eden's things. If I closed my eyes, I could almost imagine her asleep in her cot, angelic in her sleeping bag. Everywhere I looked, there were toys, photos, a large canvas on the wall of Eden dressed up as a fairy in a woodland photo shoot taken two months ago. Her room decorated to be as magical as possible.

I loved being a mother, even though the early days were hard. Eden wasn't the easiest baby and it was a bit of a shock how much she consumed me. I was no longer Ali, a writer, a wife, the only thing I had time and energy to be was a mother. Who I was before slipped through the cracks.

I'd been so smug, seeing other parents in their jogging bottoms, tops covered in spit-up milk. Determined that wasn't going to be me, I'd be different. How ignorant I'd been. Some days I barely had time to shower. I tried to sleep when Eden did, it was what the health visitor told me to do, but the messy house stressed me out.

I lost it altogether when Christopher suggested we get in

someone to help. I'd taken it as a slight on me personally. The assumption I couldn't cope. Affirmation I was failing as a wife, a homemaker and a mother, with a baby who screamed constantly and wouldn't sleep.

It passed eventually. However, my confidence had taken a knock and Christopher's patience was wearing thin. Frustrated by my insistence to go it alone, he was short-tempered with me. I couldn't be helped. My unsympathetic mother had sided with him, happy to offer an abundance of advice but no physical support. They were worried I'd dipped so low; I wouldn't be able to pull myself out.

Christopher worked long hours, trying to make his mark at the practice that had taken him on. I'd understood from the outset I was going to be the primary carer, but I had no idea how hard it was going to be and how lonely it was. In the end, with Brooke around to lend a hand with Eden, I got the break I needed.

When Eden started sleeping through the night, things got better, I felt more human, made an effort to get ready in the morning. I slimmed back into my clothes, wore make-up again and snatched time back for myself. Christopher had been neglected and I turned my attention back into us as a couple, doing things together as opposed to barely existing. But now with Eden missing, existing was all I could do.

I checked my phone, the email response I'd been so eager to receive earlier had arrived, but I didn't even open it. I was indifferent now. No longer important whether they liked my article or not, nothing mattered while my daughter was missing. I couldn't understand how the world was still turning. Thoughts of Eden smothered me. How foolish I'd been to let her out of my sight.

I called Brooke, fire burning in my belly, I wanted to know how it'd happened. She must have seen the abductor, be able to describe them to the police. The person who stole my child from me. Whoever they were, they couldn't have kids of their own. How could you inflict the most unimaginable pain onto another parent, knowing what they would go through?

The phone rang and rang. Frustrated, I hung up and dialled for a second time. Unsure whether I could ever look Brooke in the face again. It was irrational, but I was positive it wouldn't have happened if she'd been with me. There was a click and a fragile voice spoke.

'Hello?'

'Brooke? Are you okay? It's Ali. What happened?' My words rushed out at once, only to be met by silence. 'Are you there?' I said, fearing we'd lost connection.

'I'm so sorry, Ali, I don't know what happened. I was on my way back when someone hit me from behind. I didn't see him. When I woke up, Eden was gone?'

I howled to the ceiling, unable to contain the emotion surging through me.

'Ali, Ali?'

'Where are you?' I managed through sobs.

'East Surrey Hospital, they're letting me go home.'

I heard voices in the background, the bustle of a busy accident and emergency department.

'I have to go, I'll call you when I can,' Brooke said, her voice distracted, before the line went dead.

The stairs creaked and Christopher appeared in the doorway, eyes red-rimmed. Skin so pale it accentuated his freckles. He looked like he'd been hit by a truck, although I knew I didn't fare any better. Without a word, he dropped to his knees and pulled me into a hug.

'Come downstairs,' he whispered, his face buried in my hair.

'I just want her home,' I cried, clutching Eden's blankie as though someone might rip it from my grasp.

'I know.' He laced his fingers through the strands, his chin resting on top of my head. I drew into him until I was almost sitting on his lap.

'Are there any updates?' I asked, although I hadn't heard any phones ringing downstairs.

'No, nothing yet.'

'I just spoke to Brooke at the hospital, she's okay, but she doesn't know who has Eden. The waiting is unbearable. I feel like we should be out there, doing something, looking for her,' I said through gritted teeth.

'We have to stay here; we have to put our trust in the police to bring her home.'

I knew he was right, although he sounded deflated.

Christopher was a doer, he liked to be busy, so I knew the waiting would be driving him crazy. His phone beeped from his pocket; he still hadn't taken his blazer off.

'Who's that?' I asked as he retrieved it, reading over his shoulder. The message started with *Tolf*, and I knew immediately it was from the surgery. Inexplicably they nicknamed him Tolf as though the last three letters were too much of an effort to say. I was surprised he tolerated it; Christopher abhorred nicknames, anyone that called him Chris was subjected to a withering look and a formal correction.

'Henry, checking we're okay. Said to take as much time as I need.'

'Did you tell him?'

'I had to. I couldn't just up and leave.'

Henry Stoker was the partner of the practice and a well-respected member of the community. Christopher was thrilled to be offered a position at Hillcrest Surgery in the heart of Reigate, so close to our home, he was able to cycle to work.

A phone rang downstairs and both Christopher and I tensed before scrabbling to our feet. We found DC Benson trying to open the bifold door onto the patio as he spoke into his mobile. The door was stiff, and Christopher moved to open it for him. DC Benson stepped out into the wind and his voice was muffled instantly.

I chewed on my lip, hovering by the breakfast bar, straining my ears to catch any information.

'He'll tell us as soon as he's off the phone if there's any news,' Christopher snapped, and I narrowed my eyes in irritation.

Minutes later, he was back.

'Brooke is being discharged from hospital; she'll be taken to the police station to give a statement,' DC Benson informed us.

'Why? Is she involved in this somehow?' I interrupted. Should I have picked up on something from our call?

'It's routine procedure, allows us to take a formal witness statement. DCI Greene has asked me to pass on that all registered sex offenders in the area have been accounted for and eliminated from the enquiry.'

I leaned forward, gripping a stool for support. Relief thundered through my body. It was the unspoken assumption, that some monster had Eden. One I'd buried so deep it wouldn't see the light of day. 'Thank God.'

'Back at the incident room a team is trawling through CCTV surrounding the park and another team is on house-to-house enquiries. DCI Greene would like to release details of Eden to the media, to get the public involved in the search.'

'That means she has no leads then,' Christopher said incredulous.

I scowled at him.

'It doesn't,' I said, looking at DC Benson for support.

Before he could get a word in, Christopher went on, 'It's a risk. Releasing her name makes her vulnerable; whoever has got her might panic.' Christopher put his hands on his hips, eyes boring into me as though he couldn't bear my stupidity.

'Don't say that,' I whimpered, hot tears cascaded my cheeks.

DC Benson stepped forward, clearing his throat. 'DCI Greene will have factored in any risk and made a calculated decision on next steps. You have to remain positive, Mr Tolfrey; we're following every lead, doing everything we can.'

'Well, it's not bloody enough. My daughter is missing, and you've got nothing,' Christopher yelled, bringing his hand down on the breakfast bar so hard the marble shook.

13

JIMMY PEARSON

I scanned every news channel available on Freeview, staring at the small television as Eden bounced on her knees, shaking one of the rattles she'd been so quick to discard earlier. Seeming much happier after a nappy change. There was no mention of a missing child, and my face wasn't displayed on the screen as I'd assumed it might be by now. It wouldn't be long though; I was sure of it.

My stomach churned audibly, but I couldn't freak out, the worst part was done. Hurting Brooke had been a means to an end; she would never have given Eden up willingly. I'd never hit a woman before, and I felt terrible about it. I wasn't an animal. Desperation made you do things you'd never normally consider.

Getting to my feet, I took in my reflection in the mirror above the fireplace. A criminal didn't stare back at me, just the same old Jimmy. I rubbed the growth on my chin, it would have to go, as would my hair. It was the wrong season for anyone to shave their head, too cold, but it would grow back. The most important thing was not to be identified. Eden was now Eddie, in public anyway, and I was James. The names were close enough not to get confused.

I switched the channel to CBeebies and left Eden with the change bag, putting the wipes and Sudocrem on the table so she couldn't get to them. In the kitchen, the bin had no liner, but there was a roll under the sink. I put one inside and tossed in the dirty nappy.

I had five minutes while Eden was occupied to unpack. In the holdall, I'd brought a few cans of food, some fresh meals, milk and a loaf of bread for me. Eden had plenty of jars and microwave pouches, enough to keep us going for a couple of days at least. I was sure Brooke fed her proper home-cooked food normally and I would too, eventually. It was only a stopgap after all.

I put the items away in empty cupboards and made sure the fridge and freezer were plugged in. Everything in the kitchen seemed to be in good working order. I kept my ears alert but could hear Eden in the lounge, babbling to the television.

The clothes and toys I put on the dining room table, ready to take upstairs. I needed to pull the car into the garage; it was still on the driveway, but I didn't dare leave Eden alone for any length of time. I'd been lucky the chair hadn't hit her when she'd pulled it over; she'd barely been out of my sight more than a couple of minutes. Kids were a minefield, keeping them out of harm's way was a full-time job.

The house was great, but it wasn't childproof. There were no stair gates, although I could shut her in a room to keep her safe if I needed to. It would be better to buy a playpen or a bouncer, something I could strap her into to stop her wandering off. It hadn't crossed my mind I'd be so limited in what I could do while she was awake.

I scowled inwardly at why I hadn't considered a playpen before we came. It was too late today. I wasn't going to go out again. Ordering to the house wasn't an option; there was no way I could use my cards; any purchases would likely be tracked. It would lead the police straight to us.

Tomorrow I'd go out and get some more bits but pay with cash. I'd withdrawn over a thousand pounds during the week; cash would give me a little anonymity. The plan was to keep moving, hotels, places I could stay that didn't require credit cards. I hoped to get Eden – Eddie – a passport somehow. We could leave the country together. Me and her, father and daughter, or rather father and son for the time being. The best of friends.

I knew Dave had some dodgy connections; he'd got his hands on a fake driver's licence when we were teenagers to use in the pubs, but I didn't want to involve him yet. Not straight away, when a media frenzy with me at the centre was likely to commence any minute. If they spoke to him now, he'd only know I'd taken a trip. I'd told him I wanted to get away, that I'd likely visit my brother in Australia for a few months. I'd even packed my passport and bought a one-way ticket for later in the week. I wasn't planning to use it, but if I needed an escape, it would be a possibility.

I found Eden in the front room, still babbling to Waffle and Friends, a couple of cartoon dogs on the television. She kept pointing to the screen and giggling. I scooped her up on my lap and sank onto the leather sofa.

'Kiss for Daddy?' I said, eyebrows raised, and she slobbered my cheek without me having to ask twice. I squeezed her tight and kissed the top of her blonde head. She was my whole world and I wasn't going to let anything happen to her.

Brooke couldn't give me six months of parenting and take it away again. It was cruel beyond measure. I'd fallen in love with the daughter I never knew existed. She'd delivered a feeble excuse, moving away, down to the coast. Why did she need to go when I was right here? What could possibly be waiting for her there? Another bloke? I'd be fucked if I was letting another guy bring up my kid.

I'd never shirk my responsibility as a father, and I was upset it had taken her so long to tell me. If I hadn't bumped into her, I still might not have known. I'd missed out on six months of Eden's life I could have been part of. She said she'd assumed I wouldn't want the burden, but I'd deserved to know. I'd paid Brooke every week without fail for Eden's maintenance, plus more for the months I hadn't been there. I'd been more than generous, the sum amounting to just short of ten grand. Anything she wanted, she got. My daughter wouldn't go without a thing. I'd give her the world if I could. So when Brooke told me she was leaving I knew I couldn't let it happen.

'Shall we go and see upstairs?' I said, getting to my feet and carrying Eden up the steps. At the top, I lowered her onto the carpet, and she crawled away into the main bedroom.

Inside was an unmade double divan bed with a folded duvet on top. I checked the wardrobe, keeping one eye on Eden, who was already pulling open the drawers in the bedside cabinet. They were empty and she loved the motion.

'Watch your fingers,' I warned. 'Ouch,' I continued, trying to mime what I meant.

'Ow,' she mimicked, still yanking at the drawer.

The wardrobe was empty. Shit, I hadn't thought to bring sheets. Perhaps they'd be in the airing cupboard?

I left the room and Eden followed, I blocked off the stairs and she detoured into the second bedroom. There was a single pine bed, where Eden would sleep. Brooke told me she was still in a cot at home, but we'd have to make it work. I'd buffer with pillows and cushions in case she rolled out in the night. Maybe I should have her sleep in with me instead? Although she was so tiny, what if I rolled over and squashed her? The single bed was lower than the double, so it had to be the safer option.

I got lucky in the hallway airing cupboard; there were pillows and towels, as well as a few sheets and duvet sets. I pulled two sets out and threw them onto my bed. The fabric was starchy, appearing new and unwashed, but it didn't matter. I'd put them on later.

The third bedroom had been turned into an office and an empty corner desk looked out over the street. Across the road, I saw a red-faced Georgina stretching by a lamp post, obviously back from her run in the miserable weather. The drizzle had followed us north and the pavements were slick with it. All that make-up would be sliding off her face. I watched her for a second, enjoying the view.

Remembering myself, I turned around to find Eden had gone. I rushed back into the hallway before I spotted her. She'd found the bathroom and was opening the toilet lid when I got to her.

'Dirty, yuck! Let's go downstairs and get a drink and a biscuit,' I said.

Outside, the grey skies were already darkening, clouds rolling in heavy with threatening rain. I hoped there wouldn't be a storm. I could do without a night of thunder and lightning, although whatever happened, something told me I was in for a long first night with Eden.

14

BROOKE SIMMONS

'Here you go.' Janette handed me a polythene bag of scrubs when I returned, which I gratefully received. It had dawned on me; I couldn't go anywhere without trousers and the police had taken mine. Leaving the hospital in a gown would have been out of the question, but I didn't want to call Mum. She'd freak out for sure.

'Thank you,' I smiled at her weakly. I wanted to go home, crawl in my bed now the enormity of the situation had fully hit me. Talking to Ali had been awful, a knife to the back of the throat. I didn't know what to say. I had nothing to give her, but hearing her cry down the phone had been torturous. It was nothing more than I deserved.

'The doctor said you can go home; he's happy for you to take regular painkillers, alternate ibuprofen and paracetamol if you need them. No washing your hair for five days either. Have you got someone at home waiting for you?' She cocked her head to one side, waiting for my answer. I was still a little spaced out.

'Yes, my mum's there.'

'Good, she can keep an eye on you. Take it easy for the next couple of days, no strenuous exercise. Don't drive today either. If you have any problems, don't hesitate to contact your GP.' She was smiling, although already stripping the bed as I stood and ripped open the bag to remove the trousers.

Before leaving the toilets, I'd tucked the Nokia I'd used to call Jimmy back in my bra, making sure it was on but silent in case he tried to ring me. That was all I had with me, other than my iPhone. I'd had a missed call from Mum, but I couldn't face calling her back. She'd get hysterical; the best thing to do was to go home and confront her there.

The trousers were massive. I pulled them up and tightened the draw cord at the waist as much as I could before rolling up the bottoms. I looked like I'd been in a kid's dressing-up box. I slipped the iPhone into one of the pockets, further pulling the trousers down. The weight comforting against my thigh.

'Thank you for looking after me,' I said, turning around to Janette, who had already remade the bed for the next patient. Resus was like a never-ending conveyor belt.

'You're welcome. Take care.' She tucked her hair behind her ear, smiling broadly.

Pulling back the curtain, I looked left and right at the bustling corridor and headed towards the exit. Had PC Kempton gone? Would I be able to slip past him? Where was the waiting room he'd been holed up in?

I checked my phone again; it was three o'clock already. Why hadn't Jimmy called me back? Where had he taken Eden? Surely, he didn't believe he'd get away with running off with her.

'Ah, Miss Simmons, I've been asked to escort you to the station.' PC Kempton stepped out of a doorway to my left and I jumped.

'Jesus!' I took a step back, hand to my chest, heart racing beneath my sweatshirt.

'Sorry, I didn't mean to scare you.' He stifled a chuckle and I scowled.

'I've told you what I know already.'

'We need a more detailed statement,' he said flatly. It wasn't up for discussion.

I nodded and he fell in step with me as we made our way towards the exit.

I chewed the inside of my cheek, trying not to let my nerves show. Did they know more than they were letting on? Could they know about Jimmy?

'You must be hungry; we can get some sandwiches back at the station and a nice cup of tea.'

'Thank you,' I mumbled, although my hollowed-out stomach was the least of my problems.

A patrol car was waiting on a double yellow line at the entrance to the hospital. A female officer looked out at us from behind the steering wheel. As we neared, PC Kempton quickened his pace, opening the back door for me to climb in. My throat thick at the prospect of a formal interview.

The air inside the car seemed heavy, laden with something I couldn't put my finger on.

'Put your belt on please,' the female officer barked, offering no introduction.

I did as I was told, my fingers fumbling to get it into the clasp. The scrubs were so thin, they offered no warmth to my legs and I shivered.

PC Kempton slid into the passenger seat, buckling up and nodding to the driver.

She lifted the radio from its holder. 'Bravo Yankee 182 to November Papa, over.'

'November Papa received, go ahead, over.'

'We have Miss Simmons and are returning to Reigate station, ETA ten minutes, please inform SIO, over.'

'Message received, Bravo Yankee, will do. Over.'

What did they mean by 'we have'? Did they mean have in custody? My legs jiggled of their own accord. Was I going to be interrogated? Did I need a solicitor? If they searched me, they'd find the phone – it would lead them to Jimmy.

Did I give him up, expose myself and tell the truth? If I did, would I go to prison? If I kept quiet, I could still come out of this all right. Eden would be fine; Jimmy would never hurt her. He adored her, that was the problem.

I needed him to answer my bloody calls so I could talk some sense into him. I never thought in a million years he'd react like this. If only I hadn't bumped into him that day. He'd ghosted me, big deal. Why had I thought it would be a good idea to punish him for it?

I gazed out of the window, ignoring the conversation between PC Kempton and his colleague. It had started to rain again; the sky full of it. The weather was the same when I ran into Jimmy back in March. The heavens had opened just as we'd come out of the library after the sing-along baby group. I'd stood under the shelter of the entrance with Eden in her Bugaboo stroller, waiting for a break in the weather, when someone accidentally knocked the bright yellow hood as they rushed for cover.

'Sorry,' he'd said, flashing me a dazzling smile of bright white teeth, which slowly receded when he realised who I was. 'Brooke?'

I'd squirmed and pushed my hood back. Jimmy's face had peered down at me, rain dripping from his forehead into his charcoal eyes.

'Hi, Jimmy,' I'd said with a nonchalance I didn't feel. Inside, the butterflies had been going crazy. It had irritated me that, after all that time, he was still able to provoke a physical reaction. I hadn't seen him for almost a year and a half, but he still blew me away.

We'd been seeing each other for about six weeks, the first serious relationship I'd had since Karl. Only I'd been serious about us though; Jimmy, as it turned out, was just looking for a bit of fun. He'd never said he wanted no-strings, commitment-free sex, otherwise I would never have gone out with him. But Jimmy could charm the birds from the trees, and I fell for his patter, hook, line and sinker. Not realising at the time, I was going to get my heart broken yet again.

'You look well, how are you?' Jimmy had quickly recovered. He'd grinned and leaned against the library wall. Even the way he leaned was hot.

'I'm good thanks, how are you?'

He didn't answer, staring intently at the buggy, at Eden grabbing her pink soft shoes.

'Who is this little darling?' he'd asked, scraping his hand across his stubble.

I'd looked at his face, watching the frown lines on his forehead crinkle, and remembered all the nights I'd waited for his call. All the tears I'd shed, how I'd felt used when he'd disappeared from my life and blocked me on social media.

'This is Eden,' I'd said, simpering up at him through my lashes.

That's how it had begun, how the idea had grown from the smallest seed, sown in a flash. I didn't think at the time it would end, six months later, with me sat in the back of a police car and my best friend's child missing.

4PM – 7PM

15
ALI TOLFREY

The minutes ticked by, one agonising second at a time. After Christopher's outburst, he said he needed some air and left. DC Benson tried to convince him to stay, but it wasn't up for discussion and the door was slammed in his face. He needed time to cool off.

I apologised profusely on his behalf: it was a stressful time, Christopher adored Eden and we were living through every parents' worst nightmare. The words spilled off my tongue without me even being conscious of them.

DC Benson was gracious and dismissed it instantly, asking if there was anything he could do. But I didn't want food, or more tea, and there was no one I wanted him to call. His presence was meaningless, it felt intrusive and I wanted to be alone. Frustratingly his phone remained silent too, so he had no information to offer.

I sat, gazing out of the window, eyes stinging, watching the sun slowly disappear behind the back fence. It was already gone four. Eden had been missing for over five hours. She could be anywhere by now. It was cold and I hoped she wasn't outside. She didn't like the dark. We'd had a power cut late one evening and she'd woken up to a pitch-black room, screaming the place down until we'd put some battery-operated lights inside.

Was she being well looked after? Had she been given food and had her nappy changed? Was someone caring for her? I had a fleeting image of her being locked in the boot of a car and I squeezed my eyes shut, willing it away. Various scenarios kept popping into my head, each one hitting me like a vicious punch. It was like being continuously stabbed with a poker, as if I could forget, even for a second, my child wasn't with me.

I felt physically sick whenever I considered she might never come back through that door. In my mind, I imagined Christopher bringing her back from wherever he'd been, triumphantly carrying her over the threshold in his arms like a hero from the movies.

I clung onto the image, to force away the unbearable ones. It was far-fetched but no more so than having your child kidnapped out of nowhere. These things didn't happen to people like us. We were middle-class, we hadn't taken our eye of the ball; we'd entrusted Eden into Brooke's care. I just wished she could tell me more about what happened? As angry as I felt, how could I blame her when she was attacked?

'Does Christopher often lose his temper?' DC Benson broke the silence, interrupting my thoughts with his cautious tone. He'd resumed his position tucked into the corner of the kitchen, by the sink, overlooking the garden. His broad frame guarding the kettle. We weren't allowed to make our own drinks now he was here.

I awarded him a steely glare. 'No. You must know we're both under an inordinate amount of stress.' If DC Benson thought I was about to incriminate my husband in any way, he was sorely mistaken.

He nodded, deciding not to push further.

'Getting ready for Halloween?' he asked, changing the subject and gesturing to the pumpkin on the worktop, yet to be carved.

'Yes, I'm going to do Hello Kitty, Eden loves her.' I tucked my hair behind my ear and stood to turn the lights on. Chasing the shadows away.

'Are you going trick or treating?' he asked, squinting until his eyes adjusted.

'No, she's only one. Although I was going to take her out to look at the decorations. Some people around here really get into it.' I gave a watery smile and remembered the pumpkin sleepsuit I'd bought from Waitrose last week. Would she ever get to wear it now?

'That'll be fun. I'm sure she'll love it.' DC Benson grinned, and he looked boyish despite the beard. It must have been why he was chosen as a liaison officer, non-threatening, likeable even.

His phone beeped and he stared at it, reading the message. My shoulders clenched as he looked up at me.

'Local news are putting it out on the six o'clock bulletin.'

'What about national? I mean she could be anywhere by now,' I fretted.

'We've released a statement to the media with Eden's photo, hopefully it'll be run by the newspapers tomorrow. Moving forward, it may be DCI Greene's plan to arrange a press conference so you and Mr Tolfrey could appeal for witnesses.'

'Do you think that would help?' I asked, although my stomach churned at the notion of displaying my grief to a room full of strangers with flashing cameras.

'Yes, they can help an investigation, especially if we're trying to communicate directly with the person who has Eden. Appeal to them to drop her at a police station or hospital.'

I nodded. We'd do whatever we needed to, whatever it took, to bring Eden back home.

Now on my feet, I had a spurt of energy, I didn't want to sit and wallow, I needed to do something to occupy my time. To stop my brain from torturing me with pictures of Eden and all the places she could be, the people she could have been passed to. I swallowed hard, my hands on my hips.

'I'm going to clean,' I stated to DC Benson, who raised his eyebrows.

'Sure,' he replied, and I gritted my teeth. I wasn't asking for his bloody permission.

Armed with yellow Marigolds and the caddy containing dusters, polish, cloths and disinfectant, I climbed the stairs. Craving an escape from having to be polite company to the stranger in our house. Headphones in ears, I listened to loud music as I polished every surface in the master and spare bedrooms until my arms ached, before scrubbing at the family bathroom and our en suite. Periodically unplugging to keep an ear out for Christopher's return, but he seemed to have taken a long walk. My irritation grew as time went on and I chewed the inside of my cheek.

How did he get to leave? He should be here, beside me. We should be supporting each other through this hell. It was unfair to leave me here alone.

Sighing, I ditched my headphones and sat on the toilet, elbows on my knees, head bowed. I wasn't being fair; he was upset. Christopher needed to cool off, get some air, that was all. He'd be back soon, to take control of the situation and tell me what to do. I knew how much he hated feeling useless. Perhaps he was at the park searching? Maybe he'd convinced DCI Greene to let him through the cordon?

I pulled off my gloves, putting them back in the caddy. The bathroom smelt blissfully of bleach.

'Are you okay, Mrs Tolfrey?' DC Benson called up the stairs.

'Fine,' I shouted back, my voice clipped. It wasn't as easy as I thought to forget he was there.

Frustrated by the invasion of our privacy, I pulled the hoover from the cupboard upstairs. We had two: a cordless one downstairs, even though it was mostly open plan and parquet floor throughout. I used it for rugs we had in the lounge and the stairs. A spare corded one lived upstairs in the airing cupboard. I thrust the plug in and pushed the heavy hoover around, relishing in the loud noise that drowned out everything in its wake.

I'd done the entire first floor and was back in the hallway, about to switch the hoover off and carry it upstairs to our loft room, when a hand grabbed my arm from behind. I let out a yelp.

'What are you doing?' Christopher shouted over the noise, before reaching down with his free hand and turning the hoover off. The sound still rang in my ears.

'Where have you been?' I countered.

'Out, walking. What are you doing?' he repeated.

'What does it look like I'm doing?' I snapped, pulling my arm out of his grasp.

His eyes narrowed and he leaned closer. 'Are you mad? Him, downstairs, he's watching everything we do.'

'What are you talking about?' I said dismissively.

'He's not our friend, Ali, he's here to report back, to gather information. That's what family liaison officers do. Remember who he works for!' Christopher was practically hissing now.

'If you've got nothing to do with it, you shouldn't have anything to worry about,' I said, my voice scratchy.

'What the hell is that supposed to mean?'

16

BROOKE SIMMONS

Reigate police station was cold and uninviting. The pallid grey walls were speckled with dents and dirty scuff marks. Lights overhead buzzed continuously, irritating my ears.

PC Kempton gave my name to the front desk as I stared at the floor. I didn't want to be here. Shifting from foot to foot, aware I was under the spotlight, I wrung my hands together so hard I gave myself a Chinese burn.

Why couldn't they have let me go home? I wanted to crawl into bed and forget today ever happened, pretend it had been a dream. *Because*, the voice in my head scolded, *a child has been kidnapped.*

I was struggling to grasp the magnitude of the situation as I knew Eden would be fine. I'd seen Jimmy with her most weeks for the past six months and he was every part the doting father. However, in everyone else's minds, a one-year-old was potentially in the hands of a paedophile ring, being sold to the highest bidder on the Dark Web. Hence the urgency.

The officer led me into a small interview room. An oblong

table and four chairs tucked beneath left little room for anything else.

I wedged myself into the seat nearest the wall, teeth chattering.

'Cup of tea?' PC Kempton asked.

'Please. Do you have a blanket? I'm freezing,' I replied.

He gave a solitary nod and left the room.

I spied a domed camera in the top left corner and averted my eyes, wrapping my arms around myself.

PC Kempton returned with a steaming cup of machine-brewed tea. I hoped there was sugar in it.

'Here, you must be hungry. Cheese okay? You're not vegan, are you?' He squinted at me as he offered the plastic-wrapped sandwich. His hand wavering like he was going to snatch it back.

'No, I'm not, and thanks, cheese is fine,' I replied, taking the package.

'Someone will be in to interview you shortly,' he said.

Why 'someone', why not him? Wasn't he highly ranked enough? If so, what did that mean? He left, returning a minute later with a grey blanket, which I wrapped around myself.

I pulled open the packaging and nibbled at the sandwich; dry bread and bland cheese clogged in my mouth. It was tough to swallow, and I took a sip of the tea to help it go down. I didn't want to eat with an audience so persevered while I was alone, my stomach gurgling gratefully for the first proper food I'd had all day, hollowed out from my sickness in the ambulance. I'd been running on empty. My head still throbbed, although I'd gotten used to it; I'd given up waiting for it to subside.

After ten minutes of waiting, the door finally opened and a rotund man with a side parting and a wonky tie came in and sat opposite me. He had a bulbous red nose, like he enjoyed a drink a bit too much. Seconds later, he was joined by a much younger blonde female in a pale pink blouse and matching lipstick. She looked around the same age as me. I shrank lower into my seat.

'Hello, Brooke, I'm Detective Inspector Vincent and this is Detective Constable Tunstall, we're part of the team investigating the abduction of Eden Tolfrey. I understand you've had a traumatic day, so we'll try and make this as quick as possible, so you can go home.' The man smiled, the corner of one eye twitching every few seconds. 'We're going to record this statement and I'd like to go through your entire day, from the moment you woke up, minute by minute. Please don't leave anything out.'

I nodded, mustering a weak smile, before he turned on the recorder and confirmed it was Thursday, 29th October 2020, four thirty-five p.m., and who was in the room.

I rubbed my forehead and pulled the blanket up over my shoulder, shielding my neck, which I knew would turn blotchy the moment I started talking. I wished I'd worn a polo neck instead of a sweatshirt. Aware of DC Tunstall's eyes on me, heat rose on my chest, edging its way upwards like a creeping vine. Was I going to lie to the police?

I cleared my throat. Self-preservation was my priority; Eden wasn't in any danger. Once I got out of here, I'd try Jimmy again, get him to drop her off somewhere.

'Can you give me your address please?' DI Vincent asked.

'I live at 63 Yale Close, Redhill.' A nice easy question to start with.

'Do you live alone?'

'No, with my mum.'

'Okay, tell me about your day. What time did you get up this morning?'

I shifted in my seat, bringing the sides of the blanket across my lap to cover the thin material of the scrubs.

I told them about my morning; I'd got up at eight, my mum

had already left the house for her job as a teaching assistant at the local primary school. She'd left me a cup of tea and a cereal bar as usual. Something she always did on the mornings where I hadn't worked the night shift at Tesco stacking shelves.

'How many shifts do you work at Tesco?' DI Vincent asked.

'Three night shifts – Sunday, Tuesday and Friday. From midnight to eight in the morning.' It was why I was always tired, my body clock never on the right time. 'I also go to college, on a Monday and Wednesday, I'm doing a Foundation Certificate in Bookkeeping.' I wasn't sure why I'd volunteered the information, perhaps I'd wanted them to see I had direction; Tesco was a stopgap for me.

DI Vincent smiled and nodded before speaking again. 'Please, carry on. You said you had breakfast?'

I agreed, although I'd put the cereal bar back. It was Mum's passive-aggressive attempt to get me to eat in the morning when I rarely felt like it so close to waking up.

'I got showered and dressed and watched a bit of television before I left for Ali's at around nine forty. I normally get there for about ten.'

'What's your relationship with the Tolfreys?'

I told them of our history, how I'd met Ali at work and we'd just clicked, surprising giving our different backgrounds. When the company folded, we kept in touch. It was very much a sisterly relationship; she was the older sibling, giving support and advice to me. Looking after Eden was something that seemed like a natural progression. I wanted to help Ali, and I loved spending time with Eden. At first it was because Ali was desperate for a break, but then she wanted to use the time to get her career back on track. She always paid me, even when I didn't want anything. She knew how hard I was saving to move out.

'Did you speak to anyone, text or otherwise, social media perhaps?' DI Vincent probed.

'No... I mean, I logged on to Facebook, read through some posts, same with Twitter, but nothing else. My mum text me, to make sure I was up and had eaten, but I didn't speak to anyone.' I didn't mention I'd text Jimmy before I left home, confirming our arrangement to meet at half ten in the park close to Ali's house. The phone I'd used for him still tucked inside my bra, now the same temperature as my skin so I could barely feel it.

'Would you be happy for us to look at your phone? I understand a forensic investigator has already secured your DNA and bagged your clothes at the hospital?'

'That's right. So why do you need my phone?' I asked, genuinely curious.

'It's procedure. We'll check incoming and outgoing calls, messages, triangulation. Routine in a case such as this. Helps us eliminate those closest to the family, and closest to you.'

'Sure,' I said, reaching into the pocket of the scrubs and pulling out my iPhone. I unlocked it, noticing Mum had tried to call again, and passed it across the table.

'What's the pin?'

'2148,' I replied, and DI Vincent wrote it down.

Without a word, DC Tunstall placed it in a clear bag and left the room.

My eyes scanned the ceiling. There was nothing of Jimmy on the iPhone was there? No, his number had never been on there. I'd never used it to call or text him, not since we'd met up again. Instinctively, I rubbed the middle of my chest, like I had indigestion, fingering the edge of the pay-as-you-go phone still where it was supposed to be.

'Are you okay, Miss Simmons?'

My head snapped back, eyes focusing on DI Vincent. 'Yes sorry, I'm fine.'

'Good, good. Back to today,' he glanced at his notes, 'so at nine forty you left for Mrs Tolfrey's. This was prearranged?'

'Yes, every Tuesday and Thursday, I have Eden for three hours, ten to one, then I come back and have lunch with Ali. We're friends.' The last word stuck in my throat and I had to spit it out. What kind of friend would be responsible for the abduction of their daughter?

17

JIMMY PEARSON

Why was all shop-bought baby food a vibrant orange? Even so, the plastic carton retrieved from the microwave was supposedly spaghetti bolognaise and smelt delicious, despite its mushy appearance. With no high chair, I improvised, bringing the buggy into the kitchen, giving it a wipe and strapping Eden in, so any fallen food could easily be cleaned up.

She didn't put up too much of a fight. After her biscuit, she still wanted more so I decided an early dinner was in order. She loved her food, just like her dad. Although I wouldn't be going to the gym for a while, or even out for a run. I couldn't leave Eden with anybody; it was too risky. Georgina stretching in her Lycra skipped into my mind. Shame I couldn't run with her. I bet she had some stamina, I chuckled to myself. Never mind, I'd have to make sure I curbed my intake. Despite being a full-time dad, I needn't get the paunch to go with it.

Eden's mouth was ringed in a carroty glow and she smacked her lips together happily as I fed her the last spoonful. I leaned forward in the chair I'd brought out from the sitting room, digging a clean plastic spoon into a tiny yogurt pot. She opened her mouth and craned her neck as far forwards as she could, like a baby bird, ready for feeding. Clearly excited for dessert. I beamed at her, she absolutely melted me.

Once the pot had been scraped clean, I wiped her face and hands and waited for the bowel movement I knew would be coming.

Outside, the light had diminished and I drew the curtains and put on the table lamp before we sat on the floor in front of the television. We played for a while, waiting for the six o'clock news, keeping Eden entertained with some stacking cups. I built them up and she knocked them over with a squeal.

My chest hammered as the theme for the news came on and I chewed my thumbnail, waiting to hear my name. It never came; neither mine nor Eden's face was displayed on screen. I couldn't understand it, certain we'd be mentioned. My shoulders had been bunched up around my ears and they eased down, relief mixed with confusion. I'd had a reprieve, for today at least.

Eden shuffled away from me and pulled herself up against the arm of the sofa, her face growing red. The motherload was coming, my least favourite part of the job.

I stared again at the television. Had Brooke not reported it? Had she been happy to get rid of Eden? No, that wasn't possible, she doted on her as much as I did. I chewed my lip as I considered what could have happened.

A jolt hit my core, terror rippling through me. What if she was still there, lying on the grass, unconscious? What if I'd killed her or put her in a coma and maybe no one had found her yet? That's why it wasn't on the news. I swallowed hard, beads of sweat appearing on my upper lip.

I hadn't hit her that hard, had I? She'd hit the deck with a thud, but it hadn't crossed my mind to check she was still breathing. I'd had a tiny window to make my getaway with Eden and I took it. No looking back.

Surely if there was a manhunt underway for me, it would be on the news? It didn't make any sense.

A piercing scream broke my train of thought, Eden was on her knees on the carpet, tears cascading her cheeks. The cream lamp on its side but the table still upright.

'What's happened, did you fall over, poppet?' Frowning, I scooped her up, the stink from the nappy almost making me gag.

Something was wrong, Eden wouldn't stop screaming. Had she really hurt herself? Her face was bright red and scrunched up in pain. I rocked her against my chest, after checking her for any bumps. I found nothing, but she wouldn't settle, bringing her knees up to her chest, limbs rigid. I got up and walked around, trying to soothe her, but it was to no avail. Her sobs grew louder, breath catching in bursts as she sucked in air only to scream it back out.

Dropping to my knees, I sat her on the sofa to look her over properly, had she hit her head on something? The table maybe? Why hadn't I kept an eye on her?

It was then I noticed the red circle of inflamed skin on the palm of her right hand. Shit! The light bulb – she'd grabbed the bloody light bulb and burnt her hand.

My heart raced as I carried her into the kitchen, forcing her hand under the cold tap. She let out a deafening wail, trying to pull her arm out of the stream of water, out of my grip. I blinked rapidly as panic took hold.

Right, okay, a burn, what should I do? How bad is it? Cling film, do I need cling film? Surely a bit of cream would be all right, wouldn't it?

Palpitations thudded in my chest.

'Mamamamamamamama,' she howled.

Desperate to appease her, I grabbed the large plastic milk

bottle from the fridge and went back to the lounge, turning on CBeebies so she could watch Iggle Piggle dance around the Night Garden. With Eden on my lap, I put the chilled milk on its side on top of her knees and gently rested her palm flat on it. It was less traumatic than the tap and slowly Eden stopped crying as the cold relieved the pain in her hand.

Fuck, I'd have to do better. I wouldn't be able to keep her alive for a week at this rate. A rush of anger pulsed my veins and I clenched my jaw. If only Brooke had given me a chance, let me spend more time with Eden. I'd have a better idea of what I was doing.

'It's okay, baby girl, Daddy's here,' I said, cuddling her.

She'd given up the fight and seemed happy to have her hand resting on the milk, condensation pooling in sections on top. It would be soothing her hand and hopefully a few applications of Savlon would be enough, no hospital required.

We sat until *Waffle the Wonder Dog* on CBeebies finished, and I'd had enough of children's television. The red circle had dulled to a pink, and Eden let me cover it with antiseptic cream without too much complaint. She was more annoyed at having her nappy changed.

'I know, how about a bath. Eden go splish splash?' I said and her eyes widened before she gave a little yawn.

Yes, a short, shallow bath would be a good idea. She had a bath book she could play with while I shaved my beard off. I ran it lukewarm, carrying Eden around with me, going from room to room drawing the curtains and back downstairs to bring the clothes and toiletries up. I didn't want to let her out of my sight.

Ten minutes later, Eden splashed in the bath, the water covering the tops of her thighs as I stood at the sink, glancing from the mirror back to her every few seconds. Terrified she would rock backwards, but she sat upright without any problem, pulling at the pages of her book and splashing. The water might have been a touch too cold, but I didn't want it too hot. I was worried her hand might sting when she got it wet but, thankfully, she'd seemed to have forgotten the burn was there.

My shave was quick and rough, I cut myself twice, stemming the flow with a tiny bit of tissue paper. The lower half of my face was pale beneath the beard. It made me look younger than my twenty-eight years but less attractive; the George Michael designer stubble I'd managed to cultivate definitely pulled in the ladies. Although there was only one lady for me now. I glanced down at her wiggling her toes up through the water.

'Mamamamamamamamama,' she said, before patting the book and stating, 'ook.'

'Book,' I repeated, smiling.

She blinked up at me, repeating the word.

Checking out my reflection in the mirror, I ran a hand through my dark hair. I'd shave it tomorrow morning outside in the garden, before a shower.

Rinsing the mess from the sink, I put the razor and foam in the cabinet. Eden didn't seem ready to get out yet, so I lowered to my knees to swirl and splash the water as she giggled. Lathering up the sponge, I gently ran it across her arms, chest and legs. I'd never bathed her before, frightened to press her skin too hard.

I remembered the first time Brooke got me to change her; it took ages as I tried to coax her little arms into the Babygro. Brooke had found it hilarious.

'She's not going to break, you know,' she'd scolded me.

Eden tried to grab the sponge out of my hand and put it in her mouth.

'Yuk, Eden, soap,' I said.

She looked so beautiful I wanted to take a photo, but my phone was downstairs. A pang of regret hit me, knowing Dad would have fallen in love with her too, if he'd had the chance to meet her.

I had an urge to check my Facebook account. I didn't use it much and Brooke asked me never to post any photos of Eden. She said she didn't because it was too easy for paedophiles to get images of children from there. I wanted to see if anyone had posted anything about me or Eden. As soon as the news broke, it would be everywhere, but Facebook was an itch I couldn't scratch. I had to keep my head down, stay off social media and out of contact from everyone. Maybe I could ring Brooke? Check she was okay, and still alive. No, too risky. Even from a phone box the police could trace my location.

I'd had a head start; driven halfway up the country and I wasn't about to give myself away. It still niggled me there'd been nothing on the news. I'd built myself up to watch it, my heart in my mouth, positive I'd see my face fill the screen. Knowing from that moment, the heat would be on and I'd be officially in hiding, a wanted man.

It was strange there'd been no mention of it. I found the lack of news somewhat unsettling. There were only two reasons I could think of why it wasn't shown; one was Brooke had given Eden up, accepted I would be her full-time carer and decided she wasn't going to fight me on it. The other reason, I shuddered, too awful to consider, was she was dead or lying somewhere gravely injured.

18

ALI TOLFREY

'Come on, tell me. What is that supposed to mean exactly?' Christopher repeated, his forehead a mass of lines. He loomed over me, one hand on the bannister, and for the first time since we'd met, he had me on edge.

'It doesn't mean anything,' I said, shuffling backwards, realising my words had been an accusation as far as he was concerned. His nostrils flared.

'You really think I had something to do with this?' he asked, incredulous.

'No, of course I don't.' I sighed, rubbing the back of my neck. 'Where did you go, you've been gone ages.'

'Just walking. It felt, claustrophobic in here.' His voice was softer now and he seemed to shrink back to his normal size.

'I know. It's why I came upstairs.'

'The news will be on shortly. We should watch it.' Christopher took the hoover out of my hands and wound the cord around the handle. 'You go and put the television on, I'll put this back. I want to get changed out of my shirt and trousers,' he said, and I did as I was told.

The lounge was cold and soulless, as was the rest of the house without Eden's presence. Her happy giggle, even her screaming I'd settle for right now. In fact, it would be blissful to hear her relentless wailing. I sank onto the leather sofa, tucking my legs around me.

'Alexa, turn on the light,' Christopher said towards the smart speaker, appearing in the doorway wearing jeans and a T-shirt. A second later, the tall lamp next to the sofa came on, illuminating the room.

I turned the television to BBC One and Christopher closed the blinds. I hated them being open once it was dark, anyone could walk past and see in. We were exposed.

Christopher moved to sit beside me as DC Benson entered through the double doors from the kitchen. He was like a ghost, popping up silently and loitering in corners and doorways. I didn't acknowledge him, but Christopher clasped my hand in his before speaking for us both.

'Please sit down.' He nodded towards the other sofa and DC Benson smiled gratefully, lowering himself into the seat.

The news began and my stomach lurched. Every time a new story started, I assumed it would be ours and gripped Christopher's hand tighter.

'We'll be on the local news, after the national,' he whispered, but I couldn't still my racing heart. By the time the local news came on, my palms were sweaty and I wanted to pull my hand away, but Christopher held firm, eyes focused on the screen.

'*Surrey police are searching for a one-year-old child who was abducted from Bushy Park in Reigate this morning.*' The stoic newsreader looked grave delivering our nightmare to the public and I gasped when the photo I'd given DCI Greene this morning appeared, filling the screen. '*Eden Tolfrey is approximately seventy-*

two centimetres tall and weighs twenty pounds. She has short blonde hair, brown eyes and was last seen wearing grey leggings with a pink cardigan and coat.'

'They didn't mention her stripy T-shirt,' I said over the television.

'Sssshhhhh,' Christopher hissed, leaning closer to the screen.

'Anyone who witnessed the abduction or believes they have seen Eden should call Surrey Police on 01737 222289, quoting reference 4629.'

Tears fell as I stared at my beautiful daughter on the screen, wishing this nightmare would end. Head bowed, they missed my cheeks and landed on my thighs as Eden's face disappeared from view.

'The number goes straight through to the interview room, which will be manned 24/7 until Eden is found,' DC Benson said, clearing his throat as the newsreader moved on to another local story of a distraction burglary at an assisted living complex.

'Are there no other leads today? It's half-past six, surely you must have *something* for us. She's been missing for hours now!' Christopher said, straining to be polite. Pain etched into the lines of his face, which looked deeper today than they ever had. I remained silent, my chest caving in. Could you die from a broken heart?

'I should be getting an update soon, but I'll let you know as soon as I hear. In the meantime, can I rustle up some pasta for you?' DC Benson got to his feet and clasped his hands together.

'I'll do it,' I said, pulling myself up as though my legs were filled with lead. I wasn't sure how much we'd eat, but it would fill some time instead of the endless waiting.

The home phone starting ringing and we all froze.

'Would you like me to answer it?' DC Benson's eyed us expectantly. 'Now the news has been on you're likely to get calls from friends and relatives.'

'I don't want to talk to anyone right now. Tell them we'll call them back,' Christopher replied, waving his hand as though dismissing whoever was on the other end of the phone.

DC Benson picked up the receiver.

I moved into the kitchen as I heard him mumble a greeting, and put the oven on for the flatbread and put a saucepan of water on the stove, watching it until it bubbled.

'It was your mother, Mrs Tolfrey, she wasn't particularly happy,' DC Benson said as diplomatically as he could.

'She never is,' I replied bitterly, knowing she would be steaming that she'd learnt her granddaughter had gone missing from watching it on the news. It wasn't an argument I was prepared to have. She could wait.

'You may get lots of calls now, from well-meaning friends and family. Also, the press will likely try to contact you and there's a possibility you may receive crank calls. It may be wise to let me answer the phone if you're happy with that. I can field them then.'

'Sure. Should we talk to the press?' Christopher asked, his voice carrying through the open double doors into the lounge.

'We advise against it; in case it jeopardises the investigation. We prefer to control what goes out to the media if we can.'

The water boiling pulled me from the conversation, and I busied myself cooking. Twenty minutes later, three bowls of pesto pasta and a tomato flatbread were placed on the kitchen table.

'I need a drink.' Christopher sighed, bringing a bottle of red wine and the corkscrew to the table.

I held out my glass when he offered, concealing a smirk when DC Benson gave his 'on duty' response. He'd barely done anything other than lift the kettle since he'd arrived.

I knew I wasn't being fair; his job was to look after us, but one officer here was one less officer searching for Eden and she was all that mattered. The *only* thing that mattered.

I pushed the pasta around my bowl as DC Benson tried to engage us in conversation. How long had we known Brooke? How had we met her? All his questions were probing, digging for information, but we answered them without hesitation. There was nothing we wouldn't do to get Eden back.

'Thank you very much, Mrs Tolfrey, that was delicious,' DC Benson said when he was finished, collecting mine and Christopher's half-full bowls and taking them to the counter.

I smiled tightly and sipped at my wine. When would he be going home?

Christopher was already on his second glass and I considered intervening. He was no use to anyone, no use to me, if he was inebriated, but there was little point in starting a row. Instead I got up to empty the pasta into the bin and load the dishwasher. I wanted a cigarette. I rarely smoked, only occasionally when I'd had a drink, socially.

The four-month-old packet was tucked on top of the kitchen cupboard, out of view, but when Christopher saw what I was retrieving, he tutted.

'That's not going to help,' he said, rolling his eyes. He'd always been anti-smoking, but as he was a GP, I couldn't hold that against him.

'And that is?' I retorted as he took another mouthful of wine.

DC Benson looked awkward and excused himself to use the bathroom.

I stepped outside onto the patio, illuminated by the security light. The patio was dark, slick from the earlier rain. I lit the cigarette with the lighter tucked inside the packet and sucked in the smoke, blowing it out and enjoying the rush. It tasted vile, but I smoked it anyway. There was no stress-reliever like it.

When the cigarette was almost down to the butt, the back door opened, and DC Benson leaned out, eyes wide.

'We may have a lead.'

19

JIMMY PEARSON

I lifted Eden out of the bath and wrapped her in a fluffy towel retrieved from the airing cupboard. The house had warmed up since I'd put the central heating on and was almost cosy now a little life had been injected into it. It was strange to imagine Dad here, moving around the rooms, living under this roof, although I didn't think he'd ever properly moved in.

Eden wriggled as I laid her on the bathmat to dry behind her knees and crooks of her elbows, dabbing lightly at her sore hand. She didn't seem to mind too much and enjoyed me playing peek-a-boo with the towel covering her eyes.

'Right, time for milk, little one,' I said, scooping her up and taking her into her room, where I put on a fresh nappy, more Savlon to soothe her palm and a sleepsuit. I gave her 'Bubs', her favourite teddy, and left the room, closing the door behind me. Eden was crying before I even made it downstairs. Her screaming set my teeth on edge. Things would get easier once I got a playpen or something. It was always going to be a steep learning curve, but better than not knowing her at all.

Grabbing a ready-made carton of formula, I poured it into a clean baby bottle. Brooke had told me Eden has milk before bed. Shopping for it was a minefield and I just had to go by age. Eden was banging on her bedroom wall above me. Angry at being left alone. Twenty seconds in the microwave should do it. I swirled the milk around and tested it on my wrist, nope, another ten seconds. Thuds of her feet against the bed followed, she was not a happy girl.

A minute later, I was back up the stairs armed with a bib and muslin. Eden glared at me as I opened the door, face pink with exertion and her little fists clenched. Her expression soon changed when she saw the milk in my hand. I settled on the bed and pulled her onto my lap, nestling her into my arm as I offered the bottle. Without hesitating, she guzzled it down, stopping every so often for me to sit her up and rub her back until the bottle was empty.

I wasn't the best at getting wind out of her. It was something else Brooke was better at, but I just needed more practise. If I was honest, I was winging it entirely, using what I'd picked up from watching Brooke. How hard could it be looking after a one-year-old? Things were going pretty well so far, other than her burning her hand, of course.

Eden's eyelids were heavy as I laid her on the carpet with Bubs and her blanket so I could put a sheet on the mattress. She sucked her thumb while twisting the teddy's button eyes. I took the opportunity to dash back downstairs to find the music box I'd bought which doubled as a night light too, as well as her dummy and sleeping bag. That was everything, wasn't it? I mean, how much stuff did a baby need to sleep.

When I returned, Eden hadn't moved from the floor, a belly full of milk and a dimly lit room seemed to be working. I'd buffed up pillows from the airing cupboard against the bed, so if she did roll out, she'd have a soft landing. I'd put her close to the wall, to be safer.

After I'd figured out how to work the music box, a classical harmony filled the room and the night light glowed a warm yellow. I picked Eden up before she got too comfortable and put her sleeping bag on, fastening the poppers as she reached for the dummy I was holding in my teeth. She looked tiny on the single bed.

Shit, I didn't have a monitor! It was one of the things I'd forgotten to purchase. Never mind, I'd check on her often, sure Eden's crying would wake me up if I left my bedroom door open.

It was almost seven and I stayed for a few more minutes, edging closer to the door, into the hallway and eventually pulling it closed. I lingered outside, waiting for Eden to cry, but surprisingly she didn't. It had been a long day of travelling and new sights; it must have worn her out. I yawned myself, wishing I'd picked up a few bottles of beer. After being on edge all day, I could do with a drink to relax.

Later, once I'd eaten, cleared up and checked on Eden twice, I sat on the sofa as a repeat of *Top Gear* played on the television. Picking up my phone, I scrolled through the Sky News app, but there were no reports of a missing child. I chewed my lip, surely, they wouldn't be able to trace where I'd logged on to Facebook? That technology wasn't available, was it? Even if it was, wouldn't it be owned by the app? I'd take my chances. I downloaded Facebook from the app store and logged in, immediately checking my status wasn't set to show I was online to anyone who might be looking.

My settings weren't set to private; I only posted photos I was happy for others to see and that was rare. Nice cars, the occasional night out or post-workout photo. I'd had a few messages over the years from girls who'd liked my profile photo – one of me at the gym. I'd had a few good nights come out of it as a result and I wasn't about to change anything now, although I couldn't imagine I'd be going on any dates in the near future. Not now I was a family man.

I scrolled through my feed, updates from friends of friends, fellow gym goers, protein-shake junkies. Nothing from Dave since yesterday, a photo of a Lamborghini he'd driven past on the motorway. There seemed to be no buzz of news, no outrage at a father taking a child away from her mother.

I searched up a local Redhill and Reigate group, combining the neighbouring towns, and the top post, written only thirty minutes ago made my jaw drop.

Did you see on the news, that girl was abducted from Bushy Park? Awful! So close to home! Hope they find her soon.

I stared at the post, waiting for the words to sink in before a rush of anger hit me. Abducted? How could you abduct your own daughter? Especially if she was going to be taken away from you by the mother? Bullshit was what it was! I knew it was coming, everyone always sided with the mother. Anyone who believed otherwise was stupid. Eden was *home* with me. She wouldn't be going back there for sure, but I hadn't abducted her.

Comments appeared one by one, and I spent the next half an hour watching them pop up, mostly so-called well-wishers and those sending prayers for a safe return. It enraged me and I ground my teeth together the more I read. Like I'd ever hurt my own daughter. I wasn't a fucking monster. There was no mention of Brooke, no one posted about a woman being attacked or there being any violence involved. It didn't make any sense.

Switching onto the Safari app, I googled *child abducted Reigate* and found a link to the Surrey page of BBC News. The article was only a couple of lines, detailing an abduction in Bushy Park with Eden's name and description. A beautiful photo of her feeding some ducks on a lake flashed up as I scrolled down. Another day trip I'd missed out on. They'd listed Eden's last name as Tolfrey, but I was sure that wasn't Brooke's surname.

Further confusion came when I couldn't find any mention of parents in the news report, or any kind of altercation having taken place. Only the time and the location of the supposed abduction. I narrowed my eyes. Why had Brooke not told them about me? Or, if she had, why hadn't they released my name?

Switching back to Facebook, I looked Brooke up, we'd been friends at one point. Until I'd ghosted her. I'd done my usual when I'd got bored, which was to unfriend her, it saved any hassle or shitty messages. I ignored any new friend requests. They got the message eventually. I blocked her phone number at the time too, so I had no idea if she'd tried to get in touch. It was easier that way.

Brooke's settings were private so I couldn't see anything other than her profile photo and name. Brooke Simmons, not Tolfrey. Where had Tolfrey come from? Was it Brooke's Mum's maiden name? I knew her parents weren't together any more, perhaps that was it?

I frowned at the phone, a pretty head-and-shoulder shot stared back, cherry red shoulder-length hair swirling as Brooke winked at the camera. Should I try to friend her? Not knowing what was going on made me nervous. I had questions I wanted answers to, but I'd left my old phone behind and it was the only number she had. There was no way she could contact me now. I'd preloaded her number into the new phone, just in case.

As I was deciding what to do, Eden started crying and I took the stairs two at a time. I opened the door to find her sitting up, surrounded by milky-smelling sick.

'Fuck's sake, Eden,' I hissed, which made her scream even louder. Maybe I wasn't cut out for parenthood after all.

20

BROOKE SIMMONS

'Did anyone know you had this arrangement with the Tolfreys, to look after Eden twice a week, every Tuesday and Thursday?' DI Vincent asked. I shrugged, my bottom lip protruding while I considered the question.

'I guess so, my mum obviously. It wasn't a secret. I probably mentioned it to my friend, Bella, and it might have come up in conversation with Lisa, my colleague at Tesco. I'm not sure really, I don't think I've mentioned it to anyone else.'

'Did the Tolfreys receive any calls or visitors while you were there? Anything seem out of the ordinary to you this morning?'

'No, but I was only there around fifteen minutes. Ali was worried it was going to rain but I like to take Eden out so she can concentrate on work. Sometimes we go to the library, the park or soft play.'

'Who else knew you were going to the swings this morning? Were you meeting anyone? Another babysitter, or a friend?'

'No.' I willed my heart to remain steady and looked directly into DI Vincent's grey penetrating eyes without blinking, the flush on my neck in full force. All the time, guilt crushing my chest. It would be fine; Jimmy would bring her back. Ali wouldn't suffer for much longer.

'What time did you enter the park?'

'About half-ten, it's a ten-minute walk from Ali's house. I took Eden to the swings for around twenty minutes at first, in the play park, then we were going to do a lap of the park. There's a path that goes all the way around, but we only got halfway.'

'What route did you walk from the Tolfrey house, can you show me?' He pulled up a map on an iPad and angled it towards me.

'St James's road, then down Howarth Avenue – the park is at the bottom of the road.' I pointed to the small green space on the map. I didn't believe there were any cameras, although plenty of people had special camera doorbells like Ali, but I didn't meet Jimmy until I was at the swings, so I'd be seen alone, pushing the buggy.

'Can you remember anything about the attack? Are you able to describe the person who hit you?'

I shook my head, wincing as a sharp pain reminded me of my wound. 'No, one minute I was walking, the next it all went black.'

'Did you see anyone suspicious hanging around, anything strange at all?'

I could sense DI Vincent was getting frustrated; I wasn't giving him much to go on. He held his pen so tightly his knuckles were white.

'No, nothing stands out. It was a normal morning. The park was pretty empty because it had been drizzling, everything was damp. All I remember is waking up and the woman in the red coat helping me.'

'Do you have any idea who could have taken Eden?'

That was my chance to come clean, give them Jimmy's name

and try to distance myself as much as possible from the mess, but if the truth came out, everything would be ruined.

'No.' Forcing the lie out as it stuck in my throat. Holding my knee to stop it jiggling under the table.

'You can't think of anyone who might have held a grudge against the Tolfreys, someone you or they may have upset recently? No arguments at work?' DI Vincent raised his eyebrows.

'No,' I repeated, my voice unwavering.

'Are you romantically involved with anyone at the moment?'

I shook my head.

'No? Any ex-boyfriends you're in touch with then?'

I chewed my lip, blood pressure rising. Were they onto me?

'No, I'm not seeing anyone; my last boyfriend was over a year ago. I've been on a couple of dates, but nothing serious and not for a while.' That part was true at least. After Jimmy, I'd sworn off men altogether.

'We're trying to work out why you were targeted, Brooke. Who knew you were there and who has motive?' DI Vincent said as DC Tunstall returned to the room, slipping into her seat.

'I don't know who took Eden. I really want to help, I do, but I didn't see anything.' I sighed and DI Vincent pursed his lips. I could see he thought I was being uncooperative.

'You're the last person we know of to see Eden alive, which makes you a vital witness.'

We locked eyes, but I didn't speak, I wasn't sure what he wanted me to say.

'Okay, who did you see at the park? You must have seen some people during the time you were there.'

I described a mother and her son, around four years old, in the play park, who left when I arrived. Two female dog walkers, one with a spaniel and the other with a bigger dog. That was it.

DC Tunstall wrote the information down.

'We're appealing for witness on the local news tonight, hopefully it will help to identify the person who took Eden.' DI Vincent leaned back in his seat, taking me in.

'I have to say, Miss Simmons, you don't seem particularly upset Eden is missing.'

My mouth gaped at his words. I shut it and swallowed hard.

'I think I'm in shock,' I stuttered as he narrowed his eyes at me.

'Well, that will be all for now. Please don't hesitate to get in touch if you remember anything else.'

'When will I get my phone back?' I asked, trying to stave off the tears I knew were coming, now I'd been called out. My own guilt rushing to the surface, emotion bubbling uncontrollably. I'd never been a good liar.

'As soon as the lab is finished, we'll let you know.' They both stood simultaneously, as though it were a practised move, and I forced myself up on wobbly legs.

DC Tunstall left the room first and I followed, as DI Vincent held the door open. I'd left the blanket over the back of the chair; without it, I felt exposed.

When we reached the front desk, I stood awkwardly.

'Can I use the phone please? I need to call a taxi.' I had no money but knew Mum kept cash in the house, I could get her to run out and pay the driver. It seemed a better idea than asking her to pick me up, she was neurotic at the best of times, and I knew she'd arrive in a flap and bend my ear all the way home.

'Sure,' the desk sergeant replied, pushing the phone across the counter towards me. A sticker on the Perspex screen listed local cab companies and I picked the top one, Aero. I'd used them a few times to get home after a drunken night out.

'Ten minutes,' the operator said once I'd put my request in, and I hung up.

'Thanks,' I said, pushing the phone back across the counter.

Outside, I shivered in the night air, no idea of the time, but I imagined it was around six or seven o'clock. I felt like I'd been in there for hours. The urge to ring Jimmy was overwhelming, but I wasn't stupid enough to use a hidden phone in front of the police station. I wouldn't touch it until I was safely in my bedroom, out of sight of prying eyes. At least now I had an excuse why I hadn't phoned Ali back as I promised I would. With no phone, I couldn't call her. Hearing her anguish was unbearable, knowing I'd caused it.

I could fix it. I just needed to talk to Jimmy. What would I tell him? The truth? I wasn't sure how I could hide it any more. It wouldn't be long before he found out anyway. I'd nearly baulked when DI Vincent said it was going on the news. I wanted to tell him it was a misunderstanding, I'd made an awful mistake, but I could get Eden back safely. All I needed was a little time.

I had a feeling DI Vincent believed I wasn't telling him everything. I had to tread carefully. With me being the last person to see Eden alive as far as the police were concerned, they'd be watching me like a hawk.

21

ALI TOLFREY

'What lead?' I asked, discarding my cigarette into an empty plant pot and following DC Benson back inside, the hit of warmth making me giddy.

'DCI Greene just called. A dog walker has phoned the hotline and reported a man with a blonde child and pushchair being put into a dark red car near the park, at the approximate time the abduction took place. The incident room is searching the local cameras to see if we can pinpoint the car.'

'What happens then?' I asked, eager to know more.

'Once we have the registration, we can run an ANPR check, to track the vehicle's movements using traffic cameras.'

I nodded, buoyed by DC Benson's enthusiasm.

'At least that's something,' Christopher said gruffly. It clearly wasn't the breakthrough he was hoping for, but any positive news was a step in the right direction to getting Eden home.

'Did the dog walker say it looked suspicious?' I asked, the lump in my throat growing with each word. A man had taken our daughter. He'd hit Brooke and snatched Eden from her. It was incomprehensible.

'She was some distance away so couldn't say, but she heard a child crying.'

Oh God, who was this man and what did he want with my child?

'Obviously she was crying, she was in the arms of a bloody stranger,' Christopher said through gritted teeth and poured another glass of wine.

'Go easy, would you,' I said gently, but he glared at me anyway.

'It could be unrelated, but DCI Greene informs me the house-to-house enquiries haven't brought us much in the way of leads so far.'

'I knew it; you had nothing. That's why her name was released to the press.'

'Christopher, calm down,' I snapped, picking up the bottle of wine and taking it over to the sink.

He slumped forward over the table and dissolved into silent tears.

DC Benson looked first at me and then at Christopher, about to speak, but I got in first.

'You don't think there'll be a ransom?'

'We're keeping an open mind, but we would have expected some form of contact by now. In previous cases where there have been ransom demands, they've happened early on.'

I blinked slowly taking it all in. At least with a ransom they'd have reason to keep her alive and unharmed. I shuddered, trying to dispel thoughts so horrific I couldn't let them in. If they settled, I'd go mad.

The phone rang again, and DC Benson picked it up, telling the caller politely that we would not be talking to any journalists.

'Press call, first of many. It might be worth unplugging the landline if it gets too much. We have your mobile numbers if we need to contact you,' he advised.

'Okay,' I replied.

DC Benson straightened his tie and picked his mobile phone up from the side. 'I'm going to head off. I'm on call, so if you need me, I'll be on this number.' He handed me a business card. 'If there are any developments at all, I'll call ahead and come straight round. Otherwise I'll see you in the morning. Try and get some rest.'

Christopher didn't look up.

I showed DC Benson to the door, hoping they weren't giving up on Eden for the night. As he crossed the threshold onto the step, he turned back to face me.

'The incident room will be manned all night. We won't stop until we bring Eden home,' he said, reading my mind.

I gave a solitary nod, wishing I could feel some sort of relief, but it never came.

DC Benson didn't move from the step, the cold air seeped past him into the house as he cast his eyes over me. 'You'll be okay tonight, won't you, Mrs Tolfrey? If you need me, please ring. I can be here in ten minutes.'

I nodded again and smiled weakly. The whole day was like an out-of-body experience and tonight would be no exception. Nothing made sense, it was like watching a horror movie you couldn't turn off.

When I returned to the kitchen, Christopher reached out with one arm, his head still bowed, and pulled me to him. Burying his forehead in my midriff. I stroked his red hair and listened to him cry, unable to offer any words of comfort. I had none to give. We just had to pray Eden would be found before any harm came to her.

What was Brooke doing right now? Still at the station or back home? I should call her again, but something stopped me. I knew I couldn't make the call without saying things I'd later regret. Our relationship couldn't carry on as it once was. She'd never look after Eden again. No one would.

The house was stark and empty, even more so with DC Benson gone, although I'd been desperate for some privacy all day. Untangling myself from Christopher, I recovered the wine bottle and poured the rest into a glass before heading for the stairs.

'I'm going to get in the bath,' I said, my voice low.

He didn't answer.

I didn't want to be around anyone, even the closest person in the world to me, the one who knew me better than anyone. I couldn't hold him up, support him, when I was barely upright myself. Neither of us at our best, we'd never seen each other at our worst, until now. With DC Benson here, it was as though the cracks of our marriage were on show for everyone to see. I dreaded to think what he'd be reporting back, if Christopher was right and him being assigned was as much a look at us as it was an offer of support.

At the top of the stairs, I deliberately averted my eyes from Eden's room, moving ahead into the bathroom and locking the door behind me. The bath took an age to run and I stared at my reflection in the mirror, my usually glossy dark hair looked frizzy and unbrushed. Black panda-like rings caused by smudged mascara adorned my eyes. I was as pale as a ghost, the lines in my face more evident than ever. They multiplied every year.

The doorbell rang and I heard Christopher answer, calling up the stairs a few minutes later, telling me our neighbour, Catherine, had dropped around a lasagne that he'd put in the fridge. I was glad I didn't have to talk to her, I couldn't talk to anyone right now, not about Eden. I just wanted to block it out.

Lowering into the bath, the water a touch too hot, I remembered the morning. How upbeat I'd been, waiting to receive the email I hoped would be good news about the confirmation of publication of my article. Of all the doors it would open for me. Believing I could get my freelancing career back on track, looking forward to being in demand again. It seemed ridiculous. I'd been excited to order a hundred pounds' worth of moisturisers, eager to try them all for the next article. It appeared so frivolous now. There was no point to any of it.

I sank deeper beneath the water until it was up to my chin. What if I disappeared beneath the bubbles and never came up for air? What then? Would I do it if Eden was never found? Without question. I wouldn't live without her. I couldn't; it would be too painful to carry on.

Christopher would cope without me; he'd throw himself into his work. It had always been top priority anyway, the rest of us lagging behind. Perhaps I wasn't being fair, but he'd insisted we put off our life until he'd qualified as a doctor. We could have got married and had a child earlier, but everything always ran to his schedule, not mine. His career took centre stage. I knew he was of the opinion I was going back to work too soon; Eden was too young.

I was waiting for that to be mentioned. Fired at me like a shot. I was to blame as, if I hadn't been working, Brooke wouldn't have taken Eden out. There was no point in hanging on to what could have been. What I could have done differently; if I'd pushed for Brooke to play with Eden at home. If I'd said it was too cold, too damp, for the swings. Perhaps if I hadn't been so wrapped up waiting for the email, I would have taken time to wonder why they weren't home already.

Could Brooke have been in the wrong place at the wrong time? Targeted by an opportunist? It made little sense. More likely and more worryingly, Eden had been chosen, selected and followed. The idea wrenched my insides as though they were being twisted in a vice. The physical pain at being separated from my child, at having no idea where she was sleeping tonight, was torture.

Submerged so the water covered my face, I forced my eyes open, ignoring the sting. A single bubble emerged from my nose and floated to the surface. I balled my hands into fists and waited for my lungs to scream.

DAY TWO
FRIDAY 30TH OCTOBER 2020

7AM – 11AM

22

BROOKE SIMMONS

I'd spent all night trying to phone Jimmy. I must have called around fifty times, but with each try, I got his voicemail. He must have switched his phone off as it didn't even ring any more. Maybe his battery had run out? He could have disappeared and left it behind. I didn't believe he'd still be around here; he must have taken Eden and gone. I didn't leave any messages; he would know I was trying to get hold of him. What the bloody hell was he playing at?

I'd not been able to sleep a wink, instead pacing the carpet of my bedroom until the sun came up. So much I'd created a track in the pile.

I should have been getting on with my bookkeeping coursework. I had a module to submit on Monday, but there was no way I could focus on it. Not with Eden's face all over my Facebook feed. The old Nokia I used for Jimmy didn't have any apps on it, like back in the days when phones were just phones. So when I'd got home, I'd borrowed my mum's laptop to log on to my Facebook account.

The local community were going crazy and I got palpitations

in my chest every time I read another comment. Every new post was something along the lines of *'we're praying for her safe return'*. Each one was a jolt in the gut spiking my pulse and I worried my heart was going to give out as it had been racing all day.

A few people I knew had sent messages to me. Word had spread that I looked after the missing girl, but my name hadn't been mentioned in the news report. I was almost grateful I didn't have my phone, I bet it was bleeping every two minutes at the station, driving them around the bend. I hadn't text Mum when I left there to say I was on my way back home either.

She was jumping up and down when I got back. I'd banged on the door to grab a tenner from her to pay the taxi driver, and she was red-faced and wild-eyed when I returned. As soon as she'd seen Eden's face on the local news she'd freaked out, calling the hospital and police station desperately trying to locate me. She'd worked herself up, panicking as she'd heard I'd been attacked and was worried I hadn't been in touch. It took a lot of apologising and agreeing to let her reheat some shepherd's pie before she'd calmed down.

I'd disappeared upstairs under the guise of having a shower to call Jimmy. It wasn't late the first time I rang; he might have been putting Eden to bed, but after the tenth time, it was clear he didn't want to speak to me. Maybe he didn't want to talk to anyone. I'd ran through the shower, aware Mum was waiting, washing off the grime and hospital smell. I'd made sure to avoid getting my hair wet, the wound still smarted and I'd tried not to touch it, grateful I'd avoided having any of it shaved.

Downstairs I'd taken more painkillers, hoping to further dull the thud at the top of my skull. It felt as though a woodpecker was tapping to get in. A constant reminder all day of the morning's events. Mum had watched me eat, having already had dinner earlier, while pummelling me with questions about what had happened. It was exhausting and as soon as my plate was clear, I'd made excuses to disappear back upstairs.

'I'm so tired, Mum, I really want to sleep,' I'd said, eyeing the clock on the oven.

'Isn't it a bit early? Didn't they say you should stay awake as long as possible in case of concussion?' She'd narrowed her eyes, causing her crow's feet to sink into her skin.

'It's almost nine anyway, and it's been an awful day, I'm desperate for my bed,' I'd replied, imploring her to give me some space.

'Why don't you sit down, and I'll make you a nice cup of tea. Let me keep an eye on you as you've had a nasty whack.' She'd pursed her lips. I knew she wanted to me to sit and watch television with her, as we did every evening. She hovered around whenever I was home, always talking, asking questions. I loved her, but sometimes she was like a fly I wanted to bat away. I wanted to tell her to get her own life and stop interfering in mine.

'Really, Mum, I'm tired. I'm going to go to bed,' I'd said, refusing to be swayed.

'Okay, if you're sure. Shout if you want me to bring you up some hot chocolate,' she'd called to my retreating back.

You wouldn't believe I was twenty-six to hear her talk. It was one of the reasons I was so desperate to move out again. I wasn't only her daughter; I was her entertainment too. Ever since Dad had left when I was a teenager, she'd leaned on me as a social and emotional crutch. Ten years later, nothing had changed.

My mistake was moving back after Karl. When I did, she became even more clingy, almost afraid to let me out of her sight, but what choice did I have? I had no money to get my own place. I'd paid towards the mortgage on Karl's maisonette for months but walked away with nothing. Our split wasn't exactly amicable.

When I found out he was shagging the bitch downstairs, I'd trashed the place.

That was ancient history, I'd reminded myself, and I wouldn't have to put up with Mum for much longer. I had enough for a deposit on a one-bedroom flat. I would have had all of it too, if this morning had gone the way it was supposed to. Instead I'd left the park empty handed and with a hole in my head.

I'd reached gingerly into my hair, feeling the laceration.

I would never have said Jimmy had it in him. He lost his temper occasionally, but who didn't. I never imagined he'd be violent, especially with women. Most of the time he seemed in control of his emotions. Obviously, I was wrong as the little shit could easily have killed me this morning. Taking Eden and leaving me to clear up the mess, he'd confirmed himself to be the arsehole I always thought he was.

I'd crawled into bed grinding my teeth and stared at the ceiling; stomach gurgling as it tried to break down the huge amount of stodge I'd consumed. It strained against the elasticated waist of my pyjama bottoms. There would be no sleep, I knew that.

Despite being pissed off, I had to keep trying Jimmy until he answered or called me back. If Eden was returned home, it would all go away. He'd come out of it all right. No one knew he was involved except for me and I'd never tell. Even when he found out the truth, he'd have as much to lose as I would.

The only way out would be for us to strike a deal, we'd figure out a way for him to bring Eden back without being caught by the police and no one would be any the wiser. He could slip back into his normal life and me to mine. Sure, he'd be pissed, but if anyone was going to face prison time, it was him not me. I had to be smart, make him see sense. With the story now in the press, it was likely to snowball. Every day Eden was missing, it would get bigger. There wasn't much time to sort it out before there'd be no fixing it.

Unable to settle, I'd got up to pace, treading lightly so Mum wouldn't hear my footsteps. My bedroom was above the kitchen, but I could already hear the television blaring in the front room. She'd be watching her soaps, or some lame reality show I had no interest in. I'd dialled again; the phone slippery in my sweaty palm. *Damn it, Jimmy, for fuck's sake, answer your phone.* The annoyingly robotic voicemail had kicked in again and I had to stop myself launching the handset at the wall.

Perhaps I'd try another way. Going back to the laptop I searched for his name on Facebook and found his profile. We weren't friends any longer. He'd unfriended me when he disappeared from my life. When he'd decided our relationship had run its course. I sent a friend request. Maybe he wouldn't answer his phone, but he might pick that up; I had nothing to lose. Even if the police were monitoring my social media accounts, a friend request was harmless, wasn't it? We had a few friends in common, from back when we were together, so it wouldn't look unusual. With the request waiting to be accepted, I'd gone back to pacing, unable to sit still as the minutes ticked by.

My thoughts had turned to Ali and Christopher and my heart had sunk. What must they be going through? I wished I could comfort Ali; tell her it was all going to be okay. Tell them both their daughter was with someone who, through some misguided notion, believed he loved Eden as a daughter. Jimmy would be treating little Eden as the princess she was, for now at least. It was all such a mess and if I could take it back I would.

He'd been pretty hands-on as soon as he found out, wanting to get involved, change nappies, feed her whenever we were together. It was lovely to see, although I wondered how he was coping with her on his own. Eden could be a handful sometimes;

she was headstrong and knew what she wanted. Jimmy had no idea of her routine and toddlers didn't like change. Well, he deserved the sleepless night he'd probably had with her, served him right for stealing her away.

I kicked out at a cushion on the floor, my limbs aching with tiredness. I watched the sun rise through my window, waiting for contact from Jimmy. It didn't come, and I berated myself for being so impetuous. It was my fault, so like me to rush in, make a stupid statement without thinking things through. What on earth possessed me to lie, to palm Eden off as if she was my own child, and why had I let Jimmy believe she was his? I hadn't envisaged the complications of my actions. I never thought he'd do anything so reckless.

Yesterday had been a blur, between the park, the hospital, and the police station, yet the night had ticked by so slowly I felt I was going mad. Whatever happened I had to find Jimmy. Eden had been gone overnight, Ali and Christopher had likely not slept either. My head felt woolly, eyes red and stinging but I couldn't sit still. Mum's alarm had gone off; I heard her shuffle into the bathroom to shower, to get ready for the day. I stayed in my room, waiting for her to leave, unable to face the pitied look she'd have ready for me. I didn't deserve it.

23

JIMMY PEARSON

I woke with a jolt, blinking rapidly, trying to work out where I was. Easing myself up from the carpet, the room came into focus. A stiffness in my neck made me move warily and I rubbed the sore spot at the top of my spine. Eden was curled up next to me, snoring. It had to be past dawn; the sun was peeking through the curtains, although low in the sky. My mind was foggy, like I'd had those beers after all, and I rubbed crusted particles from my eyelashes. Last night had to be up there as one of the worst night's sleep I'd ever had.

The air smelt of sour milk and I wrinkled my nose. Eden had thrown up over a five-hour period into the early hours. Sleeping, then waking and throwing up every last bit of her bottle. I'd given up changing the sheets after the fourth time and put Eden down on a bed of towels, but during the course of the night, she'd got up and joined me on the floor. Her hair was matted with dried vomit and I turned away, stomach churning at the putrid smelling emanating from her.

When she wasn't being sick, she was screaming at the top of her lungs. It was so bad; I nearly took her to the nearest walk-in centre. Had something been wrong with the milk? Had I bought the wrong thing? Or was it her dinner? Was it because I hadn't burped her enough? Her body had purged it all. When I didn't think there could be any more, she'd been sick again. I was clueless, but surely it wasn't normal for a child to produce so much. I'd learned a lot from Brooke over the past six months, but I still felt massively out of my depth being on my own with Eden.

I closed my eyes, wincing as I remembered losing my temper around midnight, coming up the stairs a third time and opening the door to discover a scene which reminded me of *The Exorcist*. I'd picked Eden up, shouted in her face. I cringed at the memory; sure I'd shaken her for a second before I got hold of myself. Terrified she was poorly and overwhelmed by the stress of the situation, I'd lost it. Only for a moment, but it could have been enough to do some real damage.

Afterwards, I'd stayed with her, trying to soothe her cries, talking and singing to her softly because the way she'd looked at me broke my heart in two. Genuine fear plastered across her face. I wasn't Daddy, I was a monster.

My eyes welled up and I blinked the emotion away. I'd make it up to her today. We'd fill the day with fun things – new toys, a playpen and a trip to the nearest park once I'd got my bearings.

I eased myself up, stepping over Eden and picking up the pile of dirty laundry I'd left in the corner. It would be good to have a shower while she was still asleep. I needed to shave my head too.

In the hallway, I checked my phone; it was almost half-past seven. I'd have to move quickly to get everything done. Knowing Eden couldn't get out of her room, I whizzed downstairs and put dirty sheets and towels in the washing machine, praying it had been plumbed in. Everything else in the house seemed to work; it was ready to move in to. There were even Sainsbury's-own detergent capsules under the sink.

When switched on, the machine rumbled and through the door I could see water filling up the drum.

Straining my ears at the bottom of the stairs, I couldn't hear Eden yet; she must still be asleep. I rummaged through my holdall, on the dining room table, for my clippers, and headed out the back door into the freezing morning air.

Shivering and still wearing yesterday's clothes, I stood in my socks and began roughly shaving my head. Feeling my way over each section to check what I'd missed, using my barely there reflection in the kitchen window as a guide.

A dog barked from a neighbouring garden and I moved faster, bending over to make sure I got the base of my head and the top of my neck. It would take some getting used to, especially in the current climate, but a change was necessary. I hadn't had a shaved head since I was a teenager. Back in the Millwall days.

Turning off the clippers and brushing myself down as best I could, I stripped out of my clothes at the back door and flapped them to get rid of any leftover hair. My skin was like ice and I considered making a cup of tea, but I wanted to get in the shower while Eden was still asleep. At least I'd be dressed and ready for the day, plus my back was already itching and would stay that way until I'd washed the hair off.

It was a small victory; I'd managed to have a shower and get dressed before Eden stirred. When I heard her cry, I immediately went to her room, shrinking back as I opened the door and the smell hit me.

'Morning, beautiful,' I said as brightly as I could.

Eden looked at me warily, rubbing her face, perturbed by my new haircut.

'It's Daddy,' I beamed at her. 'Daddy's had a haircut.' I lowered my head down and lifted her hand to pat it.

She pulled away, unimpressed, bottom lip quivering.

'It's okay, Daddy's here. Up?' I said, holding my arms out.

Reluctantly she raised them, not matching my smile.

Once she was in my arms, I opened the window to air the room and put all the towels from the bed in the bathroom. I'd have to check the carpet and the mattress properly later.

'Another bath?' I said, knowing I'd need to wash her hair.

She turned away, not wanting to look at me.

Once I'd cleaned Eden up and put her in a boy's jumpsuit, her mood seemed to improve. I gave her dry biscuits and water for breakfast, fearing milk may have the same reaction as last night. She scoffed them quickly and I anxiously waited to see if they made a reappearance. We watched CBeebies in the front room all morning while she climbed over me, running the palm of her hand over my head, still unsure of my new look.

'Mamamamamama,' she called.

'Daddy,' I replied as I checked my phone. The news apps hadn't reported Eden was missing and it was almost eleven. Perhaps it still hadn't made it to the national news? That could only be a good thing. It meant no one was looking for me here, not in Nottingham.

'Mama,' Eden screeched as she whacked the top of my head. Her palm had blistered and popped in the night, leaving angry red skin beneath, but it didn't appear to bother her. I applied more Savlon, rubbing it in gently.

'Mama isn't here, Daddy's here,' I said, trying to hide my irritability.

Eden crawled away to play with her cups.

I turned my attention back to my phone, this time to check Facebook. Hundreds of comments had been added on the Reigate and Redhill abduction post but none that stood out. There was no reference to me. My name hadn't been mentioned in any of them. I scratched my chin, eyebrows squashed together.

Weird, wasn't it? Brooke still hadn't given me up, not publicly anyway, and there was no mention anyone had been hurt. If I'd caused her any serious damage, wouldn't it have been reported? Maybe she didn't want to get me in trouble, but if that was the case why report Eden missing at all? Why had it been on the local news? Nothing made any sense and up here I was out of the loop. I had no visibility on the situation, I was stuck in a bubble.

My phone vibrated in my hand, warning me the battery was running low. On the Facebook app, I noticed the tiny friends icon had a red dot beside it I hadn't spotted until now. I had a friend request. With my finger lingering over the icon, I could hear my pulse thud in my ears. I already had an idea who had friended me. I clicked the link and Brooke's profile picture popped up. The rest of her information unavailable.

I closed my eyes, letting out a long sigh. She was alive.

24

ALI TOLFREY

I sat on the cushioned window seat in the bedroom, wrapped in my cashmere shawl, nursing an espresso. It was barely seven in the morning and my eyes stung from lack of sleep. I stared at the frost patterns on the cars in the street below, silently praying Eden was safe and warm inside somewhere.

DC Benson hadn't called or returned to the house during the night. It was gone two in the morning before Christopher and I had headed to bed, but sleep was futile. Every time I'd closed my eyes, all I could see was Eden's tear-streaked face, calling out to me. I couldn't bear it and had cried until my eyes were so puffy, they were almost swollen shut.

When morning came, I'd felt like I'd been through the wringer. Christopher had slept for some of the night, no doubt helped by the two empty bottles of red wine by the kitchen sink. It would have been so easy to sink into a blissful drunken coma, but it'd be a betrayal. We had to be present, on standby, ready to do whatever the police required. Eden needed us and I wasn't going to let her down.

I scowled at the snoring lump beneath the duvet. Dependable

Christopher, so bloody good in a crisis. Except for this crisis. How he slept I didn't know. Didn't he care?

I shook the thought from my head, I was being ridiculous. Of course, he cared, he doted on Eden. Lack of sleep was sending my mind to dark places I didn't want to visit. Projecting the blame and resentment onto him because I couldn't shoulder it alone.

My mobile buzzed, it had been on all night. Messages had flooded through since the news report. Well wishes from friends and ex-colleagues, people offering help and food parcels. We'd had to take the landline off the hook. I'd even managed a strained conversation with my mother, who'd launched into the call asking how I could have been so stupid as to let Eden out of my sight.

With a sigh, I picked up the phone, expecting more texts of support. I was surprised to see DC Benson's number pop up.

Will pick you up at nine, press conference arranged for eleven.

I gasped and moved across to the bed to nudge Christopher, mouth gaping in sleep, his lips a purple hue from the wine.

'Christopher, get up, we've got to get ready,' I hissed as he moaned and rolled over. Tutting loudly, I downed my coffee, needing all the caffeine I could get and headed for a shower.

* * *

At quarter to nine, Christopher sat in the front room, on the edge of the sofa, waiting for DC Benson to arrive. We'd argued over what to wear. Initially I'd put on a black dress, but he'd sniped it looked like I was in mourning. To appease him, I chose, instead, a navy turtle-necked jumper and beige wide-legged trousers. When I descended the stairs for a second time, he rolled his eyes at me.

The Babysitter

'You look too put together,' he said flatly.

'What's that supposed to mean?' I snapped. In contrast, he looked like he'd fallen out of bed.

'We're the parents of a child who has been abducted. You look like you're going on a talk show!'

'If I were you, I would be more worried about last night's wine leaking out of your pores. Perhaps a bit of aftershave would be an idea,' I retorted, eyes stinging with oncoming tears. *Bastard.* Always so bloody concerned with our outward appearance, never mind what was going on beneath.

He stalked upstairs as the doorbell rang.

I grabbed a tissue and dabbed my eyes before opening the door. DC Benson and DCI Greene were standing on the doorstep.

'Come in,' I said, stepping aside.

When Christopher returned looking slightly less bedraggled, a waft of woody scent in the air, DCI Greene gave us an update.

'A CRA was invoked yesterday. It stands for Child Rescue Alert and means we're seeking the assistance of the media and the public in the search for Eden. Dedicated call centres have been set up overnight to filter the incoming calls as soon as the press conference has taken place. We've also issued an All Ports Warning, circulating Eden's photo and description to every airport, port and international railway station for them to be on the lookout.' DCI Greene's face was stern, her eyes focused on us in turn.

'Okay,' Christopher said, his voice strained.

'On arrival at headquarters, where we're holding the press conference, DC Benson will help you write a short statement, which I'll sign off on. Our aim is to appeal to the public for witnesses and directly to the person who has Eden.'

'Are you sure this won't force their hand?' Christopher asked, his eyes boring into DCI Greene's determined face.

'We don't believe this is a kidnap for financial gain, we're hoping to appeal to the conscience of Eden's captor,' she said, her voice unwavering despite Christopher scoffing.

'You better bloody hope so.'

I closed my eyes briefly and gave my head a little shake, squirming in my husband's rudeness.

Unaffected, DCI Greene met my gaze and gave me a tempered smile before speaking. 'I think if you're able, Mrs Tolfrey, you should read the statement. Do you think you're up to it?'

I glanced at Christopher, who nodded, my hands already shaking.

'Okay,' I managed.

'Right, let's get on our way. We're heading to Guildford to the police headquarters.'

The car journey was fractious. Christopher tried to pump DCI Greene for information on the investigation, leads that had been followed and what had been ruled out. Both of us desperate to know what was going on with the search for our child. I understood there was only so much she could say, but it frustrated Christopher that he wasn't permitted to know exactly what they were doing. I wasn't surprised, he was such a control freak. I wanted to know what was happening too, but we had to let the police do their job, we had to put our faith in them to find Eden.

DCI Greene told us they were still searching for the car, having found a number of dark red vehicles on various CCTV collected in the area. Now they were painstakingly trying to locate every car and its owner, not knowing if any of them were the one the witness had reported seeing.

It sounded long and drawn out, nothing seemed to move very fast and every hour that passed amplified the fear that we'd never see Eden again. I stared out of the window, last night's pasta threatening to make a reappearance. The last time I'd felt so dreadful was on the way to my father's funeral. I remembered fidgeting in the back seat of the car, wishing I could be anywhere else. Just like then, I had to grit my teeth and get through it.

I reached out and squeezed Christopher's hand despite my annoyance at his behaviour. He squeezed it back, reinforcing we were a team. It was us against the rest of the world and together we were stronger.

It took forty minutes to write the statement and two strong cups of coffee in a side room at the police headquarters. There were things Christopher wanted to add and he clashed with DCI Greene, who insisted we didn't want to give away too much inside knowledge of the case to the press. Some information was kept back, so if the kidnapper did contact the Crimestoppers number, they would easily be able to identify them amongst any imposters.

The closer it got to eleven, the more I began to sweat. Sick with nerves, grateful I hadn't eaten anything. Under my arms were damp, hindered by the lambswool I'd chosen to wear. My neck was itchy beneath the fabric and I kept tugging at it as Christopher frowned.

'Stop fidgeting,' he whispered, before his voice softened, 'it'll be over soon.' It was all right for him; he didn't have to say anything. He wasn't expected to cry on camera, as if any mother could convey how much they loved their child in words, or even the volume of tears.

There was a hive of activity in the corridor. The sound of heavy doors slamming in the distance and thudding footsteps that quickened as the clock edged closer to eleven. At five to, DCI Greene placed her hand on my back and smiled at me encouragingly.

'Mrs Tolfrey, we should take our seats. You'll be fine, don't worry. I'll wrap it up as soon as you've read the statement.' She appeared confident, wearing a forest green trouser suit which was much more feminine than the last outfit I saw her in.

Christopher held my hand as we left the room and my heart seemed to rattle in my chest as I walked. Steeling myself as DC Benson pushed open the door, I wasn't prepared for the onslaught of camera flashes and scuffle of chairs.

I found my seat in the middle of the oblong table, a poster-sized photo of Eden on the screen behind us. Blinking the lights away, I counted around thirty people sat in rows in front of us.

They eyed me curiously, some with expressions of pity, and I struggled to return their gaze. It was like holding a mirror up to my pain. Instead I looked down at the folded statement in my hand. The room fell silent, atmosphere electric as the press waited for someone to speak.

'Good morning, my name is DCI Greene and I'm here with Christopher and Alison Tolfrey to make an appeal to the general public for information on the whereabouts of their one-year-old missing daughter, Eden Tolfrey, who was taken from Bushy Park, Reigate, yesterday morning at approximately eleven o'clock.' DCI Greene looked at me and I swallowed the lump in my throat and spoke with a wobbly voice.

'It's been twenty-four hours since my daughter Eden was taken from us. There must be someone out there who knows where she is and can help the police find her.' I managed the first sentence before I couldn't control the wracking sobs that heaved through me.

11AM – 2PM

25

JIMMY PEARSON

I imagined Brooke was trying to get hold of me, calling the old number, and had resorted to friending me on Facebook to prod me to get in touch. I pondered whether to accept her request or let it hang. She had no idea where I was, and I wanted to keep it that way. Now I knew I hadn't hurt her badly; I could focus my energy on my daughter and keeping her safe.

'Shall we go shopping?' I asked Eden, who was busy gumming the remote control. I'd put her in a green and grey jumpsuit and a tiny fleece-lined denim jacket. She looked much more like an Eddie than an Eden in that outfit. Perfect for a trip out in public. There had been no regurgitation of her breakfast biscuits and to look at her you wouldn't think she'd been up all night being sick. The smell in the bedroom still lingered, but at least the sheets and towels had been washed and were drying in the machine.

I packed the change bag and buggy into the car, which I'd left on the driveway overnight, and we made our way into Nottingham. I'd programmed the satnav for the Intu Shopping Centre, which I'd found after googling, but I couldn't help my anxiety about our trip. I rubbed at my smooth face, the silky skin alien as I stopped at some traffic lights and contemplated whether we should be going. Exposing ourselves out in the open so early on. There were things I needed, but I couldn't pretend they were essential. A playpen wasn't life or death.

I reasoned my name and photo hadn't been released yet, I hadn't seen it on the television or the internet. No one was looking for me or Eden in Nottingham and they certainly weren't looking for a father and son. Plus, the town was massive, with a population of over 300,000 people. The shopping centre would be busy, and I'd be just another face morphing into the crowd.

When we reached the centre, I pulled on my cap and got Eden out of the car and into the buggy. The first port of call was Boots, so I could pick up more food, wipes, ready-made formula in cartons and other baby supplies. I spent ages reading the backs of the packets, making sure everything was age appropriate and I chose a different formula. I didn't want a repeat performance of last night. In the toy aisle, Eden's eyes lingered on a red fire engine, so I bought that too. It made her look more boyish, and she waved it at passers-by from her buggy.

'He's gorgeous!' A young shop assistant with pink hair and a nose ring beamed at Eden from over the counter in Argos.

'Cheers, he's a little devil, aren't you, Ed,' I said with a wink, giving Eden's cheek a gentle squeeze.

I watched as the girl retrieved the playpen and jumperoo, realising I'd have to head straight back to the car to put them in the boot. I hadn't thought through manoeuvring with large boxes and a buggy.

Everything was more difficult with a buggy. Navigating one-handed while I tried to push Eden to the lifts all the time balancing the boxes on the hood. How single parents managed a weekly shop I'd never know.

Eventually I got back to the car, a sheen of sweat on my skin, feeling like I'd done an assault course. Enough was enough, we'd head home and anything we'd forgotten would have to wait until tomorrow. It was nearly lunchtime anyway and Eden would be grisly before long if she wasn't fed.

The morning had gone well, and I was in a good mood, until I pulled into the driveway and saw Georgina, in another Lycra outfit waiting at the front door.

She turned at the sound of the car and grinned, bouncing on the balls of her feet. My heart sank, but I smiled politely and opened the car door.

'Oh, I'm so glad you're back, you don't have any jump leads, do you?'

'Umm hi, yeah sure, can't you get started?' I answered without thinking. Dad always had jump leads; he was a man of every eventuality. I should have lied, it was stupid to engage, but there was no way I could refuse a damsel in distress. Not one with an ass like that.

'No, I'm heading out to hot yoga and the bloody Lexus won't start. I think I may have left the lights on.'

'Where's your husband?' I asked, moving around to the boot, spying the gold band on her left hand.

'He's working abroad, Mexico this month, he moves all over.' She fluttered her eyelashes and I had to stifle a giggle. If I wanted an easy lay, she would be willing, that much was obvious.

I opened the boot; Eden was already whining as the car had stopped but she hadn't been let out yet. I moved aside the buggy and boxes and found Dad's jump leads wrapped neatly at the back. He always was so organised.

I turned around and looked for the Lexus, quickly spotting it on the driveway opposite.

'I'll drive up to the car.' I smiled.

'Great, thank you,' she said, turning to sashay across the road.

I watched her go, relishing the twitch from the inside of my trousers.

'Can't you think of anything other than your dick,' I reprimanded myself as I slid back into the car and put it in reverse.

Five minutes later, Georgina's engine was running, and I bent down to talk to her through her driver's window.

'Turn all your lights on, radio, fan, everything, on your journey as it'll give it a little charge. It may mean your battery is on the way out though.'

'Thank you so much, you're a knight in shining armour. Are you around later, perhaps I could bring over a bottle to say thanks?' She reached out and touched my forearm with her painted pink nails.

'Yeah sure,' I replied before I had a chance to check myself. What harm could a little action do? Eden would be in bed and I was only human after all.

Getting back in my car, I winked at Georgina as I reversed off the drive so she could leave.

'Early night for you tonight, Ed.' I chuckled into the rear-view mirror as Eden scowled. Her red fire engine had been thrown into the footwell and she kicked her legs in annoyance as I waited for the garage door to open so I could reverse inside.

It took all of five minutes to realise it had been a stupid idea to agree to Georgina coming over. This place hardly looked like somewhere a toddler lived. There was no high chair, no cot and a distinct lack of safety gates. She'd sniff a rat and there was no way some sort was going to be my downfall. I'd have to cancel, come up with an excuse why she couldn't come inside despite the prospect of some action. It was a shame but there'd be other opportunities. For once I had to think with my head.

As I prepared lunch, I remembered I hadn't bought a proper seat for Eden to eat in so resorted to the buggy in the kitchen again. It didn't matter, we'd make do. As soon as she'd eaten, we played in the front room with CBeebies on in the background, as I built the playpen and jumperoo.

'There! So, if I need to do something now, you can stay in there,' I said, lifting Eden into the playpen and scattering her cups and other toys at her feet. Almost immediately she started to cry and pulled herself up to standing, wobbling the sides, which I worried would collapse. Ignoring her tantrum, I cleared up lunch and wiped down the buggy.

The news would be on any minute and I wanted to catch it. Eden had quietened, her red face straining in the corner of the playpen as she tried to poo standing. I turned the television over to ITV and sat on the sofa. Running across the bottom of the screen in yellow capitals was Missing Child. It was happening. Saliva rushed onto my tongue and I gagged, fearing I might be sick as the newsreader introduced the press conference and four people I didn't recognise filtered in to sit behind a long table.

Who were they? Where was Brooke? I thought at first it was a coincidence until the camera zoomed in on the large poster of Eden, the same photo I'd seen on Facebook.

A woman held a piece of paper, she had long dark hair and a made-up face. Pretty, although she looked like she'd be high maintenance. As soon as she spoke, her plummy voice wobbling, my chest burned with impending vomit.

'It's been twenty-four hours since my daughter, Eden, was taken from us. There must be someone out there who knows where she is and can help the police find her.'

She broke off, choked, and they gave her a second to gain her composure.

My mouth gaped and I didn't hear the rest, only ringing in my ears as Eden screamed from the playpen and launched one of her stacking cups over the other side. I looked at Eden and then back to the screen, my molars clenching.

'Who the fuck are you?' I said to the television through gritted teeth.

26

BROOKE SIMMONS

I floated through the morning, hung-over due to lack of sleep. Thankfully, Mum left early to go to school and the once full table had been cleared. The entire kitchen had been packed with Halloween arts and crafts she'd gathered for the kids in her class to do as a Friday afternoon treat. It was the last day of term and they were excited at the prospect of trick or treating at the weekend, getting all hyped up on sugary treats. Mum said the kids were restless and needed the break; she was looking forward to a few days off too.

Halloween fell on a Saturday and I'd been invited to a fancy-dress party at Lisa's house, although I couldn't possibly go. It wouldn't be good to be seen out partying whilst Eden was still missing. A shame, as I already had my outfit in the wardrobe upstairs. I was going as Sarah Sanderson, one of the witches from the film *Hocus Pocus*. I had my dress, stripy tights, and blonde wig at the ready, but I'd have to save it for next year. At least I wouldn't have Mum breathing down my neck, telling me not to drink too much and wanting to know what time I'd be home.

I couldn't be bothered to get dressed, it was too much effort and I wasn't convinced my muscles would comply. Thankfully my head didn't ache any longer, although the skin was tight around the wound and itched a little. I sat in front of the television in my pyjamas and dressing gown, curtains still shut even though it was gone eleven. Ignoring the world outside while I worked out what to do.

Jimmy hadn't accepted or rejected my Facebook friend request, and his phone was still going to voicemail. It had to have been switched off or maybe he hadn't taken it with him?

I was supposed to be starting the night shift at Tesco later, but I'd called in sick with Lorraine as soon as I'd woken up. She was the head of our department and I'd caught her in a good mood. During our brief conversation, there was no mention of the abduction and I had no idea if she knew about it. I'd told her I'd had an accident and had been treated at the hospital yesterday but would be back for my shift on Sunday. My record was exemplary, so she didn't question me further.

I'd brought Mum's laptop down from my bedroom as, while she was out, I had no need to stay in my room. Facebook was still buzzing with Eden's disappearance; internet sleuths were on the case, coming up with outlandish conspiracy theories. I was sure it wouldn't be long before someone suggested she'd been abducted by aliens.

Around lunchtime, I ate some toast and put a load of washing on. Mum would be in a good mood if she came home and it looked like I hadn't sat around creating a mess all day; her going on was something I could do without. I was hoovering when the text from her came through.

Turn on ITV!

I ditched the hoover and turned on the television, catching the end of a press conference where Ali and Christopher filled the screen. Ali looked wretched, mascara striped her face and she looked a shell of the confident woman I knew. Christopher's eyes were red-rimmed and glazed over as though he was there in body but that was all.

A rush of guilt smacked me, seeing the grief I'd caused with my own eyes. They looked utterly broken. I'd created a tornado that had ripped through their lives. A terrible thing, which had spiralled out of control.

Now the news was national, the cat was well and truly out of the bag. Jimmy would be getting in touch as soon as he'd seen it, but I had no idea what to tell him. The planned conversation I'd had in my head where we'd been calm and I'd explained everything would be replaced with Jimmy screaming down the phone at me. Shouting that I was a lying bitch.

I looked online for a link to the press conference, which I found on the ITV website. Watching it again, seeing Ali and Christopher so visibly devastated made me sick to my stomach. How could I have done that to them? She'd trusted me, had been there for me at my darkest hour. My chest ached with repulsion. How could I ever make amends?

I stood, limbs shaky, and debated whether to walk to Ali's house. My car was still there from yesterday morning, my keys left on the window ledge in the hall, but it was around half an hour's walk and I wasn't sure I was up to it. Perhaps I could get a bus. It would mean I could get my side of the story in first, appeal to Ali's good nature. Christopher wouldn't be so easy to get around. He wouldn't understand at all, but there was a chance Ali might.

The old phone buzzed, vibrating loudly from where I'd left it on the kitchen table. A number I didn't recognise on the caller display. The back of my neck prickled. Was it Jimmy? I stared until it rung off, unable to decide whether to answer or not. Only Jimmy had the number, so it had to be him. I picked it up, bleeping in my hand. I had a voicemail message. I dialled and heard a deep muffled voice.

'What the fuck, Brooke,' Jimmy growled before the line went dead.

I swallowed the influx of saliva in my mouth, making me queasy. He'd seen the news.

The phone rang again, vibrating in my hand, and I jumped. Steeling myself to answer, I was interrupted by a hammering on the door. It sounded aggressive, like a courier on a timed delivery run or an angry neighbour. I stared at the door and then the phone. Jimmy had rung out again. In a panic, I switched the phone off and thrust it down the back of the sofa, stepping away as though it was a bomb about to go off.

The banging started up again, whoever it was, wasn't going to be ignored.

I retied my dressing gown and went to the door. An overwhelming sensation of dread clinging to me.

'Good afternoon, Miss Simmons, I hope you remember me, I'm Detective Constable Tunstall. My colleague and I interviewed you yesterday at Reigate station.' The slim blonde stood on the step, her breath producing crisp white streams in the air. The pale pink lipstick had been replaced by a nude one, but she still looked glamorous in a taupe fitted coat. Behind her, a uniformed officer I'd not seen before looked around the street, like he was her bodyguard.

I glanced down at my robe, hiding my pyjamas beneath, and ran a hand through my unbrushed hair self-consciously, wincing when my fingers skimmed the wound.

'Yes, I remember, what's happened? Have you found Eden?'

'No, not yet, but we'd like you to come back to the station to answer a few more questions.' She smiled politely and I froze, feeling like my body was shutting down as the seconds went on. 'Would that be okay; we can take you now?' DC Tunstall pushed, a quizzical look on her face.

'Umm, sure. Let me go and get dressed.'

I began closing the door, but DC Tunstall edged closer.

'Can we wait inside? It's freezing out here.' She smiled sweetly and I agreed, even though internally I was screaming. I didn't want them rummaging around while I was upstairs. What if they found the phone? Thank God I'd hidden it before I went to the door.

I took the stairs two at a time, quickly spraying deodorant and pulling on some leggings and a long jumper. I tied my hair up and cleaned my teeth in record time, trying to listen to the muffled voices below. They hadn't moved from the front room. DC Tunstall would surely be eyeing the laptop I'd left open on the sofa, the local Facebook group for Reigate and Redhill on the screen. Thank God it wasn't Jimmy's profile I'd left in view.

What questions did they have for me? Had they found something on my phone? Had Jimmy seen the news and given himself up? The hairs on my arms and neck stood to attention as adrenaline coursed through my veins. I had no idea whether the game was up and once I'd arrived at the station I'd be arrested.

I had to talk to Jimmy, but that wasn't going to happen. I couldn't risk taking the Nokia to the station, even if I distracted them out of the front room to retrieve it from the back of the sofa. What if I was searched when I got there? My stomach churned. I hated not knowing what was about to happen and had to remind myself to remain unruffled, in appearance if nothing else. I hadn't been exposed yet.

I grabbed my bag and the spare key from the kitchen and found DC Tunstall looking at photos on the mantelpiece. I met her eye and smiled weakly. The voice in my head repeating, *You don't know anything, you didn't see anyone.* That was my story and I had to stick to it.

27

ALI TOLFREY

The drive back from Guildford was quiet, no one was speaking in the car. I dabbed at my mascara-clumped eyes, overwhelmed at having to speak at the press conference. I'd always been reasonably confident, but in the face of Eden's disappearance and under the spotlight of reporters and the eyes of the rest of the world, I'd crumpled as soon as I spoke. I'd struggled through the statement, my voice breaking. Christopher had stared blankly at the crowd of press, but kept hold of my hand, squeezing it gently.

I was concerned he'd switched off emotionally as he couldn't cope with the pressure. He looked dead behind the eyes and I was glad he didn't speak. I didn't want him to come off cold, detached from the situation, and I was worried DCI Greene had come to the same conclusion. There was no point in getting angry, everyone dealt with stress in different ways. I was a crier, always had been. Christopher, on the other hand, when faced with anything difficult, opened a bottle of red wine and became a closed book.

The press had asked some questions at the end, although I didn't absorb them. All I could hear were clicks of photographs being taken. DCI Greene had answered a couple of questions but shut down the reporters quickly and we'd made our escape. I wanted to be at home, everywhere else felt wrong. I needed to be where Eden last was and I prayed the press conference would achieve what DCI Greene hoped. That whoever had her would see how her absence was destroying us, grow a conscience and bring her home.

Afterwards, as we were about to get into the car, she'd placed her hand on my arm.

'Don't give up hope. We will find her,' she'd said, eyes boring into mine. As soon as the words were out, she looked like she'd regretted saying them. Her lips had squeezed tightly together to avoid any more promises spilling out. I knew she wasn't supposed to make them, but her words gave me comfort none the less.

My mobile had been going crazy; it was set to silent but buzzed continuously. A continuous deluge of missed calls and text messages of support. I should put an out of office on the email I used for work, but I couldn't bear to log on. I had no interest in hearing from anyone except for the police, hopefully with news of Eden's discovery.

I knew she was still alive, in my heart, I knew. A mother's connection was like no other. A mother knew. She was still with me, out there somewhere. Someone had her. Eden was the brightest little star, and someone wanted her sparkle, they needed her to light up their world like she lit up ours. I refused to believe otherwise; it would kill me to contemplate any darker reason for her disappearance.

DC Benson sat in the front seat, and almost as though he could bear the silence no longer, he spoke. 'I think that went well. It was heartfelt and emotional. Anyone watching would be in no doubt how much you love your daughter.' His words were clunky and awkward.

I turned towards him and managed a feeble smile. Christopher stared out of the window, seemingly broken.

'We'll receive a massive influx of calls to the hotline as a result, more witnesses may come forward and generate new leads. With any luck, she'll be delivered to a hospital or police station.'

'What happened with the car the witness saw, the dark red one?' I asked.

'We have a list of possible vehicles, all of which were picked up on CCTV locally yesterday. The team are going through the process of eliminating them. As you can imagine, it takes time, there's a large number of owners to contact and verify their whereabouts.'

I looked back out of the window, contemplating how many dark red cars were on that list, how many could there be in Reigate?

'It's lots of knocking on doors, which is why results aren't always instant, but the team is on it. It's a good lead,' DC Benson said, injecting enthusiasm into his tone.

We arrived home just before one and I was surprised to find myself hungry. I made toasted cheese and pesto paninis for the three of us, while DC Benson made tea. We bustled around the kitchen and I had to remind myself he was an outsider in the house. Despite my reservations, I was slowly warming to him being there. At least he had a presence.

Christopher still hadn't said a word, he'd slumped onto the sofa as soon as we were through the door and put the news channel on.

'Are you okay?' I asked, delivering a panini and cup of tea to the coffee table.

'I can't understand it. Why? Why would someone do this to us? Why were we targeted?'

I sighed and wrapped my arms around myself, his words hung in the air. 'I don't know, Christopher; I have no idea, but we must remain positive. She'll be returned to us; I know it.'

Christopher looked at me scornfully before taking a bite of his panini.

Ruffled by his hostility, I returned to the kitchen and joined DC Benson at the breakfast bar.

My eyes were heavy, pure exhaustion, as I watched DC Benson tear through his lunch at breakneck speed. I wasn't sure I had the energy to lift mine from the plate now I'd sat. My muscles seemed to have turned to mush.

DC Benson frowned, taking in my stature. 'Why don't you try and get some sleep. I'll get Christopher to wake you if I hear anything from DCI Greene or the team.'

I took a bite of the panini, the Gruyère cheese oozing out.

Eating would surely make me feel better. I had to keep my energy up for when Eden was home.

'Yes, I might,' I replied, as I looked through the double doors back at Christopher, watching him frown at the television, flicking through the news channels.

'Have you heard from Brooke? Is she okay?' I asked, turning to face DC Benson and keeping my voice low.

'I believe she is back at the station being interviewed.' His tone was measured, and my ears pricked up at the change in his normal affable demeanour. He shifted in his seat; aware he was under the microscope as I narrowed my eyes.

'Interviewed for what?'

'More information gathering.'

'Didn't you do that yesterday?'

'Yes, but the team have more questions for her as I understand.'

My nostrils flared, his overly breezy tone heightening my

suspicions. What could Brooke know that she hadn't already told them? There was no way she could be involved in Eden's disappearance.

She did want a baby of her own, the voice in my head piped up, playing devil's advocate.

Yes, she did, but not enough to steal someone else's! How crazy would a person have to be? Plus, if by some mad stretch of the imagination she did, how on earth did she think she'd be able to get away with it? It was ludicrous if she was a suspect. Not to mention, she had a pretty nasty bang to the head, according to what DC Benson had said. Was I to believe that was self-inflicted?

I finished the panini, taking small bites and chewing slowly, thoughts racing. Christopher's glazed eyes stared at the television; I wasn't even sure he was seeing anything. What was he thinking about? I couldn't share the seed which had been sown with him, he'd fly off the handle, but there had to be a reason Brooke was back at the station.

For the hundredth time, I wracked my mind, going over yesterday morning's events. Brooke seemed fine; I barely saw her for more than fifteen minutes. She was her normal chirpy self, picking Eden up and swirling her into the air as she squealed. Brooke had pulled the buggy out from under the stairs as I knelt in front of Eden, holding her steady. I remembered her checking her watch. Why would she check the time? Was she meeting someone? They'd left soon after and I remembered, as guilt surged through me, being relieved when the house was quiet, so I could get on without Eden demanding my attention. I bit my lip and moved to put my plate in the dishwasher, glancing at DC Benson's back. Should I tell him? Was I remembering it right, did Brooke look at her watch or had I imagined it?

'I'm going for a lie down,' I said to no one in particular and, head whirring, climbed the stairs to Eden's bedroom.

28

JIMMY PEARSON

Eden was bawling in her playpen as I paced the room, my fingers locked behind my head. What the fuck was going on? Who the hell were those people? Pretending to be Eden's parents! They couldn't be. I was Eden's Dad.

My brain fizzed like a rocket about to launch. The room whirled and my vision blurred until I stopped moving, forcing air into my lungs.

I stared at Eden, who was shaking the sides of the playpen, snot streaming from her nose. She was my child, she even looked like me. We had the same colour eyes, although hers were lighter. I was blond as a baby too. No, she was mine. Whoever they were on the television were fake, imposters.

I lifted Eden up and jiggled her in my arms as I walked around the room. She stopped crying almost immediately, gripping my shoulders with her chubby little fingers. I'd scared her when I'd shouted at the television and kicked the change bag across the room, its contents spilling out onto the carpet. I had to learn to control my temper.

She sucked in snatched breaths, and I whispered in her ear to soothe her.

'It's okay, everything is going to be okay. Daddy's here.' I rubbed her back in a circular motion, her little body hot against mine where she'd worked herself up.

I went back to pacing, trying to calm myself, but I was all over the place, like the rug had been pulled out from beneath my feet. Why wasn't Brooke on television pleading for Eden's return? Was the photo they displayed definitely Eden, or did the child just look like her? No, it was too much of a coincidence, it had to be Eden's photo. I chewed at my lip. Something was very wrong.

Leaning down with one hand, I grabbed the phone off the sofa and dialled Brooke's number, easing Eden back onto the floor. She crawled away and found Sophie the Giraffe to chew on. The phone rang a few times before going to voicemail.

'What the fuck, Brooke!' I hissed down the phone, keeping my eyes on Eden.

There has to be a mistake. You couldn't have taken another couple's baby, I told myself. *Eden is yours.*

If I could just speak to Brooke, I was sure there had to be a simple explanation.

I dialled again, staring down at Eden's watery eyes. She looked like she was going to cry, but I needed a minute. Just one fucking minute. The contents of the change bag were spread over the carpet and Sophie the Giraffe had been discarded for the tube of Savlon. I took it out of her hands and opened a packet of cheese puffs, lifting her back into the playpen and handing them over.

I had to think rationally. What fucked-up mess had I got myself into? I wished Dad was here, he'd know what to do. Always calm in the face of a crisis, like when my brother, Eric, broke his ankle on the football field. Dad was a cool as a cucumber even though the rest of us were like headless chickens.

The call to Brooke went to voicemail again. Grinding my

teeth, I opened the Facebook app and accepted Brooke's friend request. Perhaps there was a problem with her mobile. I sent a message via the app, a simple 'hi'. I didn't want to scare her off and I didn't know who would be looking at her account. Perhaps the police were already monitoring her social media, or mine? I shuddered at the thought, any minute now I could get a knock on the door.

No, they had no idea where I was. No clue I was in Nottingham, three hours away from where Brooke lived. The house was in my dad's company's name, not even his name. It would take time to trace, although it wasn't impossible. We hadn't planned to stay more than a couple of nights anyway. The airplane ticket to Australia on Sunday was growing more appealing by the second, but I didn't see why I had to run. I didn't want to leave Eden behind. It had always been a last resort. Fuck. What was I going to do?

The Facebook Redhill and Reigate group had a new post with a link to the press conference. Leaving Eden in the playpen, I stepped over the mess on the carpet and into the kitchen, her constant babbling was driving me crazy and I had to concentrate. I clicked on the link through to the ITV web page. Eden's name in large capital letters. Her last name wasn't Tolfrey, she was Simmons. Brooke and I even talked about her taking my last name, Pearson. I wanted her to change it, to have my name. Who the hell was Eden Tolfrey anyway?

Propping the phone up against the kettle, I bent over, chewing the skin around my thumbnail as I watched the two strangers' plea for the safe return of my daughter. The woman looked grief-stricken; she had to pause mid statement to get her shit together. In contrast, the man beside her had nothing going on behind the eyes. He looked like a leaky streak of piss, and not much of a man to me. Had Brooke given Eden up for adoption or something?

Were these her foster parents? I couldn't see much of a resemblance, but the woman had dark eyes like mine, like Eden's.

I rewound the video, dragging my finger across the screen, the fire in my belly bubbling out of control. What the fuck was going on? My head spun and after the third watch, I scribbled the hotline number onto a scrap of paper, electricity surging through my veins. I was her father, no one else and I was going to fucking tell them! I hadn't kidnapped her, she was mine. I had every right to take my daughter wherever I wanted. Brooke couldn't fucking take her away from me. Those posh pricks wouldn't either, over my dead body.

Before I had a chance to consider it fully, I dialled the number and a man picked up within three rings.

'Crimestoppers,' he began in a deep throaty voice.

'She's mine,' I snarled, interrupting him.

'I'm sorry, can you repeat that?'

'She's mine. Eden is *my* daughter. Not theirs and I'm not bringing her back. She's my flesh and blood. I'm her father, not that ginger cunt on the television.' I hung up. The call only lasted a few seconds and I doubted they'd be able to trace anything.

Rage bubbled up, like a pan boiling over, and I punched a kitchen cabinet, wood splintering away, leaving a gash running through the middle. It made me feel better for a second, until I saw the blood on my knuckles.

'Fuck's sake, Jimmy,' I spat, running it under a cold tap and wrapping a tea towel over the split and tying it around my hand.

It was only then I realised how quiet it was. Too quiet, although I reasoned Eden was in her playpen, what harm could she do in there? To be sure, I returned to the lounge to check, only to find Eden on her knees, red-faced, eyes bulging, gasping for air. Her orangey fingers waving for help as she choked for breath.

29

BROOKE SIMMONS

It was the same interview room as before, just as cold, and I was glad I'd put on a jumper. A cream thread had come loose at the sleeve and I tugged at it nervously, waiting for the barrage of questions. Detective Inspector Vincent and Detective Constable Tunstall, the duo from before, sat across the table from me. Their backs straight, chins high.

'Do I need a solicitor?' I asked, unable to stop the frown appearing on my face.

The pair were pursed-lipped, shuffling paper, and it took a few seconds before anyone responded.

'That's entirely up to you, Miss Simmons. You're being interviewed as a witness, the same as yesterday.'

I wished I'd kept quiet. The way DI Vincent scanned my face, I could tell he didn't trust me, or perhaps that was his demeanour with everyone? His nose today was almost purple, broken thread veins visible in his nostrils. How much did the man drink?

'Right, let's get started shall we,' he said, before announcing the date, time and listing the occupants of the room. 'Going back to yesterday morning, who did you see when you were in the park?'

'A mother and her son at the swings and two dog walkers. That's it.'

'Are you sure?' DC Tunstall asked, raising one perfectly plucked eyebrow.

'I believe so, yes,' I replied, a deer caught in headlights.

'The reason we've called you back, Miss Simmons, is because a witness has come forward.' Detective Inspector Vincent let the sentence hang in the room as they both stared across the table at me, gaging my reaction.

'A witness reporting what?' I probed, trying to keep my voice from shaking.

'That you were in the park with a man.'

Fuck, the woman from the swings, she was with her son and left not long after I arrived. She must have seen Jimmy; she may well have passed him on the path on his way in.

'I wasn't *with* a man. A man came into the playground, he was looking for his dog, but I told him I hadn't seen it.' I crossed my arms and watched as DC Tunstall flicked back through her pad to yesterday's notes.

'You didn't mention this just now, neither did you mention it in our original interview. You said there was a woman at the swings with her son.'

'I must have forgotten about the man.'

Detective Inspector Vincent's brow furrowed, and he twirled his pen before speaking.

'Did he seem suspicious to you at the time? Did you think the story about the dog was true?'

I thought on my feet, amazed as the words flowed out of my mouth unrehearsed. 'No, not suspicious at all. He had a dog lead in his hand, and he looked panicked, so I believed him. He asked me if I'd seen a Jack Russell and when I said I hadn't, he left to carry on searching. That was it.'

'What did he look like?' Detective Inspector Vincent asked.

I had to give them a description of Jimmy, as the witness would have. It had to look like I was telling the truth.

'He was about six-foot, slim, dark hair, dark eyes. He had a short beard.'

'And what was he wearing?' Detective Constable Tunstall scribbled down my description.

'All black, I think. I didn't really take much notice.'

'The witness seemed to think he spent a bit more time with you at the swings than you suggest.' Detective Inspector Vincent leaned forward and rested his clasped hands on the table. His stomach pushed against the edge and he eased his chair back to accommodate it. 'Miss Simmons, is there something you're not telling us, because I believe you know more about Eden's whereabouts than you're letting on.'

I shook my head vehemently as Detective Inspector Vincent's steely gaze penetrated me, sending tremors down to my toes.

'I think,' he paused, 'you know exactly where Eden is. Is this about money? Are you trying to extort money from the Tolfreys?' His tone became hard, aggressive and got my back up.

'No!' I snapped, incredulous.

'You live at home with your mum, moved back in after a relationship breakdown I understand. Your ex-boyfriend, Karl Filcher, filed a complaint that you trashed his flat when he broke off your relationship.'

Karl had always been a wanker, but I was too dumb to see it at first. It wasn't until I found a cheap red thong down the side of the sofa while I was searching for my keys, that I discovered what he was up to.

'It was a difficult break-up,' I stammered. 'He cheated.' My cheeks flushed pink. I tugged at the loose thread at my sleeve, fearing I would unravel my cream jumper if I kept on, but I needed something to fidget with.

'You're saving to get yourself a place of your own?'

How did they know that? Had Ali told them? Did Ali and Christopher think it was me?

I nodded.

'Perhaps you thought the Tolfreys might be able to help. They are an affluent couple after all. I'm sure they could spare some cash, especially if the life of their daughter depended on it.'

I jumped up, my chair screeching back on the linoleum. The detectives remained still, unfazed at my sudden movement. Although I was hardly a threat, was I? I didn't know whether it was how close Detective Inspector Vincent had come to the truth or whether it was the smear against my character that caused my hackles to rise. 'That's disgusting,' I spat. 'I love Eden.' I welled up as I spoke. The words were true, I loved her.

'Then help us. Eden could be in incredible danger, someone could be hurting her,' Detective Inspector Vincent leaned even closer as I sank back into my seat.

'No,' I blurted and gasped at what I'd let slip.

DC Tunstall's eyebrows shot skyward, stare locked on my face, a missile on target. 'No what? No – she's not being harmed? How do you know, Brooke?' She glared at me and my stomach rolled. I feared I might be sick on the floor of the interview room.

I blinked, glancing at the door. Wishing I could leave, get up and run, without looking back.

'Tell us, Brooke, tell us where she is so we can return her to Ali and Christopher,' DC Tunstall implored, she was practically out of her seat, leaning forward on the table, so close I could smell her peppermint breath.

'I meant no, I don't want to believe anyone is hurting her,' I said as calmly as I could manage, trying to minimise the damage my outburst had caused.

The atmosphere in the room changed, they simultaneously leaned back in their seats, faces awash with disappointment.

'We will find out, Brooke. We will find out what happened to Eden,' Detective Inspector Vincent said, his tone measured and calm.

'I hope you do,' I replied, unable to disguise the bitterness in my voice. 'Can I go now?' I asked.

'Yes, don't go far though, Brooke. We'll be in touch,' Detective Inspector Vincent replied, a hint of menace in his voice.

DC Tunstall opened the door and I walked out of the room, the sensation I was falling off a cliff and powerless to do anything to save myself all-consuming. I continued past the desk and out of the station into the bitter air, hitting my skin like a slap. I kept walking, without turning back. I hadn't bothered to ask if they'd finished with my phone. It didn't matter. I had bigger stuff to deal with. There was no need for them to tell me I was a suspect; it was plainly obvious. They were onto me.

2PM – 5PM

30

ALI TOLFREY

I sat in Eden's room for a while, my back resting against her white wooden sleigh cot, listening to the news being played downstairs. The muffled voice of DC Benson trying to engage Christopher in conversation. The kettle being boiled for the umpteenth time.

Brooke wouldn't have taken Eden. I wanted to speak to her again, properly this time, ask her outright. Positive I'd know for certain once I'd heard what happened at the park yesterday morning, directly from the horse's mouth. It would put my mind at rest.

By nature, I wasn't a suspicious person, but we had no clue who was holding Eden, nothing made any sense and she'd already been gone over twenty-four hours. Perhaps I needed to do a little investigating of my own.

I dialled Brooke's number, but the call went straight through to voicemail as though her mobile was switched off. I left a message asking her to call me and sent a text too. I wasn't surprised if it was turned off. I imagined she'd been hounded by the press like we were being. Or perhaps she was still at the police station, being interviewed and unable to answer.

Brooke would call as soon as she could. Knowing her, she'd be beside herself at what she'd let happen. The anger that had consumed me yesterday had been buried, it wouldn't help me get Eden back. I needed answers and dwelling on the decisions I could have made provided little comfort.

I dialled one more time, to be sure, but again Brooke's answerphone message kicked in.

Afterwards, I moved up to the second floor to our bedroom where I could no longer hear anything downstairs. Cuddling one of Eden's teddys I'd brought with me, I curled up on the unmade bed and closed my eyes, dozing. Hoping beyond hope if I managed to sleep, I'd wake to find the nightmare over. It was exhausting being constantly on edge, waiting for the phone to ring or someone to knock on the door. Waiting for news to be delivered, good or otherwise.

I focused on yesterday morning, feeding Eden her apple-flavoured porridge followed by banana slices, how she'd squished them in her chubby fingers, sucking the gooey mess from her palm. Feeding her had never been a problem, she would eat almost anything she was given, and it made mealtimes a joy, albeit a messy one. I indulged in the memory until my body finally caved in and welcomed unconsciousness.

When I woke, the light in the bedroom had dimmed. My eyes were sticky from sleep, and I blinked away the woozy feeling as a loud bang rang out from below. I sat bolt upright. Someone was shouting downstairs, before the sound of smashing glass.

Throwing my legs over the side of the bed, I tore down the stairs, one set, and the next, listening to Christopher's booming voice grow louder.

'Please calm down, Mr Tolfrey,' DC Benson said, his arms outstretched like he was trying to pacify a caged tiger.

Christopher shot me a hateful look and stalked out of the

kitchen as DC Benson bent to pick up the remnants of a shattered wine glass. Red spots dotted the floor. He'd been drinking again. How early had he started? Just after lunch?

'What's happened?' I said, as the front door slammed.

DC Benson and I were both on our knees, heads bowed, carefully collecting the shards.

'DCI Greene called; she's coming over with some news. Your husband didn't want to wait, he thought I knew already and got agitated.'

I didn't respond, continuing to search the floor for glass I'd missed.

'Is he always like this when he drinks?'

I pursed my lips, irritated by DC Benson's familiarity. How dare he judge us.

'No, he's not,' I said sharply, 'he's obviously stressed, as we all are. I'm not sure what you're implying.' I stood, emptying the contents of my palm into the bin.

'I'm sorry, Mrs Tolfrey, I wasn't implying anything.' DC Benson's cheeks glowed; aware he'd said too much.

'Do you know what DCI Greene is coming over to tell us?' I asked, chin jutting forward.

'No, she hasn't disclosed it to me. But I believe she wants to talk to both of you.'

I took a cigarette from the top of the cupboard and went outside.

Bloody Christopher and his temper. What must we look like to the police? I could see the concern in DC Benson's eyes. He was worried Christopher was falling apart. I couldn't deny I was worried too. It was all too much for him, the lack of control was tearing him up inside. He was powerless to fix it, unable to take away the agony we were in. Turning to alcohol to numb himself. I knew he adored

Eden, we both did, but I was barely managing to stand upright as it was. I couldn't look after him too. He'd shut himself off from me. I could feel him pulling away, like it was all my fault.

I sucked on the cigarette, embracing the buzz as the nicotine hit my bloodstream. Through the bifold doors, I could see DC Benson doing a cursory sweep of the floor before wiping the tiles with kitchen towel.

The sky above was filled with rolling black clouds, threatening rain again. I had no idea of the time; or how long I'd slept for. Since Eden had gone, the hours all morphed into one, the haze I was in meant I was barely lucid. My brain blocking out the horror or the physical effects of lack of sleep.

It was cold, but I was in no rush to go back inside. It wasn't home in there without Eden. Not with DC Benson loitering everywhere I turned and Christopher ready to jump down my throat if I spoke. There was no privacy and I wanted to howl and scream at the sky in frustration.

'Bring my daughter back to me,' I whimpered into the air instead, hot salty tears flowed onto my cheeks. I rushed to wipe them away. I had to be strong for both of us.

With the cigarette smoked to the butt, I chucked it in the plant pot before rolling my shoulders back and heading inside. DC Benson was nowhere to be seen, but then I heard the flush of the downstairs toilet as the doorbell rang.

I didn't bother answering it. DC Benson was already there, pulling open the door to a grimacing DCI Greene, who wiped her feet before stepping over the threshold. My legs buckled as she met my eye and I lowered myself onto the chair at the head of the kitchen table. The news was bad, I could tell by her face. Saliva rushed into my mouth, swirling in the taste of ash and smoke. Was I going to be sick?

'Have you found her?' I blurted as she entered the kitchen ahead of DC Benson.

'No,' she said quickly, putting me out of my misery.

The word came as a relief. Eden was still alive.

'Mr Tolfrey has gone for a walk. I'll call him,' DC Benson said, stepping back into the hall, phone in hand.

'We've had a small development, but it's... delicate.' DCI Greene sat, interlocking her fingers.

'What's delicate?' Christopher's voice filled the room and he loomed large in the doorway, Benson trailing behind. I hadn't heard him come in.

'Come and sit down, Christopher. DCI Greene has an update,' I said, awarding him a steely glare.

He did as asked, and we waited for DCI Greene to speak.

'A man has called in. He phoned the Crimestoppers hotline and said he has Eden.'

A gasp escaped my lips and my hand shot to my mouth.

DCI Greene waved a hand to temper me before continuing. 'The man said he was Eden's father.'

The sentence floated in the room like poisoned gas and I crumpled inside.

Christopher jumped up, incredulous, already swearing and pointing his finger at DCI Greene, but I could barely hear him. Everything blurred momentarily and I clung to the table like it was a lifeboat in stormy seas. As if losing Eden wasn't enough, the rest of my world was about to disintegrate. An influx of fresh tears spilled out as DCI Greene looked at me quizzically.

'I know,' I whispered.

'Know what?' Christopher snapped, irritated at the interruption to his ranting.

'I know who has Eden.'

31

JIMMY PEARSON

I launched at Eden, roughly grabbing her out of the playpen as her eyes bulged. Choking, she was choking. Fuck, what should I do? Panic rose like a tidal wave and clouded my vision. Sinking to the sofa, I sat Eden on my lap, inserting a finger into her mouth, which was full of pulped orange crisps. She was so red; I feared she might pass out.

Once her mouth was clear, her eyes rolled back and I swiftly laid her face down across my knees, slapping between her shoulder blades hard twice until I heard a cough. An orange crisp, brittle not puffed, was fired onto the floor. Eden sucked in air as though her life depended on it before throwing up down my leg.

My heart raced so fast I expected any moment it would explode out of my chest like an alien. Sweat dripped into my eyes as I pulled her up over my shoulder stroking her hair.

'It's okay now honey, it's okay.'

She wheezed and sniffed, and I pulled her away to look at her properly. Already her colour was fading back to normal. Her eyes and face were damp and orange drool leaked from her mouth. Would she be okay?

'Drink, would you like a drink?' I asked, grabbing her sippy cup from the floor with a shaking hand and offering her a tiny amount. Her throat must have been on fire.

The vomit was pooling on the carpet beneath my sock, but it didn't matter. She was all right, she was breathing. I rocked her in my arms and pulled silly faces until she smiled. My daughter, who had nearly choked to death, grinned up at me as though it was all forgotten.

'Oh, my gorgeous girl, you almost gave Daddy a heart attack!'

'Dadadadadadada,' she said, her voice hoarse.

'No more crispies for you.'

I walked with her out to the kitchen to get my phone. I wanted to google after-effects of choking. She seemed okay but should I take her to the hospital anyway? Could I take her anywhere without being arrested? She hadn't lost consciousness, although she'd shaved a few years off my life for sure.

The press conference was all but forgotten as I took Eden upstairs for a change of clothes for us both. I wouldn't feed her again for a while, I'd wait until she complained, let her throat settle. Lots of sips of water and cuddles was what Daddy prescribed.

As she cruised around the bed, I clicked on the NHS link – *choking could cause brain damage*. Happy, happy, joy, joy. It was the perfect example of why you should never google symptoms. Eden seemed fine, she was giggling and sucking on her fingers.

Half an hour later, she still hadn't coughed or wheezed so it wasn't necessary to take her to the hospital, where I was sure I'd be apprehended. I'd cleaned up the sick, although there was an orange stain left behind on the carpet that would need some proper cleaner.

'Me and you against the world, kiddo. Tomorrow we'll move on, find somewhere else, eh. New adventure.'

She babbled back to me as though she understood.

'I know, how's about a nice walk in the fresh air?' I asked. I put on her new blue coat, hat and mittens before strapping her into the yellow buggy. It crossed my mind how distinctive it was, a bright banana yellow, but I figured with us so far away and Eden dressed as a boy, there hadn't been a need to get a new one.

Outside, the wind had picked up, orange and yellow leaves danced on the pavement, collecting in the gutters. I zipped my coat up to my neck. Despite the chill, a walk would do me good to clear my mind and distract Eden for a bit.

Being a parent was a rollercoaster of emotions I hadn't been prepared for. It was all-consuming and exhausting. I knew I'd bitten off more than I could chew taking Eden, especially as now it seemed I was a fugitive. I'd taken it for granted, how hard parenting was. There was little downtime, not when you had to keep an eye on them constantly. I had no idea how Brooke had raised Eden on her own and I guess she'd had help from her mum. Either way, I had a new respect for single parents and wasn't afraid to admit I was finding it tough. Perhaps it was why Brooke hadn't been in touch, was she finding life difficult with Eden? Did she welcome the break from her?

Why wasn't she answering my calls? I reran the press conference in my mind, struggling to understand why Brooke wasn't there. Nothing made sense and not being able to contact her, I was in the dark. I had Eden though and that was the main thing. First thing tomorrow we'd be on our way. The plan was to keep moving after all. We'd be harder to find that way. No one knew we were here; I'd only spoken to Georgina since we'd arrived, but she didn't know who we were.

Shit, wasn't she supposed to drop by later? I'd meant to cancel but hadn't got around to popping over there. I'd have to put her off, not answer the door or something. What on earth was I doing, agreeing to have her round in the first place? *You were thinking with little Jimmy is what you were doing*, the voice in my head berated.

Even as I pictured Georgina's backside jiggle in the Lycra and the much-needed stress relief an evening with her offered, it would be foolish. There was no way I could compromise myself or Eden. If we were exposed, if Georgina got the slightest whiff of why I was in Nottingham, the police could be on my doorstep in minutes. I'd never see Eden again and it was not a risk worth taking.

The street lights flickered as we walked down a side street and then another, wandering aimlessly for over an hour. I talked to Eden about the trees and we stopped when I spotted a squirrel, so she could look. Her cheeks were rosy again and she'd bounced back to her normal self.

My stomach rumbled as the first drop of rain fell, so we turned around and made our way back home. Turning the corner into Chapel Close, my heart sank when I saw Georgina loitering on the doorstep, peering up at the bedroom windows. She'd come over earlier than expected, obviously keen.

'Hi, I'm so sorry, Georgina, we'll have to take a rain check. Ed's not feeling well,' I said as I approached.

She turned to look at me, her features pinched, before glancing at Eden. 'He looks all right to me, don't you, little guy,' she said in a shrill voice before pinching his cheek.

Eden squirmed away.

Georgina clutched a bottle of red wine and smoothed down her leather jacket. She looked hot in a red shirt and black jeans, dolled up to the nines for a microwave meal and a night in front of the television. It couldn't do any harm, could it? Surely time with Georgina would be a perfect stress reliever. No, I had to be sensible.

'He's been sick a few times, so I need to try and get him to bed,' I grimaced, apologetically.

'Oh, well, if you change your mind, you know where I am. It's a shame, I was looking forward to some adult company,' she chimed, giving me a wink.

God, this girl was practically offering it on a plate! I bit the inside of my cheek and ignored the twitching in my groin.

'I know, I'm gutted, another time.'

Georgina looked disappointed. Sure she was used to getting her own way, she lingered until the silence grew awkward.

'I guess I'll see you later, James,' she said, sauntering back down the driveway, taking her red wine with her.

'Bye,' I replied, a little deflated. Perhaps it had been a lucky escape.

I winked at Eden before I unlocked the front door and wheeled her inside.

The house was warm and inviting after the brusque air on our walk. I settled Eden in her playpen, freshly cleaned with baby wipes. Entertained by her stacking cups, she was content for a while, seemingly recovered from the events of the afternoon, however many years the scare had shaved off *my* life.

Not wanting to let Eden out of my sight, I walked over to the window and dialled Brooke again. It rang four times and as I was about to hang up, I heard a click and Brooke's voice in my ear.

'Hello?'

32

BROOKE SIMMONS

A car horn beeped, and I looked over my shoulder, paranoia spreading through my veins like poison. They knew I was involved. They knew, but they couldn't prove it, because if they could, if they had any shred of evidence I'd be under arrest. Knowing what was at stake, they wouldn't mess around. I'd be interviewed for hours until they'd squeezed everything out of me. Eden's location being their priority.

I knew who she was with, but as for *where* she was, I had no idea. Would Jimmy be stupid enough to have her at his flat? I doubted it, but I had to make sure. If I had the phone, I'd call him, but it was still stuffed down the back of the sofa.

Mum would be home from school soon, finished for half-term and wondering where I'd gone. I hadn't had a chance to leave a note.

Jimmy didn't live far from me. If I jumped on the bus towards home and stayed on it, it would take me almost to his street. Turning around, I crossed the road, backtracked to the nearest bus stop and leant against the shelter, shielding myself from the biting wind.

I'd not thought to grab my coat when I left the house and the temperature was adding to the ice in my veins. I was jittery, unable to stop my eyes darting at anything that moved. The traffic was free-flowing and there were a couple of people milling around, one carrying Waitrose shopping bags filled with pumpkins ready for carving.

Some children were already out and about in full costume; it sounded like they were heading to a party. Little green faces of witches and ghosts wearing customed sheets with holes cut out for arms. I too should have been getting excited for a party tomorrow, but my life was a million miles away now from the girl who'd had the invite. Something so frivolous was inconceivable with Eden missing.

Instead I was scanning the streets for any undercover officers. It all sounded a bit MI5 in my head. If the police thought I was behind Eden's disappearance, naturally they might believe I'd lead them to her. Having me followed would be the first thing they'd do. It's what I'd do, and it's what the police did in the television shows Mum and I watched. I didn't have another option though, even if I was being followed, I'd have to take my chances. It wouldn't stop until I found Jimmy.

I held on to the fact that it wasn't over for me yet; I could still get Eden back and Jimmy and I might be able to get out of this mess unscathed. There was a glimmer of hope at least. I just had to come up with a plan, somewhere he could leave Eden safely and disappear. Somewhere busy, with lots of people.

The fact I was waiting at the bus stop, freezing without my coat in the chilly autumn air, watching the Halloween revellers, told me the police had nothing on me, otherwise I'd still be in that interview room or a cell. My iPhone was clean, I knew that. I'd been careful not to text or ring Jimmy from it. There were no photos of him on there. Often, when we met, I'd leave the phone at Ali's, so it wouldn't have location tracking stored on it.

Back in March, when I'd bumped into Jimmy outside the library, I'd dropped the biggest bombshell and left before he had a chance for it to sink in. As I made to leave, he'd stopped me, said he wanted to see us again and asked me if I still had my old number. I told him I didn't have it any more, and sensing I was wary of getting back in touch, he'd pushed me to take his instead. Pleading with me to call him.

The next evening, I'd had a rummage in the lost property drawer at work as I was sure I'd seen an old phone in there. We kept items dropped by members of the public at customer services in case someone came back to collect them. When I saw the Nokia, I took it, reasoning no one would be back to get such an old handset, it had been in there for months. I'd bought a new SIM card for it, deciding to use the number specifically for Jimmy. With the new number I was anonymous, which was what I needed for the plan that had formed in my head.

It was a stupid decision, made with a bitter heart as I'd watched him count back the months in his head as he'd surveyed Eden. In fact, he'd given me the idea. In the seconds I'd watched his brain tick over, it had occurred to me I could get him back for being such a shit. For making me fall for him, for healing my heart after Karl, then dropping me like a piece of rubbish once he'd had his fill.

Jimmy always had plenty of money, he'd loved to flash the cash when he took me out. Always paying for drinks and dinner, nothing was too expensive, and I'd been wowed at the time. Now he had a reason to pay me. Child maintenance. It would be easy money. All I'd had to do was show up.

The idea had come fleetingly. Unsure whether he'd run a mile if he thought Eden was his or if he'd even want to be involved, but the notion of buying my own place took hold. How quickly I'd be able to move out of Mum's with Jimmy's financial help. I'd be free, finally, without her crowding me. He owed me after all.

My coolness at the time had reeled him in. I'd left quickly, saying I had a health visitor appointment for Eden. When he'd given me his number, I'd promised I'd be in touch and he could meet Eden properly next time. Back when we were dating, he'd never come to the house, allergic to meeting family members, he'd said. So, he didn't know where I lived, other than the general area of Redhill. It was perfect and I could keep him at arm's-length, so he'd never find out I'd lied.

When I rang him, I'd told him I was nervous getting involved with him again, even as friends. He'd hurt me last time, and after a lot of persuading on his part, I'd agreed to let him see Eden, but there'd be boundaries he'd have to respect. If I could control the situation, it would be lucrative. I'd have to spend time with Jimmy again, but I'd know now where to draw the line. Eden couldn't yet talk; she wouldn't be able to tell Ali or Christopher where she'd been or who she'd seen. It was perfect. Stupidly I'd never planned further ahead.

In the past six months, Jimmy had given me almost ten thousand pounds in child maintenance. I told him how I'd struggled to cope financially and had got myself into debt, how child benefit wasn't enough for everything I needed to buy for Eden, and I didn't want her to go without. He bought it hook, line and sinker and gave me however much I asked for. If I wanted money for Eden's clothes and shoes, I got it. Money for the gas bill, I got it. I started small but got greedier as I got closer to being able to afford the deposit on a flat nearby.

However, I hadn't anticipated how quickly Eden would start to talk, she was already saying mama and dada and making sounds. How long would it be before she stopped calling Jimmy dada, before she understood, she had two dadas and two mamas? I quickly recognised the meetings had to stop, but I'd opened Pandora's box and I wasn't sure how to close it.

Jimmy and I got on well and our time together wasn't a hardship. He adored Eden and when it was the three of us, at least once a week, I pretended Eden was mine. It was easy, I adored her anyway and I immersed myself in the fantasy that we were a family. It was perfect until I told Jimmy we were moving away, down to the seaside.

He didn't take it well and I should have seen it coming. Our last meeting was going to be yesterday morning. The last time he'd see his daughter for a while. He must have felt helpless and desperate. Desperate enough to attack me and steal his daughter away for a new life. Unaware she was not his daughter at all and now here I was trying to clean up this godawful mess.

The bus finally arrived and I got on, glancing around at the faces buried in their phones or staring out of the steamed windows.

The stop for Jimmy was three stops past my house and I got off, looking around to see if any cars had followed, but the street was quiet. I hurried along to Jimmy's flat, seeing his black Audi A3 parked outside. The lights were off, but I hammered on the door anyway.

'Looking for Jimmy?' a voice to my left shouted; Jimmy's neighbour. A woman leaned out of her door; the noise of my knocking must have disturbed her. 'He's gone away; Australia, I think he said, to visit his brother. You a friend of his?' She squinted at me over her glasses as she puffed on a slim cigarette.

'Oh okay, no worries. Thanks,' I said, dipping my head low and scurrying away.

Australia? There was no way he'd get out of the country with Eden. Could he? Not without a passport.

I hurried along as the sky darkened, wrapping my arms around myself to keep warm until I reached home. Mum's car wasn't there, but I could see the kitchen light had been left on through the window.

Unlocking the door, I glanced over my shoulder before stepping inside, unable to shake the notion I was being followed. It could be paranoia; I hadn't slept much last night.

The phone was still down the back of the sofa and I saw a few missed calls from Jimmy. He'd seen the press conference for sure. A note on the kitchen table from Mum told me she'd gone food shopping and would be back later.

I jumped out of my skin when the phone started vibrating in my palm. I wanted to throw it from me as fast as I could, as if it was a bomb. Instead I pressed to answer, ready to face the music. To face Jimmy's wrath.

'Hello?' I said.

33

ALI TOLFREY

'Who has Eden, Mrs Tolfrey?' DCI Greene stepped towards me; eyes narrowed as Christopher looked on open-mouthed.

I turned to face him, crushed by the weight of my admission.

'I'm so, so sorry, Christopher.'

His hands trembled at my words.

'Are you telling me Eden isn't mine?' he asked, his voice barely a whisper. His face paled and eyes filled with tears as he stared at me, aghast.

'My hen night...' I began, not sure I could bear to say the words out loud.

'Un-fucking-believable.' Christopher came back to life like a clockwork toy who'd been wound up. He stalked to the sink, hand over his mouth, shaking his head.

'Did you have an affair?' DCI Greene asked gently, pulling up the chair closest to me and sitting. She leaned her forearms on her thighs, eyes drilling into mine.

'No, not an affair. It was just a stupid thing, one night. A bartender.'

'A fucking bartender!' Christopher yelled; his knuckles white from gripping the marble worktop.

'Mr Tolfrey, please,' DC Benson placated from the entrance to the kitchen.

'What was his name, do you remember?'

Christopher snorted as DCI Greene asked the question.

'His name was Jason Wells,' I stammered, feeling as though I was at the top of a rollercoaster, about to plummet to the ground.

'What bar did he work in?'

'It was the Walkabout in Brighton, I think. I mean, I don't know Eden's not Christopher's, it's just the timing…' I trailed off as I saw Christopher shoot me a look of utter disgust.

'Mr Tolfrey, could we take a DNA sample please, we can get the lab to match it against the hair we took from Eden's brush.'

'Please do. I'd love to know if the child I've been raising for the past year is the result of my wife's betrayal with a stranger in a fucking pub toilet.'

I gasped, his words like slashes of a whip. My chin wobbled.

DCI Greene ignored Christopher's comment and retrieved a swabbing kit from her bag. She'd brought one with her before my confession had been given.

Christopher didn't take his blazing eyes from me as he opened his mouth for DCI Greene to roll the swab around the inside of his cheek. I'd never witnessed such loathing. Hatred radiated off him across the room. Even if Eden was his, I wasn't sure we'd survive my infidelity. If she wasn't his, I knew I'd be homeless as soon as the result was disclosed. I hung my head in my hands and sobbed.

'I'll get this turned around as quickly as I can. Obviously we'll trace Jason Wells. I have to warn you both, it could be a crank, we do get them, but my team believe this is a strong lead.' She placed the swab back in her bag. 'Would you be able to give me a list of names of those who attended your hen night please?'

I obliged, grabbing some paper to scribble on, not even caring my darkest secret was about to become common knowledge amongst my friends. What reputation I had was long gone.

'Thank you, I'll be in touch,' she said, taking the paper, and gestured for DC Benson to see her out.

'Christopher, I'm so sorry. It meant nothing, it was a drunken stupid mistake,' I said, once we were alone, but Christopher interrupted.

'But you've always known; there's always been the possibility Eden might not be mine. You let me believe it regardless.'

'She could be yours,' I blurted, my head throbbing.

'I can't even look at you.' His lip curled, face contorted in contempt, and he stalked out of the room.

I sobbed, head bent low over the table, crying for Eden and the misery I'd caused our family, which before yesterday had been the picture of happiness. I'd done irrevocable harm to my marriage that would never be repaired, I knew it. Christopher abhorred lying, everything was black and white to him, there was nothing in between. Once a cheat, always a cheat, that's what he'd said when it came up in conversation. The guilt had stained my skin ever since, I'd never been able to wash it off, but I'd give anything to go back and change it.

My hen night had been a blur, arranged five weeks before the wedding. A simple night out in Brighton, the week before Christmas, while Christopher spent the weekend at a prestigious golf club in Wales. I hadn't wanted any fuss, but none the less Brooke had arranged L-plates, a feather boa and tiara as accessories to my outfit. We went from bar to bar and I was already wasted when we got into the Walkabout, the last pub before we headed to Coalition, a club on the seafront.

Jason served us when we arrived. He was handsome, blond hair and brown eyes with skin that looked like it had never seen the sun. He'd flirted with me and it was nice to have the attention. Egged on by my friends, I told him we were going to Coalition and he agreed to stop by when his shift was over.

Another two hours passed before I saw him again. I'd lost Brooke and the rest of the hens in the crowd on my way back from the toilet and saw him queuing at the bar. We did some shots, but afterwards I felt sick and wanted to get some air, so he agreed to take me outside to walk it off.

We'd had sex on the beach, warm bodies against the freezing wooden groyne. It was quick but passionate and, although unspoken, we both knew it was a one-off. Later, in the cold light of day, I suspected he had a bride-to-be every weekend. I wasn't sure why I'd done it. Perhaps it was the last glimpse of freedom, a chance with one more man before I settled down with Christopher. The opportunity to be someone else for the night. It was stupid and reckless, and I'd regretted it as soon as we'd said goodbye, when I'd headed back to the club to find my friends. None of them were any the wiser, not when I'd said I'd been in the toilet throwing up. I'd drank enough for it to be a plausible cover story.

The next day, all I was full of was crushing remorse and guilt, which laid heavy on my heart, sure as soon as Christopher returned, he'd see it smeared on my skin.

Of course he didn't, he returned from his golfing weekend and life went back to normal. I'd put it behind me, until a few days before the wedding my period still hadn't arrived. I'd known immediately I was pregnant and was terrified the baby was Jason's. I kept it a secret but it ate away at me throughout the pregnancy. What if the baby was born and looked nothing like Christopher? How would I explain it?

Eden came along, blonde and beautiful, with my nose and

Christopher's eyes. Immediately the worry went away, and I assumed I'd been wrong about Jason being the father. It hadn't even crossed my mind when Eden was taken, he could be involved. He'd had no idea I'd had a baby; it was likely he hadn't even remembered my name. But why else would someone call claiming to be Eden's father? It had to be Jason. He must have found out about her somehow and taken our beautiful baby girl.

34

JIMMY PEARSON

'Brooke?'

'Jimmy?' Brooke sounded nervous; her voice as quiet as a mouse.

'Yes, it's me. What the fuck is going on, Brooke? Who are those people on the news?'

'Jimmy, I'm so, so sorry. I didn't mean for any of this to happen.'

'What?' I pushed, frustration bubbling beneath my skin. What had she done?

Brooke snivelled; her voice shrill. 'She's not yours, Jimmy.'

'What the fuck do you mean she's not mine?' I snarled, turning back to look at Eden bashing her cups together.

'She's not yours and she's not mine either. She's the daughter of the people you saw on television. I'm so sorry I lied to you.'

My mouth hung open as heaving sobs rang out in my ear.

Slotting together pieces of the puzzle, they started to fall into place. Why Brooke would never let me look after Eden overnight; why I was never allowed to visit her place. Us meeting on the same days every week.

'Who is Eden to you?' I tried to remember if Brooke had any siblings. Could she be Eden's aunt?

'I look after her, for a friend.' Her voice was quiet, tone contrite.

'You're her fucking babysitter?' I lifted my hand to my forehead, unable to absorb the colossal revelation that was like a sledgehammer to the back of my head. It made sense why she was suddenly 'moving', trying to cut ties with me. 'How could you do this to me?' The words caught in my throat and my eyes prickled despite the rage frothing beneath the surface.

Brooke's words tumbled out like a waterfall. 'I didn't plan this, you assumed she was yours. I never expected you to kidnap Eden. Why would you do that? Even if she was your child!'

'You gave me no choice; you were taking her away from me. Fuck, Brooke! Why did you do this?'

'I don't know, I'm so sorry. When I bumped into you at the library and you thought she was yours, I was so angry, Jimmy. You treated me like shit at the end, you walked out of my life, you were a ghost.'

'So, this is about revenge? Fuck me. How could you use a child? How could you make me fucking believe I was her dad?'

Brooke went silent, I could only hear snuffling down the phone. Then she spoke quietly.

'How is she? Is Eden okay?'

'Of course she is.' I sighed.

'Don't do anything stupid, Jimmy, she's just a child. Don't take it out on her now that you know the truth.'

'What kind of monster do you think I am?' I said, incredulous.

Seconds passed, Brooke crying down the phone as I tried to comprehend the reality of the situation I was in. Then the penny dropped. It wasn't just about revenge. It was about money. I'd paid her child support for months, thousands of pounds. She'd really done a number on me.

'Where's all my money been going, Brooke?' My voice solidified, hardened like steel.

I waited for an answer but all I heard was Brooke's snivelling.

Sheer rage exploded out of me and my body shook. Unable to look at Eden any longer, I stormed into the kitchen. 'You fucking bitch. Do you have any idea what you've done, how much fucking trouble you've caused? I've kidnapped someone else's kid. I could get years for this. All because you felt bitter about me breaking up with you.' I raised my eyes to the ceiling, it was incomprehensible.

Bawling my hands into fists, I stared at the split in the cupboard, the urge to tear it off its hinges all-consuming. I wanted to wreck the place.

'I know, it went too far. I wanted to tell you, but you seemed so happy.'

'I fucking love her. I love her and she's not mine. I'm going to wring your fucking neck when I see you, Brooke. I'll hunt you down.'

'Jimmy, please,' Brook wailed.

I paced the room, trying to gain some control.

'Dadadaadadada,' Eden shouted from the lounge and my eyes stung with tears.

'She called you Mum, she called me Dad,' I said, sinking to my knees on the tiled floor.

'I'm sorry, I'm so sorry I lied,' Brooke sobbed.

'You're a fucking psycho,' I managed through a haze of snot and salty tears. I dropped the phone and bent my head to the floor, rocking slowly.

What could I do? Call the police and tell them where I was? Drop Eden off somewhere, a shop or a hospital? How could I get away with what I'd done? My heart had been ripped in two. That gorgeous blonde cherub wasn't mine; she didn't have an ounce of my blood inside her. It seemed too much to take in and I stayed on the floor for a minute, the world crashing around my ears.

'Jimmy, Jimmy? Are you still there?' Brooke said, sniffing.

I reached for the phone; my forehead still planted on the cool tile. 'What?'

'We can get out of this, we can, we just have to be smart.'

'Go fuck yourself, Brooke, you deserve to rot in prison. I'll tell everyone what you did.' My voice sounded strangely calm, resigned.

Brooke spoke, sounding desperate. 'Leave Eden somewhere, I can pick her up. I've not told anyone about you. No one knows who you are. It can stay that way.'

'The police are probably tracing this call right now.' I sighed.

'No, they have my other phone. They don't know about this one. No one knows you had anything to do with it. Bring her back and disappear, you can go back to your old life and I can go back to mine.'

'You're dreaming if you think that could ever happen.'

'It can, I just have to think about where. Tomorrow is Halloween, it's the perfect cover. Get yourself and Eden a costume and I'll sort out where we can do it.'

I heard a shuffling sound and Brooke muffled the phone for a second.

'I have to go, I'll call you later,' she said quickly before hanging up.

Pulling myself to my feet was more effort than it should have been. My legs were like lead. I tossed the phone onto the worktop and went back into the lounge. Eden was sucking on one of the plastic cups but dropped it and reached her arms up for me to lift her out of the playpen as soon as she saw me.

'I'm not your daddy,' I whispered.

'Dadadadadada,' she replied, and it was like a knife to my heart.

I went to the window and stared out at the dark street before drawing the curtains and switching on the overhead light. Eden needed feeding, a bath too, but I had no inclination for either. My world had imploded, everything I believed to be true was a lie.

Six months I'd been meeting Brooke, looking after Eden, paying maintenance. Was it all about the money? Money and spite. Oh, how she must have fucking laughed behind my back. I must have been a constant source of amusement. Watching me fall hook, line and sinker. What an idiot. She had me from the first moment at the library. The second I saw Eden's face. Saw similarities that weren't there. Fuck. I was going to kill that bitch.

'Nomnomnomnom,' Eden yelled and promptly began to cry.

'Fuck off,' I said, my voice quiet, the words empty. I couldn't look at her, it was too painful.

I should just get in the car, drive to the nearest hospital and leave her outside in her car seat. She wasn't my problem; she was nothing to me. Not any more.

I gritted my teeth, willing my heart to stop aching. By taking Eden yesterday I'd inadvertently ruined my life. Brooke had better come up with a watertight plan, otherwise I'd drag the bitch down with me, all the way to hell if I had to.

5PM – 9PM

35

BROOKE SIMMONS

'Help me with these bags, would you,' Mum grumbled as I ended the call to Jimmy and shoved the phone into my back pocket. She dumped some Sainsbury's bags in the hallway and went back out to the car, leaving the door wide open.

There was no time to compose myself. Jimmy was furious and I couldn't blame him. Having my actions spelt out to me only reinforced how much of a deception my money-making scheme had been. I hadn't thought it would go so far. His reaction on the phone scared me, he'd never spoken to me like that before, never threatened me.

I knew he sometimes had trouble controlling his temper, there'd been road rage incidents, or if someone took the piss, he'd be the first to call it out, but it struck me I really had no idea what he was capable of. When we met would he hurt me? Attack me again? He'd hit me yesterday and before then I wouldn't have believed he'd do that, not to a woman. It just proved how little I knew him. How far he'd go when pushed.

A bitter wind whipped inside the house and I shuddered, rubbing my swollen eyes. Collecting the bags, I tried to avoid

Mum's eye in the kitchen as I unpacked, but the woman noticed everything.

'What on earth's happened?' She stood in front of me, clutching a tin of beans in each hand. I must have looked a state, eyes puffy, red-faced.

'Nothing, Mum, just, you know, Eden, that's all,' I lied, although maybe I should start worrying about Eden. Now Jimmy knew they weren't related, would he treat her differently? He'd always doted on her before.

'Oh, love, they'll find her. I'm sure they will. You must stop blaming yourself.'

She put the tins in the cupboard, and we went back to unpacking the shopping bags.

'How's your head?' she asked.

'Okay, a bit sore still. I called in sick today,' I said.

'I would have done that for you, love.'

She probably would have written a note for my boss too. I gritted my teeth, but she carried on.

'Have a couple of days' rest. Have you got any homework to do for Monday?'

'Mum, I don't have homework, I'm not at school any more. It's coursework, and yes, I'm all up to date,' I lied, sighing audibly, but Mum brushed my irritation off.

'Here, look, I got us a bottle of Prosecco, it was on offer. Shall we put a movie on tonight? I got us some crisps too.' She seemed excited at the movie night she'd planned without asking me if I was doing anything. It was typical Mum though. All the while I was under her roof, I was there to keep her company. I found it stifling.

She hated it when I went out with my friends, leaving her home alone. She suffocated me so much I felt like I could barely breathe. Still it wouldn't be for much longer.

'Sure, movie night,' I said unenthusiastically, feeling my chest tighten. No doubt it would be *Dirty Dancing* again or some other ancient classic she'd roll out for me to watch.

'Done,' she said, shutting the freezer door. 'How about quiche for dinner?'

I nodded, although I wasn't in the slightest bit hungry.

'Stick the oven on, would you, there's a good girl.'

I rolled my eyes, she could be so patronising at times, but I did as she asked.

'I'm going to nip upstairs.'

'Okay, can you take the toilet roll upstairs. Don't sit in your bedroom too long. Dinner will be in a bit.'

I made my escape, swiping the laptop from the sofa on my way.

The battery had died unsurprisingly, but I plugged it in upstairs and Facebook sprang open when it came back to life. The local Redhill and Reigate page was on-screen and something caught my eye.

Halloween party at Mini Mischief! Bring your toddler for soft play fun. Prizes for best costume, parents wearing fancy dress get in free. Saturday 31st October only

A plan formulated in my head, something that might work.

Mini Mischief was a small soft play at the top of the Belfry Shopping Centre in Redhill. It would be busy, there were multiple exits and Jimmy could wear a costume for anonymity. Even if I was being followed, if timed right, he could leave Eden and slip away. It could be a coincidence my being there. The problem was, I couldn't be sure if Jimmy would trust me enough to come. After all, I'd spent the best part of six months lying to him.

Beneath the advert, lots of people had commented they would be attending with their child. I took the details down and sent them to Jimmy with a text.

This might work

Leaving the laptop, I looked in the money box hidden beneath my bed, pulling out the wodge of rolled up fifty- and twenty-pound notes. Counting them out on the carpet, there was a total of nine thousand, six hundred pounds. I had to get rid of it before Jimmy could make me give it back. If I'd spent it already, there would be nothing I could do other than be in his debt. After he brought back Eden, I hoped we'd never see each other again.

Returning to the laptop, I opened my email and looked at the ground-floor flat I'd enquired about. It was a beige double-fronted building that had been split into four flats, with large bay windows and plenty of parking. Although it had been two weeks since I'd been for a viewing, it was still listed as For Sale for £185,000.

The mortgage when I enquired online was around £800 per calendar month, with an eight-thousand-pound deposit, and if I upped my shifts at Tesco, I should be able to afford it. Plus, I had nearly completed the bookkeeping foundation course and once I had my certificate, then I could hopefully find an employer to take me on and maybe put me through my diploma.

It was after office hours, so I emailed the agent with an offer, figuring it would be answered tomorrow. I had to get a mortgage approval in principle, dig out my payslips and find a bank who would lend to me, but I could put an offer in. My only worry was that I knew the process of buying somewhere was slow. What if Jimmy found out where Mum lived and, even with Eden back safely with Ali and Christopher, he came for me. There was no way he'd let me walk away after what I'd done. Not with the amount of money I'd defrauded him out of. I had to make him see how risky it would be to say anything, how he could jeopardise his freedom. Maybe I could buy his silence that way?

My phone beeped, a text from Jimmy.

Work out the details and let me know. Tomorrow we do it.

Even the curt tone of his text sent a shiver down my spine.

I was in over my head I knew, but we had to get Eden back to Ali and Christopher. The only chance for us to get out of this mess was to bring her home, the sooner the better. I had no idea if the police had a clue who'd taken Eden, or if their focus was purely on me. For all I knew they could already be looking for Jimmy.

'Brooke, can you come and lay the table please?' Mum called up the stairs.

I sighed and closed the lid of the laptop; I'd have to work on the plan later. Once I'd sat through whatever movie she had planned, she'd fall asleep on the sofa and I'd be able to slope off.

I trudged downstairs, freezing on the bottom step as someone knocked at the door.

'Who's this now, at dinner time. If it's trick or treaters, they're a day early.' Mum tutted as she bypassed me and made to open the door.

'Mum, it might be the press,' I warned, but by the time I'd got the words out, she'd already opened it. I couldn't see who was outside, the door was blocking my view from the step where I'd halted.

'Hi, Mrs Simmons, I don't suppose I can speak to Brooke, can I?'

All my extremities went numb as the posh lilt of Ali Tolfrey flowed into the house along with the cold night air.

'Oh, my poor love, yes, come in. Brooke's here. I'm so sorry to hear about Eden. Awful business, it really is, although I'm sure she'll be home soon. I keep thinking any minute now we'll hear she's been found.' Mum's rambling was embarrassing.

I forced my legs to work and stepped into view.

Ali looked pale, with deep purple patches beneath her eyes despite the make-up she'd used to cover them. She was still wearing the clothes from the press conference, but it was obvious she'd been crying since.

We locked eyes and fear lodged in my throat, certain I might stumble over my words if I said anything. Positive she would see the guilt etched on my face and know immediately I was involved.

Ali remained on the doorstep even after Mum stepped back to let her pass.

'Shall we go for a walk?' Ali said, her tone ice cold.

36

ALI TOLFREY

Christopher had locked himself away upstairs, refusing to come out. DC Benson offered to cook dinner, but I had no appetite. I told him to help himself, I was going out for a walk. I needed to talk to someone and who better than Brooke. She was involved after all, embroiled in our misery. I couldn't wait any longer for her to call me, I needed to hear what had happened yesterday morning from her. Had Jason Wells hit her over the head and stolen our daughter?

DC Benson tried to dissuade me, but I wouldn't hear of it. There was no need for me to be there. I had my mobile with me, and he could call if there were any developments. Plus, I didn't want to be around for the call delivering results of the DNA test, if they were going to come today. Have DC Benson witness the disintegration of my marriage as I faced up to Christopher's wrath.

Seeing Brooke's car still parked outside, I remembered her keys and returned to the house to find them. She'd left them on the window ledge in the hall and I pocketed them to take with me.

Outside, the cold wind was bitter and I huddled deep into the cashmere shawl and thick woollen coat, hoping once again Eden was safe and warm inside somewhere. Being looked after by someone who cared about her, although that was wishful thinking. I barely knew Jason, I had no idea what sort of father he'd be, but from the little time I'd spent with him, he didn't strike me as someone wanting to settle down and have a family. I couldn't get my head around him taking Eden. It made no sense, but I was clinging onto the idea she was with someone who cared about her. It was the only thing keeping me going. My body functioned like that of a zombie as I shuffled along the pavement, beneath the street lights. It was dark and under usual circumstances I wouldn't have dreamt of walking alone at night, although it was only just dinner time, hardly late. Anyone could be lurking in the bushes waiting to pounce, but it didn't matter. No one could hurt me any more than I was hurting already. The worst had already been done. Eden was gone, Christopher would leave me soon too. I'd sooner sink into a nice hot bath with a bottle of Co-codamol and wait for the pain to go away.

The journey to Brooke's took around thirty minutes and I had to walk up and down the street twice, trying to remember which house it was. Most of the houses in her street had been decorated. Outside one a cackling witch hung from the porch, which made me jump as I passed. I found Brooke's house when I recalled the blue painted gate and her mentioning her mum had lined the doorstep with pumpkins earlier in the week, ready for the trick or treaters.

I rang the bell and listened to voices inside, unable to decipher what was being said. A few seconds passed and Brooke's mum opened the door. I'd met her once, in town whilst she was out shopping with Brooke. She was a thin, wiry woman who looked a lot older than her years, her long dark hair was always plaited Brooke had told me, and she never wore make-up. Her eyes were big but grew larger as she recognised who I was.

I enquired after Brooke and she slipped into view. A stab to the chest when I saw her, a mix of pity and loathing washed over me at the same time. Emotions pulled in two different directions. I suggested we went for a walk, knowing Brooke's mum would eavesdrop on our conversation if I went into the house. She'd told me how much her mum smothered her and how desperate she was to leave and stand on her own two feet.

Brooke agreed and disappeared to get her coat, reappearing again as her mum wittered on about how she was sure Eden would return home safely soon. I smiled politely but didn't engage. Stepping aside as Brooke joined me, we set off down the path.

'I tried to call you again,' I said, hearing my voice was pinched.

'The police have my phone,' she said. 'I'm sorry, Ali.'

It sounded like she meant it and she looked, like I did, tear-stained and exhausted.

'What happened?' I asked as we turned the corner of the street, walking aimlessly.

Brooke recalled the assault yesterday morning, citing she didn't see her attacker but woke up and found Eden was gone.

'Why do the police have your phone? Do they think you're involved?'

'I'm not!' she blurted.

I gave a solitary nod. It was what I'd been waiting to hear. For her to tell me she had nothing to do with Eden's disappearance. That my friend couldn't be responsible for hurting me in the worst possible way. A friend wouldn't cause someone they loved this much pain.

'Do you remember my hen night?' I asked and Brooke frowned, confused by my off-topic question.

'Yes, well parts, it was not a sober night.' She smiled briefly.

'Do you remember the bartender from the Walkabout? The handsome one. Jason.'

Brooke nodded and blew hot air into her hands as she walked.

My shoulders inched upwards, neck sinking into the shawl.

'A call has come into the police, someone claiming to be Eden's father.'

Brooke stopped on the pavement as though an invisible barrier had been erected in her path. 'Who? What's this got to do with your hen night?' Brooke's eyebrows knitted together and slowly released as the penny dropped. Her lips formed an O. 'The bartender?' she asked.

I nodded.

'I thought you might have got off with him, but did it go that far?' Her words didn't sound judgemental and I was grateful.

I grimaced in reply.

We carried on walking, contemplating in silence. My eyes were stinging from the wind and excessive crying.

'Does Christopher know?' Brooke asked.

'I had to tell him. I think that's our marriage finished, but I only have myself to blame. The police have taken Christopher's DNA to match it to Eden's.' I sighed and Brooke shook her head, her mouth still gaping.

'I can't believe it.'

'I don't know what to do, Brooke, nothing makes sense without Eden home.' I stifled a cry and my shoulders bounced.

Brooke pulled me to her, and I wept into the lapel of her coat as she squeezed me tight. 'It'll be okay,' her voice squeaked, choked with emotion.

'How can it ever be okay again?' I said, my voice muffled.

'It will be, I'm sure of it. Do the police think the bartender took Eden?'

I pulled away, Brooke's face was fixed, wide-eyed and incredulous. I shrugged. 'It's a lead they are following. That's all they've said, other than a car, a dark red car, seen near the park. They are still trying to locate it. I'm not sure we get told everything. There's a family liaison officer at the house, he's there all the time. It's claustrophobic. Christopher won't talk to me. I had to get out.' I smiled weakly at Brooke, who mirrored my expression. 'I'm terrified Eden is somewhere dark and cold, locked away and abused. I can't bear it.' My voice broke.

'I'm sure she's not, not with that face. Who could possibly hurt a face like that?'

'There are monsters,' I replied, walking again.

Brooke fell in step beside me, hands shoved in her pockets.

We both stared at the ground, turning the corner to walk around the block. It was good to be out in the fresh air. I felt like I'd been cooped up for ages when in reality it had only been two days. Two long days away from my beautiful baby girl. It was a lifetime.

'Let's hope they find the bartender quickly,' Brooke said. She sounded more hopeful than I felt.

37

JIMMY PEARSON

I fed and bathed Eden on autopilot. Going through the motions. My heart had been torn in two, but it wasn't her fault. She was innocent, and no matter how hard I tried, I couldn't hate her. I loved her, like she was my own, and I couldn't turn it off like a tap.

The more I went over it, the more stupid I felt. Brooke had used another phone for me altogether. She hadn't tried to reconnect with me on Insta or Snapchat when we met up again. At the time I'd thought she was still sore because I'd blocked her back when we'd finished. It didn't cross my mind that it was because I might have noticed there were no photos or posts about her daughter. Brooke was hiding me away, hiding Eden away, trying to keep the lie she'd told a secret. Surely, she must have realised it couldn't last forever.

I'd heard Eden call Brooke mama; she must have taught her, although, to be fair, she couldn't say much else. Still, how confused must the poor child be? Two mums, two dads. The idea sickened me right to my core. How could Brooke have been so callous? The revelation hit me like a tsunami, I was treading water to survive. Life would never be the same again.

I should have known when I dumped her, there wasn't something quite right. As pretty as she was, and we'd got on well, she'd become clingy. Talking about our future and settling down after only a few weeks together. I discovered her things left in the flat, like she was slowly moving herself in. It freaked me out and I'd legged it, but I didn't think she'd react like this, inventing a revenge plan that would tear my life apart.

It would be a miracle if we got out of this without being caught. The police must be searching for me, even if they didn't know exactly who I was yet. My dad's car would be on CCTV somewhere, or there was always the possibility Brooke would crack and tell them everything.

No, she had her own sorry arse to save. Self-preservation at its finest. God that bitch had a heart of stone.

I reminded myself, as I played in the bath with Eden's dolphin water squirter, every giggle that escaped her lips tightening my chest further, I still had my Australia ticket. It was now my only lifeline. The flight was on Sunday at three o'clock in the afternoon, flying via Los Angeles from London Heathrow. I could meet Brooke tomorrow, drop off Eden and head straight there, spend the night in an airport hotel, or even the lounge if I had to. Maybe there was a possibility I could change my flight to an earlier one. I'd be anonymous amongst the thousands of travellers. As long as the police didn't have my name, I could still use my passport. It would be a gamble, but there was a chance I could leave it all behind. Start afresh in Sydney with my brother.

My mind raced with possibilities as Eden splashed happily. She'd eaten an entire pot of macaroni cheese and jelly before I'd run the bath. Food always made my girl happy. I stared at her, drinking in her smile. Our last few hours together before she went back to her family. They must be beside themselves. Her poor mother had to be going crazy not knowing where her daughter was. It sickened me, but the guilt was Brooke's not mine. She'd created this situation; she'd caused the devastation in all of our lives. If she hadn't come up with her plan to extort me, I would never have taken Eden.

The familiar bubbling in my stomach returned and I gritted my teeth. How could Brooke do that to them? Knowing how much I loved Eden and she'd only been in my life for six months; I couldn't imagine what her parents were going through, their only child stolen from them. As much as I wanted to tear their faces off when they'd pleaded for her safe return through the television, it dawned on me how terrified they must be. I wanted to contact them, tell them Eden was safe and being looked after. Yes, she'd burnt her hand and bumped her head whilst in my care, but I'd never knowingly hurt a hair on her tiny head. Despite what Brooke thought.

I couldn't call them, of course, I knew that, but shame clung to my shoulders knowing their minds would be filled with indescribable horror.

'Come on then, cherub, let's get you out,' I said, reaching for a fluffy towel.

Eden beamed and tried to say bath, although it came out more like an impression of a sheep. I'd miss her, everything about her. Her smile, her laugh, the smell of her in the morning, like baby powder and milk.

I sighed, lifting her out gently and drying her on the mat.

She yawned and stuck her fist into her mouth, gnawing on it. Missing her dummy.

When she was dry, I put a fresh nappy on and then her sleep-suit, settling her in the bed. Did she need milk before bed? Perhaps I'd give the bottle a miss after last night, sure she'd let me know loud and clear if she was hungry.

Eden tossed and turned as the classical music played, lights dancing around the room, but she didn't try to get up. The walk earlier must have tired her out.

I sat on the carpet and watched as her eyes blinked slowly, eventually closing. I didn't move until my backside was numb, watching her sleep. She looked angelic, her mouth rhythmically sucking the dummy. Tears fell from my eyes and I buried my head in my hands. I was mourning a child I never had. She'd never been mine, not really. If my time with Eden had taught me anything, it was I wanted to be a father.

Around half an hour later, I sneaked out of Eden's room and went downstairs to pack. I'd have to bin the change bag; with everything I'd taken from Brooke yesterday morning. It contained a lot of Eden's things, but my DNA would be all over it and I couldn't take the risk. Even when she was returned unharmed, I doubted the police would stop looking, and even though I wasn't on any database of theirs, if arrested they'd connect me to the crime easily.

Armed with antibacterial wipes, I cleaned, washed all the surfaces and loaded the holdall with everything I wanted to take to Australia. There wasn't much, and at the airport I'd buy a bag the right size for hand luggage and dump the bulky holdall. Eden would be returned with only the clothes on her back, but I'm sure her parents wouldn't care. Everything else could be replaced.

I dismantled the hardly used bouncer and playpen and put it in the corner of the garage, along with her buggy. The house looked as though we'd never been there.

My father's company owned the house outright. There was no mortgage to pay and I believed the bills automatically came out of his company account, which was still live, with thousands of pounds in there. No one would come to the house, the things I'd left behind wouldn't be discovered and even if they were, I'd already be thousands of miles away.

I'd pick up a costume from somewhere tomorrow morning and wait for Brooke to get in touch, maybe even start the drive back down south. The sooner I dropped Eden off, the better. I wanted to get away, forget about her, mend my broken heart and where better than Australia. It would be springtime, the weather hotting up, and I was sure there'd be loads of girls who could take my mind off my worries.

My phone remained stubbornly silent. What was Brooke doing that she couldn't call me again? She'd ended our conversation quickly, as though she'd been overheard. Perhaps I'd scared her off. I'd threatened to hurt her and considered texting her but changed my mind. I'd wait until she contacted me again. She had a lot to lose too. I wouldn't remain silent if I was caught and she had to know that. It would take all my resolve not to snap her little neck when I saw her again.

I sat in front of the ten o'clock news, but it seemed Eden's disappearance still hadn't made national headlines. Instead I googled Halloween costumes, I'd need one with a mask or a hat. Eden's would have to be a boy's one too. I hoped the costumes wouldn't draw more attention to us. Only time would tell.

38

BROOKE SIMMONS

Ali's revelation had shocked me to the core, I had no idea she'd cheated on Christopher on her hen do. It was a wild night and we were all hammered, but I hadn't seen Ali go off with the bartender. I knew she was pregnant when they married, she'd told me when she'd done a test a few days before, but I automatically assumed it was Christopher's baby and she never said otherwise.

After the admission had sunk in, realisation hit, she'd handed Jimmy and I a gift. The police were now looking for Jason Wells, not me and not Jimmy. It bolstered my plan to make the swap tomorrow. They'd be looking the other way, not concentrating on me. It would be a small window of opportunity. Although as soon as they found Jason, I was sure they'd eliminate him quickly.

He was hot, I remembered, and Ali had taken a shine to him straight away. They'd flirted and I remember seeing him later at the club. The rest of the night was a blur though. Ali's tears the following day now made sense; I'd thought it had been a massive hangover but instead they were tears of regret. Back then, she never told me she'd slept with him. A pang of guilt made me wince. Not only had I been the catalyst for the kidnap of her daughter, I was to blame for the break-up of her marriage too.

We'd walked around the block twice, Ali crying most of the way. She appeared utterly broken and I felt sick being around her, the lie stuck in my throat like dry bread I couldn't swallow. Ali was distraught and barely able to get her words out through her tears. It was all my fault, all because I was desperate to move out. I'd seen a chance to make some money and I'd grabbed it with both hands, without fully considering the consequences. Shame wrapped itself around me. I'd sunk so low, caused so much heartache to Ali and Christopher, and also to Jimmy. None of them had deserved the pain I'd inflicted.

When we got back to the house, I didn't invite her inside. Mum was already peering through the curtains, watching us say goodbye. I hugged Ali tight, trying to silently convey a million apologies. Would life still carry on as before? Could I still look after Eden when she was returned? I didn't want to lose Ali as a friend. Her and Christopher had always been good to me, which made the deception harder to stomach.

Back inside, Mum followed me around, desperate to know what Ali had said, how she was feeling, was there any news? She wasn't satisfied until I told her about our walk, although I kept Ali's infidelity to myself. It was none of her business. I needed to get upstairs and work out a plan to meet Jimmy, but first I had to sit through reheated quiche and dry potatoes.

'How about *The Notebook*?' Mum asked as I pushed the quiche around my plate.

I groaned inwardly; having forgotten about 'movie night'. We'd seen *The Notebook* before; I knew Mum would have too much to drink and cry over Dad leaving her for another woman ten years ago. She'd never gotten over it and I suspected it was why she was so clingy.

'Isn't it a bit... soppy?' I said, laying my knife and fork down.

'No, well, yes I guess it is, but it's beautiful.'

I rolled my eyes and conceded. A couple of hours on the sofa with her and I'd be free to go to my room undisturbed.

By the time we'd cleared away dinner and put the movie on, it was seven o'clock. Mum drank most of the Prosecco and was three sheets to the wind by the end of the film. She snivelled into a tissue, proclaiming it was the greatest love story she'd ever seen. It wasn't my sort of film. I preferred thrillers with complicated plots and double bluffs, but ever the dutiful daughter I didn't complain.

When I crept upstairs, Mum was snoozing on the sofa. I was itching to call Jimmy but knew I had to work out a plan first. We could meet at Mini Mischief, or rather he could take Eden in and let her have fun in the baby section I'd taken her to a few times. It was soft play with a ball pit and foam-filled shapes to climb on, all age-appropriate, and she was penned in by part-cushioned walls and netting. She'd be perfectly safe if he left her there for a few minutes unattended, pretended to pop to the toilet and then left. I could swoop in ten minutes later and pick her up.

The staff were practically kids themselves; no one would bat an eyelid. I'd say I was meeting my brother and niece. As long as I paid, they'd let me in. Eden would recognise me, and she'd be thrilled. I'd be able to carry her out without a hitch. The only problem was inventing an excuse as to how I found her. It would be one hell of a coincidence I'd be the one to discover Eden. That would need some more thought. I wasn't about to incriminate myself and, anyway, it only mattered if the police could prove I was involved.

I'd go for a wander around the Belfry Shopping Centre, pick up a few bits. Should I bring Mum for cover? Would it look more natural if we were together? Perhaps we could travel in together but split up to do some of our own shopping. I pondered the idea, gently touching the top of my head. My wound was scabbing, it itched, as if reminding me of my crime.

I changed into my pyjamas and opened the laptop, it whirred loudly as it came back to life. Searching for the shopping centre, the map was slow to load, although when it did, it showed the layout I was familiar with. Never before had I paid so much attention to the locations of toilets and exits, but if this was to go right, it had to be planned to the last detail.

Timing was everything, I would have to find Eden once enough time had passed to ensure Jimmy slipped away without being seen. If he got caught, we'd both be done for; there was no reason for him not to tell the police everything. He had no loyalty to me, only contempt. I was sure he'd take great pleasure in throwing me to the wolves after what I'd done.

I ran through the options in my head. The afternoon would be quieter than the morning in Mini Mischief. Parents generally took their kids there for a play, to wear them out, then afterwards had McDonald's or Burger King for lunch before going for a wander around the shops. It was what I did when I took Eden there and we'd always queue for a while to get in. On a couple of occasions, I'd been turned away when the soft play was at full capacity. That couldn't happen tomorrow, so the afternoon would be a better time.

My palms began to sweat as I picked up the phone to call Jimmy. Two heads were better than one and I wanted to run through the plan. Find out if he had any objections or foresaw obstacles I hadn't considered. For better or for worse we were in this together and we'd have to play nice to get the job done.

39

ALI TOLFREY

I'd walked Brooke back to her door, and we'd said goodbye before I carried on the journey home. The wind whipped around my face, burning my cheeks, and I hunkered down into my coat, better for having spoken to Brooke. Seeing her pain for us reinforced what I knew. I'd been wrong to doubt her, to question our friendship. She loved Eden, that was obvious, and I couldn't believe she'd do anything that would cause her harm.

My steps were slow, reluctant to return to the house. Our beautiful family home was a cold, empty shell without Eden. Christopher would shut himself away, ignore me while he decided whether our marriage was worth saving. I'd already broken my vows before I even took them, that's how he would see it. Despite the infidelity happening before we walked down the aisle. I prayed Eden was his child.

She was, I was sure of it; she had Christopher's same shaped eyes. Hers were getting lighter by the day, a mix of my brown with Christopher's green creeping in. I'd seen his baby photos, Eden had his hair too, practically white-blonde at the same age. I blinked grit from my eyes as I walked, deposited by the wind, wrapping my arms around myself as my coat billowed behind me.

The hen night was such a hazy memory, I had flashes of Jason's image but not enough to picture him perfectly. If I was honest with myself, I didn't believe he was involved, although perhaps strangely I hoped he was. Not for any desire to see him again, but if Eden being taken from us came from a place of love, it would mean she was safe. Although how he would have found out about Eden I don't know. We exchanged names, that was it. I don't even remember telling him where I lived. No one knew about that night, I'd not told a soul, eaten up by my own guilt, so the idea Jason had Eden seemed impossible.

I chewed on it all the way home and when I reached the town house, I could see the upstairs light was on. Christopher was in our bedroom, maybe throwing his clothes into a suitcase. No, he wouldn't go, he'd force me to leave instead. With a heavy heart, I pushed open the front door and DC Benson greeted me in the hallway.

'Any update?' I asked, without looking up as I kicked off my boots and put them in the shoe cabinet.

'No, nothing from DCI Greene,' he paused, his cheeks reddening. 'No results back yet.'

I moved past him into the kitchen, to fill the kettle.

'Let me make you a tea. Are you hungry? We've had another food delivery from your neighbours across the street, Susan and Bill. I think she said it was cottage pie,' he offered, following behind.

'That's kind, but no, I'm not hungry.' I sat at the table, while DC Benson took over, retrieving a mug from the cupboard.

'They seemed very nice, said if there was anything they could do, to let them know.'

'Has Christopher come down?' I asked, changing the subject.

He looked at me with pitying eyes and shook his head. I gave a solitary nod and got to my feet.

'I'll be back in a minute,' I said to DC Benson and climbed the two flights to our bedroom, knocking on the door.

I waited for a second, but there was no response. Sighing, I pushed the door open and found Christopher inside the walk-in wardrobe. He was packing, not his own clothes but mine. Roughly shoving them into a holdall.

'Christopher, can we talk about this.'

'You're leaving. Tomorrow,' he said flatly, without bothering to look at me.

'I can't, not while Eden's missing. We need to stay here, stay together.'

He spun around to face me; lips curled back, baring his teeth. 'Together? You must be fucking kidding me. My wife shags a bloody bartender on her hen night, and I'm supposed to forget it happened?' His voice boomed around the room and I quickly stepped over the threshold and closed the bedroom door behind me.

'I'm sorry, it was a mistake. I never meant for it to happen. I never would have told you.'

'And that makes it better?' Christopher interrupted, in each hand he held the ends of a silk scarf, the fabric stretched tightly around his fists as though he was going to strangle me with it.

'No, no, of course it doesn't, but it meant nothing. I love you. I married you. I only want you.'

'My daughter might not be mine. Have you any idea the fucking bomb you've dropped on our life?'

'She will be yours; I know it,' I said softly.

'And this fucking guy kidnaps her, thinking she's his?'

'We don't know that yet.' I tried to keep my voice calm, to level out Christopher's hysteria. The scarf stretched further still; his knuckles white against the salmon-coloured fabric. It would be ruined, but I remained quiet.

'When did you last see him? Was it recently?'

I recoiled. Did Christopher think there had been some long, drawn-out affair behind his back?

'No! The last time I saw him was on my hen night. It's the only time I've seen him. I love you, Christopher, I'm so very sorry. It only happened once, it's the only time I've ever...' my words trailed off.

'Cheated?' he snapped, and I lowered my eyes to the carpet.

He dropped the scarf into the mouth of the holdall and turning back to the wardrobe viciously pulled a blouse from a hanger. He had every right to be angry. I'd be angry too if the shoe was on the other foot.

'It's over, Ali, now you can fuck whomever you like.' His words stung like a smack in the face and I sank to the bed.

'Please, Christopher, please. I'll do anything. I beg you.'

'You disgust me, you're nothing but a filthy whore. We're done. Pack your shit, tomorrow you're out. I'll be in touch via my solicitor.'

'I'm not going anywhere; this is as much my home as it is yours. My priority is Eden, not you, not us,' I snapped at the venom in his tone, he'd gone too far.

Christopher dropped the blouse on the floor and swept out of the room and down the stairs. A minute later, I heard raised voices and the front door slam.

Creeping to the window, I saw not Christopher but DC Benson leaving. He got in his car and drove away, leaving me alone with a husband I didn't recognise. My hands trembled and I placed my palms on my knees to steady them, looking around at my clothes strewn everywhere. Christopher had never spoken to me that way before, he was pompous and difficult sometimes, stubborn even, but he'd never been so brutal.

It was the stress of everything, it had to be. Eden's disappearance, my betrayal. Surely, he didn't mean those words he'd said. Once he'd calmed down, he'd see sense, take it back. Our marriage wasn't over, was it? It couldn't be. What we had was special. I loved him and I'd fight for us to stay together, the alternative didn't bear thinking about.

Without Christopher and Eden, I had nothing. I couldn't go on. Swiping away a tear from eyes on fire, I got up to put my clothes back in the wardrobe. Kicking the holdall under the shelves and closing the door on it.

Tomorrow was another day. Once Christopher had had a chance to reflect and a little time to cool off, he'd change his mind. We'd only get through this if we were together. Alone we were weak; we made each other strong.

I undressed, removing the lambswool jumper and crumpled trousers, putting them in the laundry basket. On autopilot, I took off my make-up and massaged serum into my face. The reflection in the mirror which stared back at me was that of a stranger. She looked haggard, unrecognisable. I brushed my hair, cleaned my teeth and climbed into bed, pulling the covers to my chin. Downstairs, I heard bottles clinking, Christopher rummaging in the drinks cabinet for more red wine, or maybe whisky. He wouldn't come back upstairs tonight.

I debated whether to pop a sleeping pill but decided against it. Being conscious and aware was agony, but the pain was real. I'd endure whatever I had to, to ensure Eden and Christopher stayed with me. I'd walk over hot coals to save my daughter and my marriage, I'd beg, on my hands and knees. Tomorrow, I'd do whatever I had to, as without them, life wouldn't be worth living.

DAY THREE
HALLOWEEN

7AM – 11AM

40

JIMMY PEARSON

Brooke had called late last night, and it was an effort to be civil. She'd banged on about having to work together to make sure we weren't caught. I let her do most of the talking; I wasn't sure I could trust myself to be courteous. She told me the plan and it could work. Not that we had much choice. Eden had to be returned to her rightful parents.

We'd discussed the finer details, entry and exit points, timings, where I could wait and where she'd be. She'd suggested where I could leave the car, close by, but I already had an idea. I didn't want Brooke to know my every move. It wasn't as if she was trustworthy. The last thing I wanted was to be caught with my pants down.

One of my concerns was bumping into someone I knew. Costumes would help disguise me, to others and the cameras in the shopping centre. If I got the right one, hopefully I'd be unrecognisable. Brooke told me she didn't believe she was being followed when I mentioned it, she said the police were trying to trace another suspect. It was one more reason we had to act quickly; it wouldn't be long before they'd be looking at her again.

The quiver in her voice gave me a small amount of satisfaction, spreading through me like a hot drink after a winter's walk. I hoped she'd look over her shoulder for years to come, as I would. Would she feel the hot breath of the police at the back of her neck, hear sirens and be gripped by the onset of panic? I knew I would, and she'd caused it all. Perhaps it was for the best I didn't see her face to face, if I did, I wasn't sure I'd be able to control the urge to squeeze the life out of her.

Every time I thought about what lay ahead my tongue glued to the roof of my mouth and it was hard to swallow. I had enough bravado to mask it, but inside I was shitting a brick. Today I'd be running on adrenaline alone.

Eden had gone through the night without waking, but I couldn't get off, instead I watched shadows on the ceiling cast from trees outside. Going over and over what I had to do and when. What time I had to leave and everything to remember. Trying to push down the crushing pain I felt in my chest whenever I thought about saying goodbye to Eden.

When dawn rolled around, I got up and paced the house, checking to see if I'd left anything unpacked. It was mostly done so I made coffee and waited for Eden to stir. It was gone seven when she did. I'd showered and dressed, clearing the bathroom of all our things. Eden was grizzly, she kept chewing her dummy. I knew she was teething; the front of her gum was red and swollen.

I dosed her up on Calpol and attempted to feed her breakfast, but she wasn't having any of the porridge I offered. I relented and gave her a biscuit to chew on and she chomped happily as I got our things ready to leave, loading the car in the garage as best I could. The space was tight, but I didn't want to be seen leaving so soon. Positive it would raise questions for any curtain-twitching neighbours.

Eden was left strapped into her car seat in the kitchen because I'd collapsed the playpen and bouncer and had nowhere safe to put her. By the time I'd finished, I was sweating despite the cold. Eden was screaming, her dummy spat out across the tiles, struggling to get out of the car seat. Snot streamed from her nose as I pushed the dummy back in her mouth.

I pulled the car out of the garage and closed it behind me. Georgina was across the street, dressed in her running gear and talking to a man in his fifties. She smiled and waved at me before returning to her conversation. Fervent glances as she spoke gave me the impression she was talking about me. I went back into the house through the front door to carry Eden out. The sooner I was out of here, the better.

She was having a full-on tantrum, arching her back and straining her chest against the restraints of the car seat. Her crying had started to grate, like nails across a chalkboard. How free I'd be once she was no longer my responsibility. Guilt consumed me, but I couldn't stop the bitterness. I wasn't a parent now; I was a babysitter. Eden wasn't my daughter; she was a problem. I chewed my lip as I unclicked the straps and carried her in one arm, lugging the car seat behind me out of the front door.

Georgina was still there, her hands on her curvy hips, staring straight at the house. She was frowning, deep in conversation, and I moved quickly, sensing she might come over. I didn't pause to look at the house I was leaving behind. Another piece of my dad's legacy. I would have liked to have spent more time there, tried to find out why he owned property in this village. Was it an impulse buy? An investment? I'd never know.

Perhaps one day I could come back, once the dust had settled, when it was safe. I had no idea if my name would fall into the hands of the police and there would be a manhunt. With any luck, I would have left the country by then. If Brooke was to face the music, she could do it alone.

Should I let my brother know I was coming, or just turn up unannounced? Maybe I'd call him from the airport. 'Surprise, your big brother's in town, oh and by the way, you know I told you I had a daughter... well now I don't.'

I strapped Eden back into the car seat once it was in position. My hands trembled as I fumbled with the clip. Glancing over my shoulder, Georgina was still there, although her back was to me now. It was the perfect opportunity to leave. The man she was talking to was writing something down, her number perhaps. The muscles in my neck tightened as I imagined him recording my number plate. Was he someone the lovely, lonely Georgina was trying to seduce, or was he the neighbourhood watch, suspicious of an outsider?

I started the engine and they both turned to look. I smiled tightly and raised a hand in a half wave. Neither smiled back as I drove away, and I swallowed the lump in my throat. Had the news of Eden's kidnapping gone national? Was my picture on the front page of every newspaper? My heart slammed against my chest and sweat beaded on my forehead. I barely heard Eden's babbling in the back as my mind raced.

I had to get a costume for Halloween and fast. I indicated at the roundabout and headed towards town, trying to still my whirling thoughts. Panic turned to anger as I gripped the steering wheel tighter and shouted at Eden to quieten down. Her bottom lip wobbled. Brooke had done this to me, she'd turned me into a neurotic freak. As much as I'd miss her, the sooner I got rid of Eden, the better.

41

BROOKE SIMMONS

I'd barely slept a wink, spending hours going over every possible scenario that could arise; Jimmy not coming, or him getting arrested before he'd even set foot in the shopping centre. How did I know the police weren't already onto him? Had I not spoken to Ali last night, I would never have known they were searching for someone else. Maybe I was being paranoid, but I was unable to shake the feeling I was being watched whenever I stepped outside the house.

Would they have put me under surveillance? I couldn't imagine so, but I was their only link to Eden, and I knew they suspected my involvement. If Jimmy was caught, he would take me down with him, he'd told me as much on the phone. His manner was short, curt and I could tell he was forcing himself to talk to me. I'd tried to ignore the hostility; it wouldn't get us anywhere. He could be as hostile as he liked when he was on the run from the police. It gave me a small jolt of pleasure I quickly dismissed. What had happened to me? What had I become? Was I that bitter I wished that on him? Karl had turned me into someone I didn't recognise, he'd completely messed me up and left me broken. Then when I was starting to heal, to trust again, I'd unexpectedly fallen in love with Jimmy, but he'd buggered off and pretended we'd never met. It seemed I had little luck with men.

Even now, I was unable to move forward, I'd forever be stuck in the past, waiting for the next man to hurt me. I was going to be stronger. If we got out of this, I'd change, move out and start afresh. Leave all the baggage behind, the guilt too. I'd make it up to Ali and Christopher somehow.

The estate agent hadn't got back to me, although they weren't yet open. I kept refreshing my inbox anyway. Mum was already awake and moving around downstairs; I could hear the kettle whistling from below and my stomach growled. As much as I didn't want to deal with Mum, I needed to eat so made my way down to the kitchen.

'Want some toast?' Mum placed a mug of tea in front of me at the table.

'Yes please,' I replied. When had I got so lazy as to let Mum prepare all my meals? She enjoyed having me there to look after, she'd told me as much. Still, it wouldn't be long before I'd have to do my own cooking and washing. Would she cope all right on her own? I knew she'd be lonely, perhaps I could suggest she get a dog. It might be good company for her.

I already dreaded the conversation we'd have, if I was lucky enough to get my offer accepted to buy the flat. There would be floods of tears, she wouldn't understand why I'd want to live anywhere else. Not even that I was a few years shy of thirty and still living with my mum.

'Here you go,' she said, smiling as she delivered hot buttered toast and strawberry jam, cut into fours, like I was a child.

I smiled tightly, refusing to comment.

'I'm going shopping today, into Redhill, want to come?' I asked, mid-chew.

Mum's eyes immediately lit up which was a kick in the ribs. It was something we never did. I never spent more time with her than I had to. 'Yes, I'd love to!'

'I need to get a few bits and I'll buy us lunch, okay?' I said, reinforcing I was an adult who earnt her own money. I wasn't clinging to my mum's apron strings.

'That sounds wonderful, I can wear my new coat. I need to get some toiletries from Boots and there's a couple of books I'm going to have a look for. Ooohh, and we need to get some more sweets for the trick or treaters tonight.'

She carried on, but I zoned out, chewing my toast but finding it hard to swallow. Bringing Mum with me felt shitty. I was using her for cover, so she could plead my innocence, if for whatever reason we were caught. A simple mother-and-daughter shopping trip. Like we did those so often! I couldn't remember the last time.

Before I knew it, Mum had whipped upstairs to have a shower, excited at the prospect of an outing. I was as terrified as she was enthusiastic. Only a few more hours. As soon as I had Eden in my hands, I could phone the police, in fact I'd get Mum to. I was still trying to work out how I'd explain finding out where Eden was. Worried I'd be giving myself away. I had to come up with something and fast.

I had thought about getting Jimmy to call the Crimestoppers number on his way out of the shopping centre, but I didn't want Eden left for long. I had to come up with something, there wasn't any time to delay. In a matter of hours Eden would be back where she was supposed to be, and the police would be chasing a ghost.

As I put my plate in the dishwasher, there was a knock at the door. Wrapping my dressing gown around me and tying the cord into a knot, I went to answer. As soon as I pulled open the front door and saw the blonde policewoman on the step, terror gripped me and I froze, glad I could hear the shower running upstairs.

'Brooke, Detective Constable Tunstall, can I come in?' she asked, holding out her warrant card and already moving across the threshold as I staggered backwards. Her again.

'Sure,' I managed, my voice upbeat although the tremor remained.

We went into the kitchen and I was relieved she was alone.

Although her eyes were piercing, she plastered a smile onto her face. 'We're looking at a line of enquiry in reference to Eden Tolfrey's disappearance and are speaking to all of Mrs Tolfrey's friends who were invited to her hen night a little over a year ago.'

'Oh?' I replied, not sure if I should let on I'd spoken to Ali or not.

'Yes, could you tell me, would you happen to remember a Jason Wells?'

'There was a bartender called Jason at the Walkabout. I remember as he was flirting with Ali. Are you saying he could be involved in Eden's disappearance?' I pressed my hand against my chest. Mock horror. *Too much?* It was a little.

Blondie's eyes narrowed. 'We're not sure yet. Do you remember if he said where he lived, or anything that might help us find him?'

'No, I'm sorry, I barely spoke to him. I think one of the other girls, Kelly, spoke to him a little.'

'Okay, no problem. I'll put Kelly next on my list. Thanks for your help. Sorry to have bothered you so early,' Detective Constable Tunstall said, smiling tightly. 'I almost forgot, here's your phone, the lab is finished with it.' She handed me the phone in a plastic evidence bag.

'Have you any updates on Eden?' I asked, as I held the phone, enjoying the familiar weight of it in my hand.

'I'm afraid any information can only be divulged with Mr and Mrs Tolfrey. I'm sure you understand.'

I nodded, no closer to knowing what was going on in the investigation. Only that they hadn't found Jason Wells, yet anyway. That was positive enough. All the time they were looking at him, they weren't focusing on me.

We smiled politely at each other before I could no longer hear the shower upstairs running or the pipes rattling. I took a step forward towards the door, willing the detective to leave before Mum came. Following my lead, she passed me, moving quickly, her blonde hair whipping behind her, reaching the door before I did and pulling it open.

'Thanks again for your time, Brooke.' She didn't pause but carried on down the path, gracefully avoiding the pumpkins Mum had laid out, the ones I always tripped over.

See ya, blondie.

42

ALI TOLFREY

The morning sky was an apocalyptic red, the sun in flames as it saw off the night. I woke, staring straight at the skylight above where I'd neglected to close the blind the night before. Sweating under the thick duvet, I threw the cover off, heart racing from a nightmare I couldn't remember. A nightmare which had spilled over into real life. I rolled onto my side, taking in gulps of air, my chemise sticking to my skin. The house was quiet, Christopher not yet awake. The bedside clock read a little after seven, but I made no effort to get up. Was there any point? What was left of my life had disintegrated last night, it was damaged beyond repair.

Wrong attitude, my inner voice interjected. Eden would be home today, I had to think positive. The police would find Jason and she'd be returned, although I didn't really believe it to be true. He didn't have Eden.

Despite knowing that deep down in my gut, I consumed the fantasy, imagining twirling her around in my arms, listening to her precious giggle. I knew it wasn't reality. As if a shadow fell across my mind, the image fragmented. Eden had been missing for two days and nights; I knew the statistics. It was more likely my baby would be brought home to me dead not alive.

My gut wrenched at the thought. I wouldn't believe it. Not until I knew it to be true. I had to have hope. Eden was out there somewhere. I still felt her, she had to be alive. I was sure I'd know if something happened to her, by some kind of maternal connection, one so strong it could never be broken.

I never knew it was possible to hurt so much. My insides twisted like a knife, and I brought my knees to my chest in a foetal position. Grief swamped me, like a tidal wave, relentless despite my belief Eden was alive.

Swallowing it down, I reached for my mobile, the battery almost dead. I had ten missed calls from my mother last night, texts from her too. More messages had come in overnight from friends and acquaintances. Too many to count and I deleted them without reading. I couldn't bear their heartfelt sympathies and I couldn't speak to my mother either. I wished I had a better relationship with her, but whatever I did wasn't good enough, I had enough guilt without her laying it on. I knew for certain when Eden grew up, I'd always be on her side, no matter what.

Forcing myself out of bed and into the shower, I grimaced at how prominent my collarbones were. My hips jutted out accusingly too. The jeans I pulled on were looser and I covered up with a chunky jumper, not bothering with any make-up. I twisted my hair into a bun, secured with pins, and sighed into the mirror.

Unable to put off going downstairs any longer, I winced when the bedroom door creaked as I pulled it open.

On the first-floor landing, Eden's bedroom door was open. Christopher's feet came into view as I rounded the bend from the stairs. Inching closer, I saw he'd fallen asleep on her rug. The room smelt musty; sweat and alcohol permeated the air and an empty bottle of red wine lay on its side. Blood-red spots had leaked from the bottle, staining the pink carpet where it had been discarded.

Incensed, my nostrils flared, molars clenching together, jaw locking as I kicked the soles of Christopher's feet.

'Get up!' I hissed. 'Fucking get up!'

Stepping over him, I snatched the bottle from the floor, as he groaned. I threw open the window to let fresh air in, seething so much my hands shook. How dare he desecrate her room.

'Get up!' I yelled and his hand moved to his head, eyes squinting at the light.

He slowly lifted his head, taking in his surroundings and blinking rapidly.

I brandished the wine bottle in front of me. 'In here? Look what you've fucking done. Get out, get out!' I yelled, stamping my feet.

Surprised at my outrage, he crawled to his feet and rushed to the bathroom, throwing up over the side of the bath. I followed him, my eyes boring a hole into his back. Pink liquid stark on the gleaming white tub.

'You're pathetic,' I blasted as he wiped his mouth on his sleeve, straightening up.

Before I had time to react, he launched at me, catching me off guard, his hand around my neck, squeezing tightly. Disgusting breath hit my face as he held me fast against the hallway wall.

'Do it,' I wheezed, so livid I no longer cared what he did.

He released me almost at once, shoving me to the floor, returning to the bathroom and locking the door.

I coughed, my throat burning. What had happened to us? Christopher had never raised a hand to me before. Losing Eden had ripped us to shreds, so much so we had no idea who we were any more.

Refusing to cry, I stalked downstairs, gulping in cold water straight from the kitchen tap. Messages blinked accusingly on the answering machine on the kitchen worktop. The landline had been plugged back in yesterday afternoon, but the phone had the volume turned right down so the constant ringing hadn't driven us mad. I hit the play button before rummaging in the kitchen for something to tackle the wine stain.

There was another message from my mother, one from my friend, Kelly, sending her support, two from journalists, although how they'd secured my number I'd never know, and the last was the dentist letting me know I'd missed my appointment yesterday afternoon. Under the circumstances I'd hope they'd waive their missed appointment fee. Normally I'd be on top of everything, but I barely even knew what day it was.

Donning rubber gloves, I got a mix of baking soda and cold water and went back to Eden's room to try to remove the stain. I dabbed at first, then scrubbed as hard as I could, releasing all my anger onto the carpet, but even though the stain lessened, it wouldn't disappear completely, having sunk deep within the pile and left to fester for hours.

I clenched my jaw. The carpet would need replacing; Eden's room had to be perfect again.

As I sat back on my knees, behind me I could hear the shower running. Perhaps Christopher would be so hung-over he'd slip. The fleeting thought provided me with intense pleasure. How had we gone from love to hate in a matter of days? All of our emotions magnified in our hellish situation.

The doorbell sounded from below and interrupted my macabre mullings. Hurrying down the stairs, I opened the door to a pink-cheeked DC Benson, his blond beard looking more Viking-esque by the day.

'Mrs Tolfrey,' he greeted, eyes bright.

'Morning,' I replied, not quite meeting his cheerful tone.

'Are you okay?' he asked, stepping over the threshold.

My hand instinctively moved to my neck; the skin tender.

'Yes, yes, I'm fine,' I muttered, turning away to let DC Benson close the door.

'Is Christopher home?'

'He's upstairs, in the shower,' I replied, still walking towards the kitchen. DC Benson followed behind.

'I spoke to DCI Greene on my way here,' he said to my back.

'Do you have news?' I asked, spinning around, heart leaping into my throat. DC Benson almost walked into me I'd stopped so abruptly.

'They haven't managed to trace Jason Wells yet; he left Brighton three months ago, according to his most recent flatmate. We think he might be in the Worthing area.' He paused. 'Also, the DNA results have come—'

'And?' I interrupted before DC Benson could finish his sentence.

'Eden is Christopher's daughter.' DC Benson smiled as though he'd handed me a gift. In a way he had, although I feared it was already too late. Was I as desperate to save my marriage this morning as I had been last night?

My shoulders sank, knees buckling beneath me as I lowered myself into a chair.

'I'm sure Mr Tolfrey will be relieved to hear the news.' DC Benson's tone was cautious, respectful, although I almost expected him to add, 'It's a shame his wife is still a slut though.'

I sighed, head in my hands. Christopher need never have known. If only I'd kept my stupid mouth shut. After all, did I honestly believe Jason had taken Eden?

'Did I hear my name?' Christopher bristled into the kitchen, the wine staining around his mouth now gone. He was composed, stoic, his shower having washed away his sins. It wouldn't wash away the bruising around my neck that was sure to appear in a few hours though. I could barely look at him.

'Eden is yours, Mr Tolfrey, it's been confirmed by the laboratory this morning.' DC Benson rolled forward onto the balls of his feet as if he wanted a high five.

Christopher shot him a disdainful look. 'Well that's good to know. Thank you,' he replied stiffly, rubbing his freshly shaven face.

DC Benson reiterated what he'd told me to Christopher while I picked at a loose thread of my jumper.

'Do you mind if I use your toilet?' DC Benson asked politely, even though he'd been here for the best part of two days and we were beyond niceties now.

'Of course,' I said, and DC Benson left the room.

'The DNA result changes nothing,' Christopher said to me flatly as he sidled to the table.

'Fine,' I retorted, 'only know that when Eden comes home, if I'm moving out, she'll be coming with me.' I'd found a resolve I didn't know I had, the fury of being manhandled, the way I'd been spoken to, it masked the pain inside. It was all bluster, but he wasn't to know that.

Christopher scoffed, amplifying my bravado. 'I'm sure the courts won't see it that way.' His smug face loomed over me, but my voice remained icy cold.

'Know many cases that have awarded fathers sole custody, do you? You'll never paint me as an unfit mother, Christopher, in court or otherwise. Not when DC Benson has seen what a temper you have. I'm sure he'll be my star witness. Especially when I take photographs of the marks you've left on my neck.'

43

JIMMY PEARSON

The roads were relatively quiet as it was early on a Saturday morning, the shops having only just opened. I'd googled a business park where there was a Sainsbury's I could nip into. When I parked, I considered leaving Eden in the car but had visions of returning to find irate people had smashed my windows, like passers-by do in the height of summer when dogs are left to roast. It wasn't hot, but I knew I shouldn't leave her. An angry mob was something I could do without; I didn't want to draw any attention to either of us.

I'd dressed Eden in a blue jumpsuit with brightly covered trucks and a navy hoody. The last outfit I'd bought, not realising toddlers could be so messy and go through so many changes of clothes. The rest of her things were stuffed into a carrier bag, which I disposed of in the large recycling bin outside. The only thing left to get rid of was the change bag and the car seat, but I couldn't do that yet.

'If you have an accident today, girl, you'll have to wear it,' I said to her quizzical face.

Eden wriggled in my arms as I carried her to the supermarket, propped on my hip. I'd left the buggy in the garage, as it was one less thing to get rid of, but juggling Eden wasn't easy and I sat her in a trolley. She kicked her legs excitedly as I pushed her along.

We headed straight for the clothes, the Halloween costumes were at the back, and luckily, they had plenty of choice. I wanted a dinosaur onesie, but they didn't have it in Eden's size. In the end, I settled on a pirate outfit, tiny cut-off trousers and a top with skull and crossbones on the front. It came with a bandana, secured with Velcro for safety. A spark of inspiration hit me, I could add to the costume, to disguise us further.

I bought a similar outfit in adult size; it came with a white shirt, thin waistcoat and sash and billowing trousers. The accessories were a hat and eyepatch. Sure I'd freeze as I fingered the thin material on the hanger, but being cold would be the least of my problems, my adrenaline would keep me warm.

But was this really a good idea? Surely walking through the Belfry dressed in costume would draw attention, Halloween or not. Brooke had better be right about Mini Mischief's Halloween competition, and she better hope I wouldn't be the only one dressed up. I was aware that I had way more to lose than my pride.

I grabbed the costumes and walked to the make-up aisle. A few years back when I was seeing Lucy, the curvy, olive-skinned girl from Brazil, we went to a Halloween party. She wore a black catsuit and looked smoking hot. We'd ended up having sex before we even left the flat. She'd complained I'd smudged her whiskers she'd carefully drawn on with black eyeliner.

Selecting the cheapest one I could find, I hurried to the tills. Eden was chewing my keys, dribbling down her jumpsuit. At the self-service tills, I scanned the costumes and eyeliner, keeping my head low. I'd put the England cap on before I'd left the car, anything to make it harder to identify me on the in-store cameras.

Struggling to feed the notes into the machine, I gritted my teeth when one kept being spat out.

'Come on, for fuck's sake,' I muttered.

Eventually it went in and I pushed the trolley towards the exit.

As soon as I passed the security barrier, the alarm sounded. I rolled my eyes as a tubby security guard practically leapt on me from my left, his hand on my shoulder.

'Easy, mate, I haven't robbed anything,' I said gruffly, holding out the costumes.

'No need for that tone, sir. I don't want to have to call the police.'

'Take your hand off me.' My voice quivered as I buried the urge to punch him in the face deep in my gut. He did as I asked and took the costumes from my outstretched hand.

'Looks like one's still got a tag on it. Have you got your receipt, sir?'

I scowled; I'd left it at the till.

'It's still at the till, I didn't take it.'

'Step over here, sir, and I'll go and take a look.' He led me to the customer service desk, where a smiley lady in her sixties took the costumes and searched for the tag on the adult costume, unlocking it with ease using a tool on the counter.

Tubby had gone back to the tills to look for the receipt I'd neglected to take with me.

'Is it his first day or something?' I said, voice terse.

'He's a bit eager is Patrick. Ah, who's this lovely lad, hello poppet!' She grinned at Eden. I got a kick out of it whenever someone mistook Eden for a boy, it was too easy. Dress kids in blue and people assume.

'Eddie, my son.' The word stuck in my throat as I gazed at Eden's gummy smile, pleased with the cashier's attention. She reached out a saliva-covered finger, pointed and began jabbering.

The assistant waved back and spoke to her as I looked around, trying to find the security guard. I wanted to get out of the shop and on our way. There was no telling what the M1 would be like.

'There you go, sir, all done.' Patrick appeared out of nowhere. He moved faster than I'd anticipated for a chubster.

I took the receipt out of his hand. 'Cheers.'

'Bye,' waved the assistant as I left; I didn't turn around.

The car park was slowly filling, parents who looked like they'd rather be anywhere else were pushing empty trolleys towards the store. Should we get changed into our costumes there? No, I'd stop at a services, somewhere halfway. Eden would likely want a snack and nappy change at some point, maybe some more Calpol too. She was practically drooling, and I needed to put more Savlon on her hand. The skin had peeled right back, and it looked angry, but it was impossible to keep a baby's hands clean and dry.

I listened to her cry for around twenty minutes as I drove along the A46 towards signposts for the M1. I turned the volume louder, drowning her out with Capital radio. She wasn't impressed and flapped her arms.

'Eden, stop it, come on,' I said, my grip on the steering wheel tightening as I looked over my shoulder at her.

The traffic was slowing ahead, and I eased on the brake. As I came to a stop behind a Vauxhall Astra, I saw in my rear-view mirror a green Nissan haring down the lane.

'Slow down, you idiot!' I said, turning to look out of the back window.

The driver was young, early twenties maybe and I saw the shock in his face as he realised the traffic in front was at a standstill. He'd left it too late and braked hard, tyres squealing.

The next few seconds seemed to take an eternity. Stuck in traffic with nowhere to go, I unclipped my seat belt and pushed my body through the gap between the seats, throwing my top half over Eden's legs, covering the toy bar and bracing her seat for impact, trying to provide her with as much protection as I could.

I gripped the car seat as the Nissan shunted into the back of us. The car jolted and Eden's head snapped forward, her chin hitting the top of my head with a crack and she let out an ear-piercing screech.

44

BROOKE SIMMONS

'Who was that?' Mum asked as I closed the front door, giving me a fright.

'God, Mum, you scared me!' I scowled, rocking backwards.

'Was it the police again? They're not hounding you, are they?' The towel on her head wobbled like she was wearing a heavy ancient headdress.

'No, just bringing my phone back, nothing to worry about. Go get dressed, I'm going to get in the shower,' I said, climbing the stairs, forcing her to turn and go back the way she'd come.

The water was tepid, not the steaming hot I'd wanted. Was the boiler on its way out? I grimaced, the sooner I was out of here, the better. Mum never did any decorating or upkeep of the house. I mean, I didn't expect a show home, but it was so drab. The walls once a fresh magnolia had dulled to a dirty cream, the carpet a seventies brown. The building itself was old; pipes rattled every time the central heating came on, and in the winter damp patches appeared above the windows, causing the wallpaper to peel. Mum didn't seem to see it, or if she did, she ignored it.

When I had my own space, everything would be tidy and clean. The flat as I remembered was pretty neutral anyway, but I'd paint everything white and grey. I wanted clinical, I wanted modern. *It's not even yours yet*, the voice in my head piped up. It would be soon. I needed out of here.

Stopping the shower, I rushed to my room wrapped in a towel, eager to check my emails on the laptop while my dead iPhone was charging on the bedside table. Still nothing from the estate agent. Chewing my lip, I bit the bullet and dialled their number using the old Nokia. I could be running out of credit and needed to make sure I had some saved for today, in case Jimmy got in touch, so I would make it quick.

The voicemail kicked in and I glanced at the time, it was a little past nine but perhaps the office didn't open until late on a Saturday. I left a message, mentioning my email and confirmation I wanted to place an offer of £175,000. My blood pressure shot skyward at the amount. It was so grown-up, my first bid on a new home. It was something I would have talked through with Ali, but I could hardly do that now. Surely someone would get back to me, unless it was already under offer. I didn't want to believe I'd left it too late.

I left the phone on the bed and got dressed, pulling on black jeans and a jumper. I looked like a cat burglar, but it was Halloween after all. Maybe I was channelling my inner criminal. All I needed was a swag bag and an eye mask. The humour helped ease my anxiety whenever I considered what could go wrong today, and a lot could.

Although I didn't think I had too much risk, not with my part; Jimmy had that. I would merely be in the right place at the right time. The police couldn't prove I'd been involved in Eden's abduction. If they could, I'd have been arrested already. They'd seen me enough over the past couple of days to know I didn't have her stashed anywhere.

I thought of Eden's little chubby cheeks, I'd missed her and couldn't wait to see her again. I hoped Jimmy had still doted on her, even knowing the truth. I couldn't bear to think otherwise. Additionally, I hoped there wouldn't be any long-term effects of her being away from Ali and Christopher. No, she was only a year old, she wouldn't remember any of it. However, I knew Ali would bear the scars for years to come and I'd always be sorry. I could never explain how easily the lie got out of hand. If I ever told her I'd palmed Eden off as my own child, she'd turn her back on me for sure.

Someone like her, with her good fortune, money and a stable family would never be able to understand how someone like me could stoop so low. In truth, it wasn't even solely about the money, more about hurting Jimmy. Hurting him as he'd hurt me. I'd punished him for both his and Karl's crimes. It had become a perfect storm, pain for Jimmy and an escape route for me.

'Ready?' Mum pushed open my door without knocking and I pressed my lips together, holding in my complaint. Another reason why I wanted out, no bloody privacy.

'Yeah, I'll be there in a minute.'

'Okay, I'll go and write my list.' She turned and trotted down the stairs, plait bouncing on her shoulders. I hadn't seen her hair loose for years. I didn't want to tell her the plait she always wore made her look like a schoolgirl. A very old schoolgirl.

I packed a small cross-body bag with the Nokia I used for Jimmy, now switched off, and my iPhone with about thirty per cent battery and a million notifications on the home screen I hadn't looked at yet. I took some cash – twenty quid – a scrap of paper and a biro, shoving them in, in case I needed them. Scanning the room to see if I'd forgotten anything. We only had one shot to get it right, and it was all about timing.

Eden couldn't be left alone too long in case someone noticed and called the police. But if I was too early, there was a chance Jimmy and I might bump into each other. The shopping centre had cameras so that wouldn't do. In my head I'd figured out the route to take around the centre, I'd be able to steer Mum if I had to.

My underarms dampened, despite the recent shower. As the minutes ticked by, the more nervous I was about the whole thing. Maybe it was a mistake? Jimmy would have disappeared, and I'd be the one to face the rap. What if I caved under questioning? *You didn't before*, the voice inside my head bolstered me on. I had to do it, I had to end Ali and Christopher's nightmare. Eden had to be returned. Once she was back everything would go back to how it was before. It would have to, wouldn't it? Maybe there was even a slim chance Ali would let me look after Eden. At the house initially, then maybe she'd feel safe with me taking her out?

I glanced in the mirror before going downstairs.

'It's all going to be fine,' I whispered to my reflection.

Downstairs, I could hear Mum on the phone, I found her in the kitchen and frowned.

'It's Betty,' she hissed, her hand over the mouthpiece.

I rolled my eyes. Betty was our next-door neighbour, in her eighties and mad as a box of frogs.

'Okay, no problem, Betty, we'll see you in a minute,' Mum trilled in her sing-song voice.

'What? We're supposed to be going shopping,' I complained, hands on my hips as Mum hung up.

'Sorry, love, as soon as I said we were going into town, she said she needed a few bits, what could I say?' Mum slid her arms into her coat, and I stood staring, incredulous.

'So, she's coming?'

Mum shrugged and smiled apologetically as my heckles rose.

'For God's sake!' I muttered as a light tap came from the door, spritely for an incapacitated old woman, wasn't she?

45

ALI TOLFREY

Empowered by my conversation with Christopher, I was buoyed on witnessing the shock on his face as I stood up to him. For the first time since Eden was taken, I had fire in my belly, a reason to fight instead of collapsing in a puddle of tears. Wanting to keep momentum and out of the way of DC Benson, I took to cleaning again. Hoovering first, then scrubbing the bathroom Christopher had been sick in, trying to eradicate everywhere he'd been as though it was a crime scene. I had another go at the stain on Eden's carpet, but it still wouldn't budge. I'd have to get it replaced; every time I saw it, it would be a reminder of Eden's disappearance. The darkest time of my life.

Every so often, I paused to glimpse in the mirror at the small circular imprints of Christopher's fingers growing darker on my neck. I pushed at them, prodded the tender skin beneath. Teasing the bruising out as much as I could. Hopefully they'd be nice and purple when I reappeared downstairs.

I'd left them to it. The *men* had found a common ground over breakfast, in golf of all things. I'd raised my eyes to the heavens when they started talking about their handicap. As much as I wanted to hurt Christopher right now, our marriage wasn't over, not for me anyway. What I'd said about the courts awarding custody, it wasn't true. I'd never take Eden away from her father. I'd been so angry at his spitefulness I couldn't help myself but bite back. He'd been stupid, arrogant and callous, saying vile things and even laid his hands on me, something he'd never done before. But our daughter had been kidnapped and his wife had been unfaithful. I had to make allowances for all of the catastrophic news he'd had to absorb over the past seventy-two hours and how he'd dealt with it. He was angry and I couldn't blame him for that.

There was no doubt he'd been a shit this morning though, and I wasn't going to let it go lightly but I still loved him. I believed we had something worth saving. We'd talked recently about having another child, a brother or a sister for Eden. It was something we were both keen to do soon, before the age gap between siblings grew too large. Having Eden had put a strain on our marriage in the beginning, with the struggles I had as a new mother, but we'd worked our way back to each other again.

'Mrs Tolfrey,' DC Benson called up the stairs as I wiped the bannisters with a damp cloth.

'What is it?' I asked curtly. If it was another offer of a cup of tea, I'd shove that kettle where the sun didn't shine.

'DCI Greene is here. Do you want a tea?'

I stifled a mirthless laugh and peeled off my rubber gloves. I had been so absorbed in my thoughts I hadn't heard the bell.

DCI Greene was already seated at the table with Christopher as I entered the kitchen with my chin high and eyes focused, while DC Benson stood, guarding the kettle. Her eyes instantly clocked the faint blotches on my neck, her initial smile of greeting quickly fading.

'Hello,' I said, sliding into a spare seat.

'Mrs Tolfrey, how are you both?' She looked from me to Christopher and back again.

I smiled tightly and Christopher answered for both of us.

'I'm sure you can imagine, DCI Greene,' he said bluntly.

'Yes. I've come to give you an update. I know DC Benson has given you the results of the DNA test, which must come as a relief.'

In my peripheral vision, I saw Christopher's mouth twitch, but he remained silent.

'We have managed to locate Jason Wells to a flat in Worthing. My team are on their way there now.'

'Do you think he has Eden?' Christopher asked, his voice catching in his throat.

'We're not sure at this moment, but we'll quickly be able to determine his involvement and whereabouts over the past few days. The team will corroborate any information they are given.'

'Have you had any more calls?' I asked.

'We've had an influx of calls overnight and are following every lead, every description and name put forward.'

'It's been over forty-eight hours now, two nights away from home,' I whimpered, tears welling.

DCI Greene reached over and placed her hand on my forearm, resting on the table. 'We won't give up, Mrs Tolfrey, not until Eden is back home. The team are working day and night to find her.' DCI Greene's stormy grey eyes were imploring. I believed her. 'The CCTV hasn't given us much, we have a couple of vehicles of interest still to rule out, ones where we haven't located the owners as of yet. However, Eden hasn't been found on any of the CCTV in the surrounding area at the time of her disappearance. A witness has reported seeing a man at the park and given us a description, which is being turned into an e-fit. We will be appealing for him to come forward.'

I tried to take in the influx of information. It wasn't real life; these were things they did on television crime dramas. Talk of witnesses and e-fits seemed alien and other worldly.

'I know the past two days have been unimaginable, but the best thing you can do is to stay here. Don't talk to anyone, certainly not the press. Lean on each other, and DC Benson of course, for support. Anything you need. It's what he's here for.'

'He makes a good cup of tea,' Christopher said, and I snorted at his attempt to charm DCI Greene.

She smiled and her eyes wandered to my neck again.

Christopher followed her gaze and stood from the table.

'Well, I'm sure you've got lots to do,' he said, eager to see her out.

'DC Benson, if we could just have a chat,' she said, nodding to Christopher and leaving him standing idle at the table as they both left the room.

He glared at me when we were alone, but I remained impassive, not wanting to take the bait.

'You think you're so clever, don't you,' he hissed. 'You could have changed into a polo neck or something for god's sake.'

'Why, are you ashamed?' I asked, turning to go back upstairs without waiting for an answer, feeling the irritation radiate off him in waves.

On the first floor, I eased open the bathroom window, positioned above the front door to listen to the conversation outside. I caught DCI Greene's soft voice, mid-sentence.

'You need to keep an eye on him. She's got bruising on her neck. Has there been any evidence of violence towards her? Do we need to intervene?'

'No, I don't believe so, mam, he's got a temper, but I've not seen any physical violence whatsoever. In fact I wouldn't have said he's got it him before now.' I stiffened, Christopher had clearly charmed DC Benson this morning, perhaps he'd even suggested meeting up for a round of golf once this was all over.

'Well, clearly he has. Keep a record of it. Any other information?'

'Mrs Tolfrey left the house yesterday around dinner time for a walk, she didn't say where she was going. Was out for around an hour. They've argued, understandably, because of the revelation about Jason Wells. He asked me to leave last night. I thought it best to give them some space.'

'Hmmm, those marks look fresh, maybe from this morning. Anything else?'

'The only calls to the house have been from her mother, a couple of friends and the local rag. A few reporters were hanging around outside this morning, but I've warned them off. Nothing untoward through the post.' There was a pause in conversation, and I was tempted to look out before DCI Greene's voice started again.

'I don't think the Tolfreys are involved, there's no evidence to suggest it. We're keeping a watch on Miss Simmons. Something not right there. DC Tunstall is convinced. The team are stretched thin, Benson. We'll keep plodding away though. I'll be in touch with news on Wells.'

'Understood. Thank you, mam.'

I heard DCI Greene's footsteps click down the garden path and the front door shut before the muffled voices of Christopher and DC Benson came from below.

Who was DC Tunstall and what hunch could they have about Brooke? She hardly hit herself over the head. I saw the wound with my own eyes last night. No one in their right mind would do that to themselves. No, she had nothing to do with Eden's abduction. They were on the wrong track there. As the thought entered my head, another struck me like a sledgehammer around the back of the neck. Maybe they didn't believe Brooke had Eden but were convinced she knew who had.

11AM – 2PM

46

JIMMY PEARSON

Eden's screams rang in my ears as my head throbbed. I lifted my head up from Eden's lap.

'Are you okay?' I asked, touching her legs and flailing arms. Her mouth was red, a small amount of blood smeared down her chin. My insides recoiled like a tightly wound spring, ready to go off. 'Let me have a look,' I said, pulling her lip down with my thumb. It looked like she'd cut her gum. The bleeding having stopped already. It could have been a lot worse if she'd smacked her face on the toy bar across her seat.

A rush of anger surged through my body and I pushed myself back into the front seat and launched out of the car onto the tarmac.

The young guy approaching had his hands raised in apology, but the red mist descended over everything and, without speaking, I swung my right arm back and punched him straight in the face. My knuckles gave a satisfying crack and the expulsion of my anger was euphoric. He staggered back, knocking into his wing mirror. I watched as it bent inward. His eyes were wide, the swagger gone.

'I've got a fucking kid in the car,' I hissed through gritted teeth, my hands clenching into fists as I took a step towards him.

'Hey, hey, come on. No need for that.' A woman in her thirties tugged at my upper arm.

I shook her off and spun around, she took a step back, arms outstretched in front of her, fear coated her face.

I bent to survey the damage. The rear of my dad's car had a long dent across the bumper, but it looked like it could be knocked out. The Nissan had come off far worse, its lime green bonnet crinkled upwards, in a concertina fashion.

'I'm sorry, I didn't brake in time.' The man, who was barely more than a kid himself, cupped his hand over his bloody nose.

Traffic crept past, beeping their horns as they manoeuvred around our convoy. Rubberneckers staring from their windows, taking a long look at us, at the man bleeding, then at me and my car. I turned away from the onlookers, my heart thumped like a drum. It was no good, I had to get out of here.

'You were driving too fast,' I growled, moving back to my car.

The woman who had tugged my arm was the driver of the Vauxhall Astra in front. She was looking at where my car had brushed hers. Thankfully, it appeared there was barely a scratch. It was no matter, as long as the car was driveable, I didn't care. I had to get back to Redhill.

Ignoring the man's apologies as he hovered around like a fly, buzzing annoyingly, I opened the back to check on Eden. Grabbing a baby wipe from the change bag, I dabbed away the blood from her chin and checked the skin wasn't broken. She continued to wail, her tiny chest convulsing every time she took a breath.

'It's okay, darling, all better now. Want your dummy?' I gave it to her, and she sucked on it hard. The rage which had coursed through my veins only minutes before melted away when I looked into her watery eyes. Her gum was red, but no blood remained, the injury no doubt caused from her chin hitting the top of my head. A dull ache left behind where she'd struck me.

'Is he all right?' The man peered over my shoulder, into the car.

I stepped back, bumping him onto the grass verge.

'Fuck off,' I snapped as I slammed the door and made my way around to the driver's side.

'Where are you going? We need to swap details,' the woman chimed, her hands on her hips.

'I'm taking my son to the hospital to get him checked over. Call the police if you want.'

I started the engine, chucking the baby wipe I was still holding into the passenger footwell. My heart hadn't yet returned to a normal rate, I was wired, adrenaline peaking in my system as I thrust the car into gear and pulled out into the traffic, forcing a black BMW to let me in.

'You can't just leave,' the woman shouted. Already digging into her pocket for her phone and brandishing it over her head. I watched her get smaller in the rear-view mirror as I drove away.

She would likely call the police, which was exactly what I was afraid of, but I needed to push on. We had one shot and if I missed it, well, I'd have no other option than to dump Eden somewhere. My hands trembled on the wheel as I weaved in and out of the traffic until I reached the M1.

Within twenty minutes, Eden was fast asleep, all cried out, her mouth hanging open and the dummy threatening to fall out from between her lips. I could smell she'd messed her nappy too, but I didn't want to stop until we'd reached Toddington services.

I knew the services; and we could get changed into our Halloween costumes there. It also meant I could feed Eden something and get back on the road. But what if the police were looking for my car? What if the woman in the Astra had called them and given my registration number? They'd see it as a hit-and-run or leaving the scene of an accident or something. Not to mention the assault.

Fuck, I needed to get a better hold on my temper!

I glanced in my rear-view mirror at the rows of cars behind, searching for the blue flashing lights. Sweat prickled at the back of my neck, making me itch. I was being paranoid, but even as I tried to convince myself, I kept looking. If the police pulled me over on the motorway, it was goodnight Vienna.

I had no choice, I couldn't wait until Toddington, I had to pull off the motorway at the next junction and see what I could do to the number plate. Did I have any black tape in the glovebox? I doubted it. Fuck, I hit the steering wheel, my knuckles white as I ground my teeth.

I had enough time, and even if I was late, Brooke would have to wait. She hadn't been in touch today but told me when we spoke yesterday she'd only contact me if there was an emergency. That suited me fine. I didn't want to speak to the treacherous bitch anyway. She'd been enough to put me off women for life. Although I knew the fine fillies on the Australian beaches would turn my head in an instant. I'd be twitching in my shorts watching them play volleyball.

I snorted and my throat crackled dryly. I reached for the stale bottle of water in the driver's door, my knuckles sore as I wrapped my hand around it. The change bag had a fresh bottle in it, but I couldn't reach it without twisting my body around and we'd had one accident too many today. Taking a slurp and letting the musty-smelling water slide down my gullet, I saw an exit up ahead for Leicester – change of plan, it would have to do.

Indicating to get into the inside lane, a few minutes later I pulled off onto an A road, following a dual carriageway until I found an exit at a roundabout for a newly built housing estate.

Turning in, the main road was lined with speed bumps and I slowed to find somewhere to park in one of the many residential streets.

Eden was blinking, having woken up as we went over a bump a little too fast.

'Hey, wakey, wakey.' I smiled at her as I parked on the corner of a quiet cul-de-sac.

In the back, I gave Eden some water in her sippy cup and another biscuit while I got out and rummaged in the boot for something to disguise the number plate. Frustratingly the boot was empty, and the glovebox held only tissues and plastic gloves for using the petrol pump. Shit.

I walked around the car, fingers interlaced behind my head, cooling off and trying to think. My sweatshirt sticking to my back. Eden's eyes followed me as I walked, chewing the inside of my cheek. *Think, Jimmy, think.*

Sighing, I slipped into the back next to Eden and pulled the sweatshirt over my head. Now was as good a time as any to get into our costumes. That's when the idea came, as I slipped on the shirt, and spied the black eyeliner on the car floor.

Twenty minutes later, we were both wearing our costumes. Eden had eaten half a jar of apple pudding as well as her biscuit and had a clean nappy on. I had used the eyeliner on the number plate, turning both Is into Es and the 3 into an 8. No idea if it would last the journey, although the eyeliner was apparently waterproof.

I'd be lying if I said it didn't look fake, but it messed with the number plate enough. I made sure to cover one corner of it with mud too before we headed back on the M1 to go south. Every little helped, and I'd need all I could get.

47

BROOKE SIMMONS

I tutted loudly as Betty shouted from the doorstep. The cold air seeping into the house as Mum concentrated on doing up the zip on her coat.

'Thank you, love, so kind of you to offer.' She was hunched over, the way old people's spines began to curve; everything about her irritated me.

My shoulders inched upwards, creeping towards my ears. Should've gone by myself, I knew it was a mistake to invite Mum, I berated myself. She was a fucking liability anyway and now, with Betty along for the ride, it was like care in the community.

As we all shuffled out to get into Mum's car, mine still outside Ali's house, Betty chatted about the weather. Like a sullen teenager, I was stuck in the back, drowning in fumes from Betty's hairspray.

'Put your seat belt on,' Mum said, and I bit my tongue, fighting the urge to snap that I wasn't a child. Instead I took the opportunity to go through my recently returned phone. My notifications had blown up, so many comments and messages. People offering support, with their 'I'm here if you want to talk to someone,' but really seeking gossip on what had happened to Eden.

The number of true friends I had I could count on one hand and that included Ali, if we would remain friends after this. I hoped that would change when I moved out and was no longer embarrassed to invite people over. I'd be able to entertain in my own home without Mum hovering, wanting in on the action. It struck me, as I was about to close Facebook, a post on my whereabouts might do me a favour. I typed quickly.

Desperate to get out, shopping trip with Mum

As I hit post, I considered it might draw attention; should I be shopping when a child in my care had been abducted? Was I opening myself up to hateful comments from keyboard warriors who had nothing better to do? No matter, I didn't care what people thought. Now anybody who bothered to look would know where I was going to be.

'There's a car behind us,' Mum said, as she turned right at the roundabout.

'What car?'

'That black one. I've seen it since we left.'

My stomach churned and I turned around to look out of the back window, trying to conceal myself behind the headrest. Maybe the police were following me after all, or the press.

The toast threatened to make an appearance as we went around the bend. I rummaged in my bag for a tissue to blow my nose and glimpsed the Nokia I used for Jimmy. That was it. An anonymous text from the Nokia sent to myself. That's how I would know where Eden was. The idea formed quickly; surprised I hadn't thought of it before.

I looked again at the car behind us, a male driving and a female in the passenger seat. They looked innocent enough.

We were on a shopping trip, taking our elderly neighbour to the shops to pick up a few bits. We were good, charitable neighbours after all.

Mum changed the subject back to Halloween and Betty said she didn't put any pumpkins out any more.

'I switch all the lights off and sit upstairs to watch television, I don't answer the door after dark.' Her voice was high, almost a squeak.

My iPhone rang, drowning out the conversation and making me jump. I lowered the volume, recognising the number and knowing I'd have to answer.

'Hello?'

'Hi, is that Miss Simmons?'

'Yes, it is,' I replied, trying to ignore Mum's inquisitive eyes in the rear-view mirror.

'It's Emma from Whites Estate Agents, we got your message and are pleased to let you know the flat is still available. I see you've visited before; shall I arrange another viewing?'

'No that's fine, I'm happy to proceed,' I said, choosing my words carefully.

Emma went on to ask if I was a first-time buyer, which I said I was, and asked if I had a mortgage offer in place. I lied and said yes, stupidly realising I should have got that sorted before I put an offer in. No matter, I was sure it was something I could turn around quickly if accepted.

I squirmed in my seat as Mum's eyes flicked from the road to the rear-view mirror again, but Emma carried on. She confirmed the amount I was offering and told me she would pass it on to the sellers and let me know their response. I thanked her and wrapped up the call, Mum's concentration now on trying to find a suitable parking space on the ground floor of the car park.

Internally I beamed and struggled to stop the smile forming. I was so close to being free, finally having my own place and able to do what I wanted, when I wanted. I was desperate to get out from behind Mum's apron strings, where I'd been tied for so long. Living with Karl had given me a glimpse of freedom and since I'd moved back, I felt I couldn't breathe. She didn't want her daughter to grow up and stand on her own two feet, she didn't want to feel lonely again.

'Who was that?' Mum asked as I put the phone back into my bag.

'It was work, might be a promotion on the cards,' I lied.

'That's wonderful, dear,' Betty chipped in, and I smiled.

'Yes, it is.'

We parked in one of the few remaining spaces on the ground floor, which would mean easier access for Betty, without the necessity to wait for the lift, which was always packed with parents and their buggies. I wasn't due to meet Jimmy for a couple of hours yet but already I was scattered. With Betty's shopping to get too, I wouldn't have to make excuses to prolong our trip, it would take us ages to get around at her speed. The planned route was out of the window.

Maybe I'd have a look at Robert Dyas, or Dunelm Mill, there was bound to be some home bits in there. I couldn't buy them, not with Mum about, but the idea of shopping for my new home filled me with joy. I knew I was getting ahead of myself, but things were looking up. My bookkeeping course was almost finished, which would increase my prospects for job hunting. Eden would be back with Ali and Christopher, and I'd have a fresh new start with Jimmy out of the picture.

I really felt like life was moving forwards and I wouldn't have been able to do it without Jimmy's cash, but despite how awful I felt for the situation I'd put him in, I held little guilt about taking his money. He owed me for all the misery he'd caused, certain he wouldn't be so quick to ghost another girl that was for sure.

Buoyed by the news, I found I had a spring in my step and had almost forgotten about the black car until I saw a couple outside Boots who looked familiar. Was it them? Had they followed me to the Belfry? Reminding me I wasn't in the clear yet.

'Here, Betty, let me take your bag for you,' I said as I passed them. They kept their heads low, looking in a carrier bag at items bought, seemingly uninterested in me. Betty had purchased some athlete's foot cream and bath salts from Boots.

'You're such a lovely girl,' Betty said, her crinkly eyes glistening.

'Can we pop into Marks and Spencer's? They've got a sale on,' Mum asked.

'If we start on the top floor, we can have a look at the home stuff,' I suggested.

Mum shot me a quizzical look.

'I want to look at the bedding,' I mumbled, which seemed to satisfy her curiosity.

We turned in the opposite direction, up the escalator and made our way towards the end of the centre. By the looks of Betty trailing behind Mum, it wouldn't be long before we'd have to stop for a coffee and a rest. That worked out fine, I had some time to kill.

It was hot inside the centre in our layers and sweat further dampened my underarms. Hardly anyone in the centre was dressed for Halloween. I was on edge, mouth as dry as sandpaper whenever I thought about why we were really here. As we got closer to Mini Mischief, I saw a small queue forming outside. There were few parents who had made the effort, but all the children strapped into their buggies wore costumes. Mostly princesses and skeletons, the odd pumpkin thrown in for good measure.

I breathed a sigh of relief; it had been a good decision to use the cover of soft play to make the swap with Jimmy.

I kept my head down, not wanting to let my eyes linger too long on the brightly coloured entrance, not if I was being watched.

48

ALI TOLFREY

I sat on the closed lid of the toilet, going over the conversation I'd overheard between DCI Greene and DC Benson. Brooke? What did she know? I'd agonised over every detail, every spoken word during our walk last night. She hadn't given me any impression she knew more than she was letting on. The thought of it made me sick. Brooke wouldn't do that to us, and for what gain? There hadn't been a ransom. No one had contacted us to ask for anything.

I couldn't believe Brooke had anything to do with it. Jason neither; why would a guy pop up almost two years later to claim parental rights to a daughter born from a one-night stand? He hadn't even asked for my number at the time. We both knew what it was.

The guy who called into Crimestoppers had to be a crank. After all, the police were clutching at straws and hadn't given us one credible lead. Although after eavesdropping on their conversation, I knew they weren't telling us everything.

I stood to open the bathroom cabinet, spying the bottle of

prescription painkillers Christopher sometimes took when his back was sore. He'd slipped a disc years ago, playing squash, another reason why he'd moved to the gentler sport of golf. I could take them. I could take them all now, run myself a bath and slip away. Christopher hated me, our marriage was on the rocks and without Eden there was nothing left for me in this life. There'd be no more pain, no more guilt. Every minute that passed without Eden was agony. The only way I'd been able to deal with it was to shut it out, but it wouldn't last forever. My beautiful baby girl had vanished and as the hours ticked by, although I didn't want to admit it, it was becoming less likely she'd ever return home.

As tempting as the idea was, I'd never be able to do it, what if Eden was returned and she had to grow up without a mother. No, I had to stay strong. Christopher and I had to work through our problems and stay together. Eden deserved to have two parents that loved each other. She needed a happy home full of love to come back to.

Staring wistfully at the pill bottle, I was jolted back to reality by the sound of the doorbell, carried from outside through the open window. Whoever it was was impatient as they rang again, the shrill sound filling the room. Without bothering to look out, I closed the window and locked the bathroom door, taking my seat back on the toilet.

Despite wanting to take a couple of Christopher's painkillers and drift into nothingness, I had to be aware of every slice of agony her abduction had caused. As a mother I should bear the brunt of it. It was me who wasn't there, it was my penance.

'Mrs Tolfrey.' DC Benson's voice was accompanied by a gentle knock on the door.

'What is it?' I snapped. For goodness' sake, I couldn't get a minute's peace by myself.

'Your mother is here,' he said, apologetically.

'What?' I jumped up and unlocked the door, wrenching it open.

DC Benson struggled to meet my eye and I could already hear her downstairs, barking at Christopher.

'Christ, that's all we need,' I muttered, trudging down the stairs, already feeling the tension in my shoulders.

I heard her before I saw her. The posh high-pitched lilt like crashing cymbals to my ears.

'No one bloody answers the phone any more. Alison barely replies to any of my messages. I'm going out of my mind with worry. My only granddaughter!'

'Your only granddaughter whom you hardly see?' I asked, unable to keep the sarcasm out of my voice as I entered the kitchen.

'There you are, darling, how are you?' She air-kissed me, wafting her flowery perfume and frowning as she took in my bedraggled appearance. The woman looked immaculate in a grey woollen jumper dress and flat riding boots; hair pulled into a chignon with a full face of make-up.

I lifted a hand to touch my greasy hair, a flush creeping up my neck. Before I let it take hold, I rolled my shoulder back. I had every right to look terrible, my daughter had been abducted.

'What are you doing here? I said I'd call when there was news. There is no news, so I haven't called.'

'Tea?' DC Benson interjected; his face flushed too. Likely he'd been admonished by my mother as soon as she crossed the threshold.

'That was days ago!' she exaggerated.

I sighed, pulling out a chair and slumping into it.

'Do you have any Earl Grey?' my mother turned to ask DC Benson, her nose wrinkling as though she smelt something bad.

DC Benson's eyes darted to me.

'Cupboard above the kettle, behind the peppermint,' I said.

'I'm here to help, what would you like me to do?'

'There's nothing you can do, Miranda, unless you can bring Eden back to us,' Christopher grumbled, his voice weary.

They both sat as I got up from the chair.

'Where are you going?' Mum looked at me incredulously.

'For a cigarette,' I snapped as all eyes fell on me.

Ignoring them, I rescued the packet from the top of the cupboard and wrenched open the bifold doors.

I lit up and inhaled the smoke, instantly calmer. My mother always rattled me, and now she was here, in my kitchen. Given half the chance, she'd take over, whisk in and out, claim she'd rescued us when we were at our lowest. I flicked my ash so violently it came away altogether and I had to light my cigarette again.

The door slid open behind me and I heard the thud of her riding boots on the patio.

'That isn't going to help.'

I spun around, fire in my cheeks. 'What would you have me do, Mother, walk the streets? I don't know where to look,' I sobbed and she patted my shoulder mechanically, as though it was as much physical contact as she could bear. Why couldn't she be like every other mother, hold me until I felt better, wipe my tears and tell me everything was going to be all right?

'What have they told you?' she asked.

I relayed everything DCI Greene had told us, while Mother picked flecks of cotton off her dress, discarding them into the air.

'Did Christopher do that to your neck?' she asked causally, as though it was expected.

I berated myself for not putting a scarf on before I came downstairs, having forgotten about the marks.

Ignoring the question, I turned on my heel to go back inside, speaking over my shoulder. 'There isn't anything you can do. Go home. We'll call you when there's news.'

Back the kitchen, the tea had been made and DC Benson had vacated.

'You clearly aren't coping,' Mother said, continuing the conversation.

'We're fine,' Christopher replied, squaring his shoulders.

'Really, so fine you've been manhandling your wife?'

He gasped and shot me a look, as though I'd told her.

'Did your daughter tell you she screwed someone else on her hen night? Oh yes, Miranda, I had to do a bloody DNA test to see if Eden is mine!'

Mother gave Christopher a withering look, his words rolling off her back. 'Is she yours?'

'Yes,' I interjected.

'Well then,' she replied quickly, her voice a little too high.

Christopher scoffed. 'I'm supposed to just accept it, am I?' Christopher's voice grew louder, and I cringed.

'Oh, stop being so ridiculous, you knew what you were marrying into.'

I gasped as though I'd been slapped. 'What the hell is that supposed to mean?' Hot, resentful tears pricked my eyes. Why couldn't she be on my side, for once?

She glanced at me, fleetingly, then back at Christopher, continuing to talk about me as though I wasn't there. 'Our darling Alison is fanciful, like her father, always has been. She has big ideas; her head is in the clouds and she's easily swayed. If you can't control your wife, Christopher, that's down to you.'

'Get out.' My voice was low, almost a snarl.

'I beg your pardon?' Mother turned to look at me, her cup raised to her lips, pinky extended.

'You heard me, get out, you're no longer welcome in this house.'

49

JIMMY PEARSON

The closer I got to the M25, the more anxious I became; my knuckles were white on the steering wheel as Eden's mood deteriorated and she cried for almost an hour. The wailing was like torture, and I screamed at her to stop twice. Unable to control my outburst. It only made her notch up the volume. I guessed her mouth was hurting; she was teething, and her gums were sore even before the impact with my head.

My eyes were on a rotation; road, Eden, road, Eden, making sure to keep checking behind us for any sign of a police car. Every time a traffic officer, or the cone police as I liked to call them, went past, my heart skipped in my chest. That was the intention, with their vehicles designed like police cars, everyone slowed down.

Although cooler dressed in the cheap flimsy pirate's costume, perspiration still peppered my back. Agitation made me shift in my seat. I just wanted to get there and get rid of Eden. If she screamed any more, I'd go mad. The sound was so cutting, but I remembered Brooke telling me the noise was designed to make you act. It made me want to bang my head against the steering wheel.

Joining the M25 and seeing the signposts for Heathrow spurred me on, but then the traffic slowed to a crawl and Eden kicked her legs restlessly. I was sure her chin was discolouring. She'd be returned to her parents with a burnt hand, a cut gum and a bruised chin. Some father I'd turned out to be – or rather not to be. Couldn't even keep her out of harm's way for a couple of days. Maybe I wasn't cut out to be a dad?

The crying finally stopped, and her eyes wandered around the car before she chewed at her T-shirt, the skull and crossbones crinkled, flashing a slice of pink skin from her tummy. As we came to halt, I risked a grab at the change bag, thrusting the first thing I could find into Eden's lap. She snatched the rattle and shook it, spinning rings reflecting in her eyes. The journey seemed to be taking forever and for once the way back seemed longer than the way there.

I cricked my neck, easing it from side to side, trying to relieve the tension in my shoulders. I felt like warmed up dog shit. My stomach rumbled, I'd missed breakfast and lunch, but the thought of eating made me queasy. The dull pain from where Eden's chin collided with my head had grown into an ear-splitting throb and all I wanted was to go to bed.

'Look. Eden, a plane!' I pointed out of the window at the low-flying aircraft, smiling as she followed my finger with wide eyes. If I was lucky, I'd get a seat on one of those today. I just wanted to get to the airport, where I was within reach of an escape route, putting myself thousands of miles between me and the police. Once there I had options, I had my passport and a credit card, if I couldn't leave for Australia today it wasn't the end of the world. I could go anywhere. But I had to return Eden first. She had to go home, where she belonged.

Another hour and we'd be there, I just had to hold on, keep it together for a bit longer. The traffic sped up and I put my foot on the accelerator, jumping as a police car overtook me on my right, blue lights flashing and the siren blasting as they passed. I automatically shrank lower in my seat. Cars slowed ahead and I could see the passenger making hand gestures to pull over. Were they motioning to me?

They were two cars ahead and I slowed down, indicating to move from the middle lane to the inside. Sirens still blaring, I swallowed hard, tongue glued to the top of my mouth. Positive I made eye contact with the male policeman in the passenger seat. He kept pointing, gesturing to pull over.

My hands shook on the steering wheel, was this it? Game over.

I indicated to move to the hard shoulder but couldn't bring myself to pull in. I could put my foot down, speed away, although I was sure they could easily outrun me. Could I put Eden at risk like that?

As I debated, unsure what to do, the police car manoeuvred into the inside lane and onto the hard shoulder. Seconds later, an old blue Escort XR3i with spoiler followed it in. I hadn't seen the car because it was in front of the Transit I was behind.

'Fuck,' I said, flicking off my indicator quickly and letting out a low whistle, swiping at the beads of sweat that had appeared on my forehead. That was close, too close. In my wing mirror, I saw them get out of the car and walk back to the driver of the Escort.

For a second, my life had flashed before my eyes, I was convinced the game was up. I drank the remaining stale water stashed in the door, the adrenaline leaving my body and taking every last ounce of energy with it.

'Dadadadadada,' Eden babbled, slobbering over the rings of the rattle.

'I know, you'll see him soon.' I sighed.

The rest of the drive was uneventful. Traffic moved continuously, albeit slow at times, and after the panic, I zoned out, turning the radio on and concentrating on the music. Anything to take my mind off what was going to happen in the next couple of hours. I stopped to fill the tank with petrol at the nearest station once off the M25, my hat still on.

The guy behind the desk smirked and commented on my costume, which I'd forgotten I was wearing. I'd left the waistcoat and sash in the car and the bandana and eyepatch were still in the packet, so I wasn't surprised he remarked on it. I looked strange in a white shirt with a deep V-neckline and billowing trousers, like I was auditioning for a part in *Poldark*.

I paid quickly and left, keeping my head down. Within twenty minutes, we were in Redhill, my blood pressure instantly shot up knowing we were so close. Brooke would likely be in the shopping centre already, counting the minutes to our quarter-past two exchange time. I'd leave at two and she'd be there fifteen minutes later to collect Eden. That was the plan. It gave me a fifteen-minute head start if nothing else.

Not wanting to risk parking in the Belfry Shopping Centre, I carried on past and pulled into Linkfield car park, a minute further down the road. I had visions of alarms in the centre going off and having to drive through a lowered barrier like something out of an action movie to get away. No, it would be far easier if I was on foot. I could jog back to the car in minutes and be on the motorway before the police had even arrived.

Once parked, I put on the rest of my costume, the bandana around my head and eyepatch, which was extremely uncomfortable. Then I drew on my beard using the black eyeliner, swishes of black to represent the hairs. It was a pretty good disguise, you couldn't tell my exact hair colour, and for once I was grateful I didn't have a hairy chest as the shirt was so low-cut.

Moving around to the back seat and checking the time, we had an hour to go. I gave Eden another biscuit which she munched happily, then a drink before I changed her nappy again. I rubbed some Savlon onto her palm, which still brandished a circular red mark, and gave her some Calpol. Once she was content, chewing on her dummy, I attempted to draw her beard on. It was smudged and messy within minutes, but the general idea was there. The red spotted bandana had been hard to secure, but after a few attempts I got it on over Eden's curls.

She looked like the perfect little boy. My Eddie. Brooke's Eden. I left her in the car to put the change bag in a bin across the other side of the car park, as well as Eden's clothes and coat. Baby paraphernalia had worked its way into the footwells and pockets of the car I found as I cleaned it. I knew her DNA would be inside the vehicle and mine would be all over the bag, but I didn't have time to dispose of it any other way. It was the best I could do.

Now it was just the two of us. Me with my phone, car keys and wallet and Eden with her dummy. I hoisted her onto my shoulder, wrapping my arms around her. Aware it was too cold for her in only her costume as I shivered, bracing the wind. We'd be inside the centre in less than ten minutes. It was a short walk to the Belfry.

'Come on then, poppet, time to go and play,' I said, holding her close to me. Warmth from her body spreading into mine. My heart chipped away with every beat of hers.

Each step felt heavy, closer to saying goodbye. Did I really want to do this? I could turn around and put her back in the car, keep running.

She's not yours to keep.

The voice in my head whispered. It didn't matter, it still felt like my heart was being stamped on. I loved her, but it wasn't about me. Eden needed her parents, her real parents, and I had to do the right thing.

50

BROOKE SIMMONS

We sat in the Marks and Spencer's café, nursing cappuccinos. Betty and Mum had gone for a toasted sandwich and a slice of millionaire's shortbread, but I couldn't face it. Instead I glanced apprehensively at the customers around us, as if they knew why I was there. I hadn't seen the couple for a while, the ones I believed were police, although now I was doubting they were police at all. Could it be paranoia had got the better of me?

'Why do you keep checking the time?' Mum asked, her brows furrowed as I tapped the screen on my iPhone to reveal the time again.

'No reason. How's your sandwich?' I asked, changing the subject and pulling my mouth into a smile.

'Lovely, thank you, so nice of you to treat us,' Betty replied, hers already half eaten. She must have been sweating under her layers of clothing. I'd taken my coat off but could still feel the flush of heat around my throat. I pulled at the neck of my jumper, wishing I'd worn something else.

A text came through on my iPhone, shaking the table. Ali's

name popped up as the screen came to life. I quickly swiped to see the message.

The police think you're involved, tell me it's not true.

It was a jolt straight to my gut and my legs jerked under the table. The police were following me, I'd been right. It wasn't paranoia.

Jumping up from the table, the cups rattled on their saucers.

'What's wrong?' Mum frowned.

'Umm nothing, I've got to go to the bathroom.'

I rushed away from the table, clutching my phone and bag as Mum and Betty talked in hushed whispers. I had to send a message to Jimmy. I couldn't go through with it. Not now. There was too much of a risk. He'd have to take Eden somewhere else, a police station or hospital. Somewhere there was no connection to me. The plan had been stupid, and I was going to get caught. If Ali suspected my involvement, it changed everything. She wouldn't fight my corner against the police, assure them I loved Eden, I'd never hurt her. The truth would spill out and I'd be unable to stop it.

Assaulted by the smell of bleach, I hurried inside the beige café toilets and locked myself inside a stall, aware the one beside me was occupied. Someone rustling with their clothes as though they were doing a complete outfit change. I pulled the phone I used for Jimmy out of my bag. Fumbling with the handset, it slipped from my fingers and clattered to the floor sliding under the partition.

'Whoops, here you go, love.' A hand appeared underneath from next door; phone clutched in wrinkled fingers.

'Thanks, sorry, clumsy today,' I muttered, taking it back.

I punched out a message to Jimmy, frustrated at the old phone where typing took so long, hitting each key multiple times to get the letter I needed.

It's off, can't do it here, being followed.

I waited a minute, listening to next door flush and leave their stall as another person entered the bathroom. It wasn't long before I got a reply.

Too late, I'm already here.

Cold unease swept through me and I shivered from the perspiration sitting upon my skin. He was here, in the centre already. It wasn't a surprise, there was less than an hour until the drop-off.

I lingered, not knowing how to respond.

'Is someone in there?' I heard a voice, realising there was a queue and I'd been in the cubicle for a while.

'I'll be out in a sec,' I stammered, flushing the toilet and slipping the phone into my back pocket.

The old battleaxe tutted as I unlocked the door, brushing past me to get inside. God, people were so rude.

I washed my hands, rinsing my wrists under the scalding water, trying to relieve the chill in my bones. My reflection was ghostly, so pale I was nearly transparent. As I dried my hands, my pocket vibrated. Another message.

I'm leaving her as arranged. Come, or not. I don't give a fuck

Jimmy's words gave me jitters, strangling my thoughts. What choice did I have? I couldn't leave Eden to be found by someone else. Especially not the same time as I was in the shopping centre, it looked even more suspicious than what I'd originally planned. He was angry, and he had every right to be, no doubt he wanted to be as far away from me, and Eden, as possible.

The bathroom door opened again and more ladies filed in, so I took my leave and returned to the table to find Mum and Betty with empty plates in front of them.

'You're as white as a sheet, Brooke,' Mum said.

'I'm fine, I just came over a little light-headed that's all,' I grumbled.

'Because you never eat anything,' Mum berated, rolling her eyes and fingering the plait laying limply across her shoulder.

I gazed into the distance, scanning the crowd once more for the police I now knew were following me.

Should I respond to Ali? She would have seen I'd read her text, but I didn't want to get into a dialogue with her now. Not with everything else going on.

'Shall we go home?' I suggested. Hoping Mum would give me an out, give me a reason not to stay and follow through. My knees knocked together under the table, cup trembling slightly as I raised it to my lips to sip the lukewarm cappuccino.

Her eyes darkened and Betty grimaced, it was obvious the shopping trip was not going to be cut short.

'Finish your drink and we'll go for a wander. I've got to get a birthday card.'

That was that, the plan was back on. In forty minutes, Jimmy would be leaving Eden at Mini Mischief alone and making his escape. My stomach churned, the smell of coffee filling my nostrils and I pushed it aside.

'I'm ready.' I pushed my chair back and stood, taking Betty's shopping bag from the floor and putting my handbag over my shoulder. Mum took the receipt and handed it to me. I scrunched the paper up inside my pocket, using it like a stress ball as we left the café.

The Belfry centre was busy, people milling about, chatting and standing in awkward places, blocking shop doorways. I saw a few more people in costume but no one took much notice. The shop windows were decorated with pumpkins, spooky spiderwebs and witches' hats, as if any of us could forget how commercial Halloween had become.

Mum stopped and pointed, cooed at the orange sweet buckets and mannequins dressed in costumes. I tried to keep track of hers and Betty's conversation, but my mind wandered, convulsing every time I spotted someone who could be Jimmy. Sick at the prospect of bumping into him, of us exchanging words, or worse. I had no idea if he was still mad, whether he'd explode on sight if he saw me.

Shrinking into my coat, trying to make myself as small as possible, I dodged the shoppers, trailing behind Mum and Betty. We reached the card shop and I let them both go in, choosing to wait outside with the bags. I leaned my shoulder against the window, keeping my head low, eyes locked on my phone, contemplating responding to Ali but with no idea what to say.

Suddenly I was shoved from behind, my shoulder lurching forward as a dark figure brushed past, my iPhone dropping to the floor with a sickening crack.

'Bitch,' came the hiss from his retreating back, a toddler over his shoulder gazed at me, stretching out her arm. It was Eden. Seconds later, they were gone, disappearing into the crowd, and I crouched over, hand to my chest, watching the world spin.

51

ALI TOLFREY

I stared at my phone through teary eyes, waiting for the confirmation from Brooke. I needed to see it in black and white. That, despite what DCI Greene had said, Brooke wasn't involved. Could I trust anyone? My heart was in a vice, slowly being crushed. Did I have no one in my corner?

Mother had been gone for an hour and I'd been upstairs in my bedroom ever since she'd left. Or rather, after I'd thrown her out. She hadn't caused a scene, just finished her Earl Grey and got up to leave. How dare she speak about me that way, in my own home. It was the final straw.

Even at the age of thirty-three, she still had the ability to make me feel useless, unable to stand on my own two feet. My confidence dipped whenever she was around. It was as though she'd passed the burden of looking after me on to Christopher when we met, confirming it the day we married. I was no longer her problem, although she liked to be kept in the loop. Offering her opinion whenever she deemed it necessary. It was no wonder she was still alone. No man could stand that level of management.

Christopher had gone out for a walk, licking his wounds

because he'd been unable to gain leverage by exposing my fling to my mother. I'd heard him say to DC Benson he was going to the shop to get some bread and milk. I would normally have done the shopping on a Friday, but there was no way I could face the supermarket, or the pitying faces of anyone locally who might recognise me.

DC Benson had offered to go, wanting to make himself useful, but Christopher needed to blow off steam. I came upstairs soon after, escaping DC Benson's surveying eyes. It was hard not to feel observed whenever he was around. No doubt running back to DCI Greene to give her an itinerary of our movements, our every argument.

I was hollowed out, an empty shell. I just wanted Eden back, everything else could go up in smoke. If we had to stay in a hostel, if we were chucked out by Christopher with only the clothes on our backs, I'd bear it. As long as I had Eden with me.

Moving to Eden's room to be closer to her, I glared at the red wine stain on the carpet before taking one of her teddies from the shelf and holding it to my chest. It didn't smell of Eden. Panicking, I grabbed the muslin hanging over the cot, it smelt of slightly soured milk but not Eden. Running to the bathroom, I tipped the washing basket on its side, the lid flopping open and clothes sprawling onto the tiles. Grabbing wildly at anything of Eden's and thrusting it to my face, trying to inhale her scent. It was there in snatches, but I couldn't consume enough.

'No, no, no, no,' I wailed, tears streaming down my face.

'What is it?' Christopher appeared at the top of the stairs, for once his voice without scorn. I looked up through my haze, I hadn't heard his approach.

'I can't smell her, on anything.' I buried my head in her clothes and sobbed.

Christopher reached over and laid his hand upon mine, a

gesture of kindness, of comfort. When I looked at him through blurry eyes, he was crying too. He sank down on the bathroom floor and wrapped his arms around me, resting his chin on my head, clothes strewn around us.

My body heaved, wracking sobs, until I had nothing left to give.

'She'll come back,' he whispered into my hair, although we both knew his words were barren. Neither of us knew if we'd ever see our daughter again. Life wasn't worth going on if we didn't. We had nothing to live for, no other children and our marriage was crumbling beneath us.

We stayed on the cold tiles for a long time, our legs slowly growing numb. As much as I hated Christopher for the way he'd treated me, as I'm sure he felt the same way about me, we needed comfort only the other could give. There was no way to explain the nightmare of losing a child to anyone else. They could never understand the torture, the misery we were unable to escape from.

When we untangled ourselves from each other, I was aghast at Christopher's appearance. He looked not just pale, but grey. His eyes were lifeless, blank. We both looked like shells of ourselves. His bravado about the infidelity was nothing but that; he was running on his anger, holding on to it as though it was all he had left.

'Benson's probably rooting through our things downstairs,' Christopher said, his voice low.

'I overheard him and DCI Greene talking, they think Brooke has something to do with it,' I said.

His head snapped around to look at me, eyes sharp.

'What?' I shrugged, conveying I knew no more than that.

Christopher reached out a hand towards me and I flinched

automatically. He sighed, shaking his head, and tried again, fingers brushing the bruises on my neck. 'I'm sorry I hurt you.'

I bit my lip and remained perfectly still, but he didn't examine me for long, quickly turning away and lowering his head. The image of contrition, but it had little impact. We'd both crossed a line that could never be uncrossed.

A phone rang downstairs, not my ringtone or Christopher's. It stopped and we heard the muffled voice of DC Benson. We looked at each other, hopeful there was news, and hurried down the stairs. DC Benson paced the kitchen, eyes cast to the floor.

'Understood, mam, I'll let them know.' He hung up and turned to Christopher and me, waiting expectantly. 'That was DCI Greene. Jason Wells has been found and ruled out of the investigation.'

My shoulders slumped, body imploding into itself. If he didn't have Eden, who did?

'So, what now?' Christopher barked; his annoyance obvious.

'DCI Greene is going to call another press conference this afternoon, to appeal for the witness she mentioned yesterday to come forward. The man was seen talking to Miss Simmons at the swings, we have an e-fit now and are trying to locate him.'

'Talking to Brooke? She never said!' I blurted.

'You've spoken to her again?' Christopher shot me an incredulous look, as though I'd deliberately withheld information for him.

'Yes, when I went for a walk. Well, I walked to her house. I wanted to hear what happened from her.'

DC Benson's mouth twitched, and he began dialling.

'What? I don't see what the problem is?' My mouth dropped open, like a fish.

'You could have told her something, about the investigation,' Christopher explained.

'I... I... didn't,' I lied, remembering our conversation about Jason Wells. 'Anyway, whatever happened to innocent until proven guilty?' I continued.

'I don't give a shit about that, all I care about is getting Eden back,' Christopher snapped, waving a hand to dismiss me.

I balled my hands into fists, pushing my nails into the fleshy skin of my palm.

DC Benson finished speaking, to who I assumed was DCI Greene. His full attention back to us.

'Is Brooke a suspect in Eden's abduction?' Christopher demanded.

DC Benson seemed to visibly recoil at the question. 'She's been helping us with our enquiries.'

'Oh don't give me that old bollocks! Is she a suspect?' he asked again, enunciating each word in the question.

DC Benson pursed his lips, his blond beard moving ever so slightly as he did. No reply came, although he'd told us all we needed to know.

'Right, I'm going around there. I want to talk to her myself. I'll find out the truth.' Christopher marched to the front door, snatching his keys from the console table in the hall.

I hurried after him, DC Benson a few steps behind.

'Mr Tolfrey. Christopher, I really must advise against it.' His voice grew to a near shout as he tried to catch us.

Christopher was already out the door and climbing into his Range Rover as I exited the house, rushing around the front of the car to get to the passenger side as he started the engine. I'd left the front door wide open, DC Benson gesticulating at us on the front step, already on his phone as we pulled away.

2PM – 3PM

52

JIMMY PEARSON

It took all my self-restraint not to grab Brooke by the hair and scream into her face, when I spotted her. Rage boiled in the pit of my stomach and Eden complained, trying to wriggle out of my grasp before I realised I was holding her too tight. My muscles clenching around her tiny frame, subconsciously reacting to the sheer hatred that consumed me when I recognised Brooke.

Every inch of me wanted to give that bitch what for. I imagined myself shaking her, scaring her. In the past, I'd been no angel, but I'd never hit a woman, even if provoked, and fuck, no one had provoked me like Brooke! It was unimaginable, what she'd put me through, what she'd put Eden's parents through. All because she was pissed off at being dumped and saw me as a cash cow.

Fucking psycho. The world was full of them and I seemed to attract them in droves. I'd show her. I'd make sure it would come back to bite her on the arse, all of it. I couldn't let her walk away scot-free, no chance.

A small shove to her shoulder as I passed gave me a surge of pleasure. No looking back. I heard her gasp and the phone clatter to the floor. Knew she'd recognise Eden over my shoulder, even with the smudged beard and bandana. I wanted her to be scared. I wanted to fucking terrify her. She deserved nothing less. Perhaps I should have opted for a Grim Reaper costume.

I looked an idiot in my pirate outfit, as I knew I would, but some people had dressed up, not many though. It didn't matter. It served a purpose. There were only a few who gave me a second glance or stifled a laugh, like I was some fucking comedian. Fuck them, fuck them all. I was going to drop Eden off and get out.

Adrenaline rushed around my body, gearing me up. Like I was going to do something crazy, a parachute or bungee jump. The fear was real, it made my muscles pulse and twitch. Fight or flight, that's what they called it, wasn't it? I could see why. Energy surged through me, a massive transformation to the exhaustion I felt in the car.

I found the end of the queue for Mini Mischief, which snaked out of the reception area and onto the main drag of the shopping centre. I had to get a space inside. They couldn't be full. It would fuck everything. But I quickly realised it wasn't a problem of capacity but how slow the girls were to check customers in. My bicep throbbed, aching with the weight of Eden, I'd been carrying her for so long. I switched arms as the build-up of lactic acid took hold. Stretching out the muscle, I caught the eye of a mum further ahead in the queue.

She smiled at me; her eyes wide. I winked and she giggled, whispering to her friend pushing an identical buggy. I was supposed to be keeping a low profile, but carrying a child made you even more attractive, it seemed. It was a good distraction from Brooke and by the time I reached the front of the queue, I'd calmed down.

I could see through the doors there were tables still available and my shoulders rolled back. It was a hive of activity. Parents chatting, toddlers stumbling about and screaming with excitement. At least I didn't have to tolerate it for long.

'Here we go, Ed, time to play,' I said, jiggling her in my arms as I handed over a ten-pound note to the girl behind the counter. She was barely sixteen but had already cultivated the resting bitch face. Her hair pulled up into a pineapple.

'Nice costume, thanks for making the effort. You only need to pay for your child today. Competition winner is announced at three for this session. Here's a white band, your call-out time will be three thirty.' She attempted to smile but it didn't reach her eyes. I could tell she hated her job as she reeled off the information with the enthusiasm of reciting a shopping list.

'Thanks,' I said, shoving the change and the band in my pocket and pushing the turnstile into the main soft play area.

My eyes and ears were immediately assaulted by the bright colours and shrieking children, even the drum of conversation from the adults was loud, trying to compete. Eden was already wriggling, trying to get down, eyes bulging at her surroundings. The most fun she'd been offered since I'd had her. Regret pinched me; we'd wasted our time together hiding, when we could have been having fun.

At a table near the back, I slipped off my desert boots and removed Eden's trainers before carrying her to the toddler section. Babies, some not yet able to walk, were playing with the plastic balls and pulling themselves up on the edges of the foam walls, wobbling on their feet. As soon as I sat Eden down, she crawled away, spying a bright yellow foam shape she wanted to climb on.

I knelt on the carpet, fascinated. Her gummy smile stretched wide across her face, beard now barely intact, one big charcoal smudge, bandana askew.

'Ah, he's gorgeous,' said the mum from the queue. Her

daughter had one of those stupid hairbands with a flower on it. Ridiculous on a baby with no hair. I wasn't surprised. The girl had fake everything, from her tan to her extensions, her nails to her eyelashes. She was a bit of Mona Lisa, not as pretty up close.

'Cheers,' I replied, getting to my feet and heading back to the table, not wanting to engage any further. I could see Eden from there but wanted to get us both a drink. There was a tuck shop of sorts at the back wall and I bought a bottle of water and an apple Fruit Shoot. Her sippy cup was in the change bag, left in the bin by the car park, but we'd give it a go.

I returned to the side of the toddler section, the mum with the hair extensions carrying her crying daughter around on her hip, trying to console her. Eden was still playing happily in the ball pit, kicking her legs. I held out the bottle of juice and her hands opened and clenched in a 'give me' motion before crawling towards me, babbling.

Lifting her out, I carried her back to the table, placing her on my knee as I fumbled with the nozzle. Unsurprisingly when she took a drink, a little of the juice escaped her tiny mouth and dribbled down her chin, dampening both of our trousers. I scowled, looking at the time on my phone as she got to grips with the bottle. It was almost quarter past, time to go.

Stroking Eden's curls popping out from the bandana, I held her close to me for a second, kissing her head and absorbing her scent. I didn't think when the time came, I'd get choked up, but my stomach plummeted knowing it was time to say goodbye.

'Bye, poppet, I'll miss you,' I whispered into her ear.

She turned her head quickly, sticky lips across my face. A toddler kiss.

Leaving the bottle on the table and pocketing my water, I carried her back to the ball pit, my heart shrinking with every step. She wouldn't even know I was gone. Laying her down gently, she crawled away without a second glance.

Without giving myself a chance to change my mind, I turned and headed for the door, slipping the white band out of my pocket and onto my wrist.

'Toilets?' I asked at the counter, raising my arm to show the band.

The girl, busy serving a family, barely looked at me as she replied. 'First left.' Her hand touched a button and the turnstile gave. I swallowed hard, forcing down the lump in my throat. Head bowed, I strode away, past the toilets and towards the escalator.

53

BROOKE SIMMONS

'Mum, I've got to go to the loo,' I said, shoving the bags at her as soon as she came out of the card shop.

'Okay, we'll wait here,' she said, looking me up and down with a grimace. I knew she was wondering what was wrong with me today. Hopefully she'd assume it was a bad stomach. It wasn't a lie; my stomach was tied in so many knots I wasn't sure it would ever recover.

'No, don't wait, I'll find you. There's a couple of shops I want to go to downstairs.' I was already walking away, so I didn't hear her answer. I had to get to the toilets and out of view of the cameras.

I hurried down the escalator and towards the main shopping centre toilets, which were bustling. Once inside the locked stall, I retrieved the Nokia phone I used for Jimmy and composed a text.

Eden is here. Mini Mischief. Now

Then sent it to myself, to my iPhone and waited for it to come through. Once it did, I opened the old phone and took out the

SIM card, wrapped it in toilet paper and flushed it. I waited for a few seconds to make sure it didn't reappear in the bowl. To ensure it didn't float to the surface like all the secrets I had been burying over the past six months.

The Nokia was a flip-style silver design and I bent it backwards against its hinges until it snapped it in half, putting the bits into my pocket. I left the toilets, after a quick wash of my hands. There was a cleaning trolley outside, and I dropped the two halves of the phone into a white rubbish bag tied to the handle, watching it fall beneath reams of toilet paper.

Wiping my already clammy hands on my jeans, perspiration collected beneath my bra strap, seeping into the fabric. The back of my neck was damp, hair clinging to my skin. I'd never felt so sick with dread; it lay upon me like a shroud. I made my limbs move faster, aware every minute I delayed, Eden was on her own.

When in view of a camera near the exit of the centre, I took out my iPhone and opened the message, trying to convey a shocked expression before hurrying towards the escalators to go back upstairs. I kept my head low, staring at the phone open-mouthed. Not daring to look up. Terrified in case I saw Jimmy pass me by. I had visions of him lunging at me on the escalator, arms flailing as I fell to my death, a broken neck from hitting the marble floor.

Pushing Jimmy out of my mind, I reached the top. The upstairs floor was busy, lots of people milling around and queuing for food from the various outlets. I squeezed past them, my heart galloping so fast I could barely catch my breath until I saw the entrance to Mini Mischief. As always, there was a small queue to get to the counter. Should I barge to the front? Say it was an emergency? What would someone do in a real scenario?

I hopped from foot to foot, at the back of the line, growing impatient. I was so close to getting Eden back. I'd be the hero of the hour; returning Eden to her parents. Doing what no one else could. I imagined Ali rushing towards me with open arms, face awash with relief, beaming at me and Eden. Thanking me through her sobs.

Everything would go back to normal. Ali would trust me again, our friendship stronger than ever. I'd still be able to look after Eden, be a part of their extended family, which I'd taken for granted this past year. With Jimmy gone, I wouldn't have to look over my shoulder. With his money, I could buy the flat and finally break free of Mum's smothering. It was all within my grasp, a few minutes away. Terror turned to wild excitement, palpitations rippled through my chest and my fingers pulsed.

'Where's your child?' the young girl at the counter frowned at me.

'Oh, no, sorry I'm here to meet my sister and her daughter,' I lied, thinking on my feet.

'That'll be four pounds, please,' she pointed towards the card reader and I tapped my phone against it, waiting for the ping.

I heard the click of the turnstile unlock and pushed through, eyes scanning the adults standing around and seated at tables. I couldn't see Jimmy; there were barely any men there at all. Shrieks of raucous children filled my ears and my heart burst with the sound. Eden was somewhere, I just had to find her.

Moving towards the shallow ball pit, I saw some toddlers crawling through the balls and then, there she was. My eyes brimmed with tears as I saw her, dressed as a pirate with black smudges all over the lower half of her face and a lopsided bandana on her head. Even dressed as though she was a boy, there was no mistaking her chubby cheeks. She was chewing on a ball, oblivious to having been left alone.

I surveyed the surrounding parents, but they were deep in conversation or absorbed in their phones. No one had seemed to notice a toddler had been abandoned. No one had noticed me without a child either. Moving casually closer and lowering to my knees beside the soft wall of the pit, I waited for Eden to recognise me. It took a minute or so. She glanced my way, looked around the room and then back again. Taking in the enormous smile stretched across my face, her eyes lit up with recognition.

I thought my heart would burst with the influx of love that rushed to the surface as she crawled towards my outstretched arms. Her lip looked a little swollen, although it was difficult to see amongst the black smudges of her drawn-on beard.

'Eden!' I said, picking her up and holding her to me, so close I could feel her heart beating against my chest.

'Mamamamamamama,' she babbled, fingers in her mouth.

I rocked her gently, stroking the back of her hair, unable to believe she was real.

'Where are your things?' I asked, knowing I wouldn't get a response.

I scanned the tables, finding an unoccupied one at the back, and heading towards it. On the table was a discarded Fruit Shoot bottle, sat in a small puddle of yellow liquid. A blue pair of tiny soft trainers had been neatly arranged on the chair. I looked around the floor for Eden's change bag, but it was nowhere to be seen.

'Are these yours?' I said to Eden, searching for who else they could belong to. After a minute, no one had even looked in my direction. Surely if it was someone else's table, they would have come back to it, especially as I was loitering. Parents got territorial around tables at soft play, there were never enough and always someone at the side lines ready to pounce when one became free.

I sat on the chair and put Eden on my lap, the front of her trousers felt damp, but her nappy wasn't full. I stared at her, thrilled to have got to her before anyone else. She babbled, pulling on my jumper, when I noticed the red mark on her hand. It looked like a burn.

'Let me look, poppet,' I said, holding her hand to look closer, it was healing and didn't appear to be bothering her. Putting on the trainers, I looked around for a coat, but there was none. Jimmy had left Eden but nothing else. 'It's okay, I'll buy you another coat when we get out of here,' I whispered into her hair.

She smelt amazing, a mix of Johnson's baby wash and nappy cream. She smelt comforting, like home, and I wished I could bottle it.

'I've missed you so much,' I said, standing and hoisting Eden onto my hip.

She smiled at me, her fingers already wrapping around a chunk of my hair, tugging on it like she always did.

I moved towards the exit so I could go outside and call the police. It was so noisy in the soft play; you couldn't hear yourself think.

'Right, let's get you home.'

54

ALI TOLFREY

Christopher drove too fast and I clung onto the overhead handle as he tutted.

'I'm not going that fast!'

'Feels like it,' I replied as he swung around a corner and I leaned into the door.

'Do you think Brooke has got Eden?' Christopher asked, looking ahead at the road.

'No,' I said quickly. The whole idea was ridiculous. As if Eden was at Brooke's house, stashed in the cupboard under the stairs like Harry Potter.

'Do you think she might have become too attached to her?' Christopher stopped at traffic lights and turned to me. He looked pasty; eyes sallow. The stress of the last few days etched onto his face, which was usually a picture of health. Something he always prided himself on, being a GP. 'I've got to look the part, Ali,' he'd say. 'How will people believe I can look after them if I don't look like I can take care of myself?' Would either of us ever recover?

'She adores Eden, but I don't think it's that,' I replied.

'Why are the police so interested in her then?' he pressed.

'I don't know, they don't tell us anything.' I sighed and rubbed the back of my neck, as the lights turned green and Christopher pulled away.

A few minutes later, we turned onto Brooke's road and Christopher slowed to a crawl, trying to locate the house amongst the low row of terraces.

'It's there, with the blue gate,' I pointed, and Christopher pulled over opposite, unbuckling his seat belt and jumping out. I quickly followed, trailing him as he crossed the road. 'What are you going to say?' My heart quickened. The last thing I wanted was a showdown on the doorstep like some episode of *EastEnders*. Even at our worst, we were better than that.

'I'm going to find out why the police are so bloody interested in our babysitter,' he hissed. I was grateful his voice was low, for the time being anyway.

The gate was stiff to open, and Christopher tripped on one of the pumpkins which decorated the path, kicking it across the flower bed and swearing. I cringed behind him. Reaching the door, he rapped loudly on the wood with his knuckles. Nobody answered. Stepping back and looking up at the house for a second, he knocked again. Peering through the downstairs window when no one came. Inside, all was quiet.

'They've taken my mum shopping?' came a voice from my left.

We both turned to see a scruffy man in his fifties coming out of the neighbouring house.

'I beg your pardon?' Christopher said, tilting his chin skyward.

'She left me a note, my mum. She's in her eighties, they've taken her shopping apparently,' he repeated.

'Food shopping?' I asked.

'No, I got her food in yesterday. They've gone into town, I think, the shopping centre.' He took a handkerchief out of his pocket and blew his nose.

'Thanks for your help,' Christopher said, already marching back down the garden path to get to the car. I smiled at the scruffy man and he shrugged.

'Where are we going?' I asked Christopher as I caught up with him.

'Shopping,' he replied flatly and before I'd barely had a chance to close the car door we were off again.

Christopher's mobile rang from the pocket in the centre console, but he barely glanced at it.

'Want me to get it?'

'No, it'll only be Benson, calling us back home.'

He was right as a few seconds later my mobile rang too, a withheld number, and then again, but this time our home number filled the display.

I itched to answer it. What if it was Eden? What if they'd found her?

'It won't be about Eden,' Christopher said, as if reading my mind. His hands gripped tightly around the steering wheel as we queued onto the roundabout before the main road into town.

For a second it felt good to be out, to do something relatively normal and also to help find Eden. Free from house arrest. But the guilt seeped in. A reminder that without Eden, we weren't allowed to feel normal, we couldn't feel anything but misery. It was our punishment for losing our daughter.

I pushed the notion away and stared out of the window at the houses rushing by.

'What are we going to do, Christopher, wander around window shopping?' I sighed. Every inch of me wanted to curl up in bed. It was too much.

'We're going to look for Brooke,' he said in a tone reserved for his most difficult of patients. I could see he was agitated, and I worried if we found her, he'd make a scene in the shopping centre.

I remained quiet, not wanting to fight; we were only just talking again. Since the moment in the bathroom, there was a chance for us to move on. It would be a lengthy process. I had to know he wouldn't hurt me, that he'd never put his hands on me again. He hadn't before and I knew I'd pushed him to his limits, but I had to feel safe. Christopher would have to promise. He would take a long time to trust me again, I'd have to earn it, but we could be happy. As long as Eden came home, we could. Eden was the bond that bound us together.

We arrived at the shopping centre, parking on the third floor, the roof, where wind whipped under the structure and I nearly lost control of the car door as I opened it.

'Shall I text her? See if she's here?' I asked, struggling to hold my hair out of my face.

'No, not yet. The element of surprise might be a good thing,' Christopher replied.

Perhaps he was right; without the chance for Brooke to prepare her answers, we could catch her off guard. Although it hadn't made a difference when I turned up on her doorstep yesterday. It was a wild goose chase; I was sure of it. If Brooke was a suspect, surely she'd be in custody, being questioned, not wandering around the shops.

The sheer volume of people stupefied me as we pushed through the double doors of the car park into the shopping centre. It was overwhelming and I lurched forward grasping the rail.

Christopher frowned at me. 'Are you all right?'

'There's a lot of people here,' I muttered, straightening up, my cheeks burning under his disdain. Christopher's easy bedside manner was mostly reserved for his patients, not his unfaithful wife.

We moved down the escalators to the bottom floor, watching people scurrying around like ants. The noise was a constant buzz of footsteps, chatter and laughter. I clung to Christopher's side, unsure why I was so wobbly. Stepping off the escalator, I began to wheeze, unable to get enough air into my lungs, the world closing in.

'Ali, Ali, you're having a panic attack, breathe slowly in and out.' The voice came from above; it sounded like we were in a tunnel. There was pressure on my shoulders before everything went dark.

I came to on a bench, Christopher's thumb and forefinger attached to my wrist, counting silently in his head. He looked grave, as though he was going to deliver bad news. Was I dying?

'There you are, welcome back,' he said, forcing a smile.

A lady sat the other side of me, holding out a bottle of water. I shook my head, blinking rapidly, a flush crawling up my neck to my ears. Had I passed out here? In front of everyone? I put my hands over my face to shut out the onlookers staring.

'We shouldn't have come, it was too much,' Christopher said, putting his arm around me.

I eased my hands away from my face. The crowd had started to disperse, the show was over, although my mortification had just begun. Closing my eyes again, I listened to Christopher thanking the lady offering the water before footsteps carried her away.

'Ready to go?' he said, his voice gentle this time.

'Yes,' I murmured and felt him guide me upwards until I stood on shaky legs. What use was I to Eden when I couldn't even hold it together, especially when she needed me the most. I hadn't even managed a trip to the shops without a panic attack. My tongue felt thick, mouth filled with revulsion. What sort of mother was I?

55

JIMMY PEARSON

Without making eye contact with anyone, I hurried through the shoppers towards the exit, the crushing sensation in my chest swiftly replaced by icy unease. Head low, I was vaguely aware of a commotion on the ground floor. Someone had fallen over by the looks of it. A crowd had formed, and everyone was staring, allowing me to slip past unnoticed, but I didn't run until I got to the automatic doors and the crisp air touched my skin.

I made it back to the car in a couple of minutes, skin slick with sweat from the sprint. Inside, I wiped my face with a serviette stuffed in the glovebox, the moisture allowing me to remove most of the drawn-on beard. I stripped off in the tiny space, roughly pulling on jeans and a T-shirt from the holdall and balling up the costume to bin later. I left the cap on, even though my head was steaming. My wish for comfort didn't outweigh the need for anonymity.

The clock on the dashboard read twenty-five past two, Brooke would be with Eden by now. I had to get going; lingering for a second, my fingers on the keys ready to turn. What if Brooke hadn't come? What if Eden was there by herself, at the mercy of strangers? Someone would realise she was alone.

She was surrounded by parents, the safest place to be. But what if someone took her, or hurt her? My imagination ran wild before I reined it back in. Eden would be fine; Brooke would be there. As much as it pained me, Eden wasn't my responsibility any more.

The engine took two attempts to start as I turned the key, pumping the accelerator furiously on the second try.

'Come on, come on,' I said through gritted teeth until the Mondeo spluttered to life. I whispered a silent prayer as I pulled out of the car park and into the traffic, heading towards the M25.

Eden's face, her gummy smile and chubby cheeks invaded my mind as I drove and I couldn't help but well up, berating myself as I batted the tears away. I didn't even have any photos, a couple on my phone which I'd left behind. So many little things I would miss; how she always rubbed her ear when she was tired, or when she'd get so excited if offered food.

Get a fucking grip, she wasn't even yours, the voice in my head sneered, ridiculing me.

However, knowing I wasn't her real dad made little difference to the ache in my heart.

Getting away spurred me on. It was about survival now and I wasn't going to prison because of Brooke's lies. It had occurred to me I could come clean and take my chances. Surely the police wouldn't put me away because of a misunderstanding. Sadly, I believed otherwise, someone would be made to pay, and I was the one who had committed the worst crime. Whether or not I knew I was doing it was beside the point. It wasn't a risk I was prepared to take. What would I get for kidnapping, ten or fifteen years? I'd be a few years shy of forty by the time I got out, with nothing to show for it.

Because of Brooke I'd had to abandon my life. Leave my home, all my possessions and the job I loved. I hated her for what she'd done to me. She'd more than got her revenge and what was worse was that I had to walk away, there'd be no retribution for her, not unless the police locked her up.

Inside I was stewing, but I ploughed on, hitting the M25 towards Heathrow, which at first slowed due to sheer weight of traffic before it seemed to ease. After passing Leatherhead, I sailed through the traffic onwards to Heathrow without seeing a single police car or traffic officer. It seemed almost too good to be true. The tightness in my chest eased with every mile passed, putting distance between me and Eden.

I felt free. Free of responsibility without Eden in the back. On my Jack Jones again, only having to worry about number one. There was a lot to be said for that. It didn't change the fact I'd miss her. For six months I'd believed she was mine. She'd won me over, and I'd fallen for her hook, line and sinker.

Gripping the steering wheel, I clenched my jaw. I'd even considered getting back with that bitch, so Eden could have a family. Not once had I felt trapped, it seemed right almost straight away. We got along fine. At times I even thought I'd been stupid to break it off with Brooke at all. Within weeks, I was living for Tuesdays and Thursdays when we'd all be together, our own little family unit. I was besotted and knew there was no way I could let her go when Brooke announced they were moving.

She'd gone cold and at the time I thought it might be about commitment. That I hadn't done enough to prove I could be trusted not to hurt her again. I snorted at the memory; resentment lodged in my throat like a bitter pill. I'd considered fucking proposing, even went so far as to look at rings. Brooke had done a number on me and I'd been stupid enough to fall for it. I had paid dearly for my unexpected encounter with Brooke that day, both emotionally and financially. Well, never again.

Now I had to focus. Concentrate on the next few hours. Pour all my energy into making my escape. Initially I'd considered leaving my car in the long-stay car park, but I'd need to register a card, I was sure. When I didn't return, they'd charge it, and I didn't want to draw any attention when the owners looked into why a car had been dumped at the airport. It was better to drive into Hounslow and park it somewhere residential. Anywhere would do; it wouldn't matter if it was vandalised or towed away. It was worth very little, especially now with the damage from the crash. I had no use for it any more. I'd changed the registration plates and even when discovered, it was in my dad's name, not mine. I could call an Uber to take me to the airport and drop me off.

The only problem was if they were searching for me, if Brooke identified me as the person who took Eden, the police would check tickets out of the country for sure. It would be easy for them to see I had a flight booked, but it was a chance I'd have to take. I'd try to change the one I had booked, even if it wasn't to Australia. Money wasn't an issue, getting out of the country was, and you couldn't put a price on freedom.

My mind raced as I drove, excited at the prospect of not having to hang around. I had to hope Brooke would keep quiet, out of guilt at least. Leave my name out of the investigation, she owed me that. Although nothing would surprise me; she'd let me take the fall for all of it if the heat got too much. By then I hoped I'd be long gone, sitting on a beach with a can of Fosters, living my best life. That was the plan.

56

BROOKE SIMMONS

'Excuse me.' The grating voice came from behind me, as I nudged the turnstile. It remained stubbornly rigid.

I shifted Eden onto my other hip, I'd forgotten how heavy she was.

'I'm sorry but...' the voice trailed off and I turned to see it was coming from the girl behind the counter, she frowned first at me and then at Eden.

I stepped back from the barrier, having realised my mistake. I'd got so caught up in finding Eden, it escaped me how it would look. I'd walked in minutes before without a child, only now to be leaving with one. All the moisture in my mouth evaporated, my tongue lodged inside, too large for my mouth as I tried to speak.

The girl moved around the side of the counter and stood in front of me, blocking my exit. She was young, still in her teens. More of a waif than I was, but she puffed out her chest regardless. Did she think I was going to launch myself over the turnstile and make a run for it?

'I'm sorry, there's been a misunderstanding. My brother has gone to the toilet and I'm meeting him outside with my...

nephew.' I chuckled awkwardly, jiggling Eden up and down. Pleased she was smiling and not screaming her head off, which would make the whole situation more difficult to explain.

'Right. Only you said a minute ago you were meeting your sister.' Her forehead crumpled further, a mass of lines. I could see her looking around for the manager.

My cheeks flushed as I registered the queue of customers now staring at me like I was a lunatic, or worse, a criminal.

'I... I meant my brother,' I stammered. Holding Eden tighter still, she wriggled, and my arms throbbed.

'Can I see some identification please? Are you able to prove this child is your nephew?'

'That's ridiculous,' I snapped as sweat trickled beneath my armpits, seeping into the wool of the jumper.

'I'm very sorry. Can you call your brother, ask him to come back?' Her polite tone was becoming strained and red blotches dotted my neck, hot flush in full swing. If anyone looked guilty, it was me.

'I need to leave. Open the turnstile,' I said, voice wavering, knowing full well I was sounding desperate. I pushed the metal bar with the front of my thigh, which refused to budge. It was too high to get my leg over, not without dropping Eden. I was snookered.

'Nicola, call security,' the girl shouted over her shoulder.

The queue was snaking out and around the corner now, lots of disgruntled onlookers with their whiny kids, shifting from foot to foot, annoyed at the delay but also mesmerised by the scene unfolding in front of them.

'Fine, fine. Call them. I need to call the police anyway,' I said, moving back from the exit, shoulders sinking.

'Why don't you wait over here and we'll get this sorted out,' the girl directed me back inside the soft play to the table I'd just vacated. Unbelievably, it was still empty.

I sank onto the seat, the muscles in my arms pinging. Eden wriggled down onto the carpet and crawled towards the toddler section, happy to be back. I watched her go, shoes still on, no energy to stop her.

Pulling out my phone, I called the police through the noise of the play area to report I'd found Eden Tolfrey. The call took less than a minute. I was asked to remain where I was, and the operator said they would send officers directly to my location.

The girl continued to watch me from the entrance, making sure I didn't attempt to leave. I could see she thought I was mentally unstable.

My muscles slowly relaxed, although I was still a hot sweaty mess. It was over. Eden was back, and she looked to be fine. Other than her hand, which didn't seem to bother her, she hadn't changed in her time with Jimmy. I watched her play in the ball pit, through the legs of adults standing in the way of my view.

Towards the exit, I saw two security guards in conversation with the cashier who'd stopped me from leaving. I couldn't make out what they were saying, it was far too noisy, but everyone looked serious, brows tightly knitted together, eyes narrowed. The girl was gesticulating wildly before pointing over at me. I looked away from their judgemental stares.

When I returned my gaze, the three of them were joined by the couple I'd seen in the centre earlier. The ones who had followed me here. I sniggered; it was the tiniest victory. I'd been right after all. They were police and I was being watched. I always believed when I'd watch television shows with Mum, I'd be able to spot undercover police. They always looked so uptight and nothing like the credible couple they were pretending to be.

Before I knew it, they were coming towards me, flanked by DI Vincent, who had miraculously appeared.

'Miss Simmons, DI Vincent,' he said, although no introduction was necessary, 'We've had a report you have Eden Tolfrey?' He loomed over me, buttons straining on his shirt, stomach flighting to get free.

'Yes, she's here,' I stood and pointed. 'The pirate in the ball pit.' I moved to recover her from the play area. She wasn't as happy to leave this time, kicking her legs and letting out a wail when I gathered her up.

'How did you know she was here?' the female plain-clothed officer with large almond-shaped eyes asked brusquely.

'I had a text from a number I didn't recognise, saying she'd been left here.'

'Right okay, we need to stop everyone leaving,' DI Vincent said, directed at his colleague.

Within minutes, the soft play area had been closed to new customers and more officers arrived on scene to take contact details and statements of everyone inside. I jiggled Eden on my knee and the girl behind the counter delivered a bag of tiny gingerbread biscuits and another Fruit Shoot. Eden was getting restless, gazing at the bright colours of the ball pit and wanting to play.

All of the parents were staring at me, trying to work out what had gone on. Why the police had arrived and so many of them. Why their contact details, movements from this morning and arrival time at Mini Mischief was being recorded. The manager of the centre was asked to provide a printout to one uniformed officer. It was a hive of activity.

'Can I take a look at her?' the female officer held a phone to her ear and did a quick check of Eden, her head, her neck, lingering on her hand, where I'd spotted the red welt in the centre of her palm.

'Oh, Eden, you'll see your mummy soon?' I said into her hair.

The officer walked away, talking into the handset.

'Hello, Miss Simmons,' came a chirrupy voice and I turned my head to find Detective Constable Tunstall had arrived to join the party.

I stiffened.

'Detective Constable Tunstall is going to take Eden to the hospital, get her fully checked over before she will be reunited with Mr and Mrs Tolfrey,' DI Vincent instructed.

Instantly my arms locked, I didn't want to hand her over to anyone, not when I'd just found her. Why couldn't I give her back to Ali and Christopher? I wanted to be the hero.

'It's okay, Brooke, they'll take good care of her.' DC Tunstall placed a hand on my shoulder, pale pink nails to match her lipstick. Her voice was soft, comforting, and I let her take hold of Eden under the arms and lift her off my lap.

'She needs a nappy change,' I protested.

'We'll make sure she has one,' DC Tunstall replied before carrying her away.

'Miss Simmons, you need to accompany us to the station.' Detective Inspector Vincent laced his fingers around my upper arm, guiding me to my feet as though I weighed nothing.

'Why?' My voice was weak.

'Brooke Simmons, I am arresting you on suspicion of child abduction, you do not have to say anything, but it may harm your defence if you do not mention when questioned something you later rely on in court. Anything you do say may be given in evidence.'

57

ALI TOLFREY

Christopher helped me back to the car, via the ticket machine. My head was still swimming, and my limbs were like jelly. I leaned back in the seat, taking large gulps of air and waiting for the world to come to a standstill.

'You're not eating enough,' he said flatly when he opened his door and climbed in, leaning over to fasten my seat belt. Locking me into place. 'It's why you feel weak, you're not consuming enough calories.'

I rolled my eyes and looked out of the window. The doctor was in the house.

Christopher's phone rang, but he ignored it, continuing to stare at me as though he was waiting for me to speak. His eyes boring into me.

'We'll get through this.' He placed his hand on mine, squeezing my fingers as a single tear trickled down my cheek. I'd never felt so out of control, nothing was in my power, not even, it seemed, my own body.

'I'm sorry,' I said, 'for everything.' The blanket term to cover so much. My indiscretion, letting Brooke take Eden, every time I'd taken my family for granted.

His mouth twitched as though I'd said a dirty word, but he didn't reply.

The background music for our heart-to-heart at the top of the multistorey started again, first Christopher's phone and mine straight afterwards.

'Benson really wants to find us, doesn't he,' I said, chewing my lip and resisting the urge to reach for the phone.

Rain fell, fat splodges hitting the windscreen and blurring the outside world.

Christopher sighed and leaned back in his seat, hand still on mine. His warm palm atop my icy fingers.

'Let's sit here for a while.' He closed his eyes, both of us exhausted as the grey clouds rolled in above.

I could have fallen asleep; cocooned in the car, the patter of rain on the roof. In fact, I was nodding off when the phone rang again. Mine first this time. I snatched it up, patience wearing thin.

'What?'

'Mrs Tolfrey, it's DC Benson.' He sounded breathless, excited, but it didn't register straight away. I was too annoyed at the relentless calling.

'We'll be home soon,' I interrupted, my voice clipped.

Christopher shifted in his seat, sitting upright and slotting his key into the ignition.

'We've found Eden,' Benson said, his words rushed out as though he thought I might hang up.

A shriek erupted from my mouth, making Christopher jump. He turned ghostly pale watching in horror as my tears turned to laughter.

'They've found her,' I gasped when I was able to speak. Christopher and I clutched each other, eyes like saucers. 'I'm sorry can you repeat that,' I said to DC Benson who'd been giving me instructions, but I hadn't been able to take them in. Unable to comprehend anything because my heart was bursting out of my chest. I'd never experienced such elation or relief in a single moment. Those three words meant more than anything.

DC Benson told us to drive, slowly, to East Surrey Hospital where Eden had been taken. There was nothing to worry about, reports were that, physically, she appeared fine but would need a routine examination due to the circumstances.

'Okay, we're on our way. We'll see you there?' I asked.

'Yes, I'm leaving your house now.' I could hear rustling in the background, imagined DC Benson shrugging on his coat, phone pressed against his shoulder.

I ended the call, turning to Christopher, my heart still pounding.

'She's okay, she's safe!' I squealed.

He leaned over and kissed my lips, faces pressed together as our tears mixed. His hand gripped the back of my neck and he rested his forehead on mine.

'I knew she'd come home to us. We just had to keep the faith.'

I didn't tell him I'd started to lose mine. That as the hours ticked on, I expected DC Benson to be calling to tell us they'd found a body. A tiny lifeless bundle that had once been my daughter.

Christopher plugged in his seat belt and started the car, driving out of the car park much slower than he'd driven in. I was surprised at his level of restraint. If I'd been driving, I would have had my foot to the floor to get us there faster.

'It's over,' he said, grinning, eyes on the road ahead.

'It will be, when I've got her in my arms, it will be.' I rested my hand on his thigh as he drove. Something I hadn't done for a long time.

My stomach squirmed, like eels wriggling around. I wanted to get there, to hold Eden, to never stop holding her. I wanted to look at her beautiful cherub face and absorb every inch of it in the flesh. Never would I be parted from her again.

The drive seemed to take forever until the looming white building came into view and my anxiety spiked. Trying to find a parking space was never easy, especially not with a big car and I gritted my teeth as Christopher drove around looking for a bay. Tempted to throw open the door and sprint to the building ahead of him.

Last time we were at East Surrey hospital, we'd left with Eden in her car seat, only a day old. She'd been born there on Rusper Ward, delivered by two young midwives. Christopher carried her out of the hospital as though she was the most precious thing in the world. I'd waddled beside him, elated but also feeling as though I'd been run over. We'd never been back to the hospital. Hadn't needed to. Christopher being a GP meant he was who I turned to if I had any concerns about Eden's well-being.

I stared at the automatic doors across the road, opposite to where we'd parked, watching people milling around. Patients came out with hoodies over their gowns, cigarette packets clutched in their hands. As I opened the car door, I spotted DC Benson's bearded face waiting at the entrance. He'd driven faster than us.

It occurred to me I had no idea where we were supposed to go – accident and emergency? Paediatrics?

'Benson's there,' I said, gesturing towards the figure staring at his phone, his tie crooked and the collar of his jacket turned inward where he'd been in a rush to get it on.

Christopher stretched his legs, marching ahead, pausing for an oncoming car. DC Benson looked up and clocked us both, his smile blossoming.

'Great, you're here. Eden is with Doctor Ahmadov at the moment and my colleague, DC Tunstall, just being checked over.'

'Have you seen her?' I asked.

'Not yet, I've said I'll bring you both to the waiting room.'

Christopher shifted from foot to foot and DC Benson took his cue and headed inside, with us hot on his heels.

The paediatrics waiting room was decorated with trees, bumblebees and butterflies. Boxes of books and toys were scattered around, and one particularly loud child was a whirlwind of destruction everywhere she went. Tearing around the tiny chairs and shouting at the top of her voice.

We sat in the opposite corner, huddled together as DC Benson filled us in on what information he had.

'Eden was reported to the police as having been found at the Belfry Shopping Centre today.'

'We were just there!' Christopher said, incredulous.

'Have you apprehended anyone?' I asked.

'An arrest has been made. That's all I know right now.'

'Mr and Mrs Tolfrey?' a voice called across the room. Dr Ahmadov smiled and shook our hands as we rushed over. He had kind eyes and a soft voice. 'Eden is through here. We'll need you to make a formal identification of course, but I'm sure she'll be thrilled to see you.'

He pulled the curtain as my shoulders clenched, and there she was, sat on the bed playing with her toes, with who I assumed to be Detective Tunstall. I rushed forward and scooped her up, pressing her warm body to my chest and planting kisses on her head.

'Oh, my baby girl,' I whimpered, tears pouring uncontrollably.

'She has a minor injury, what looks to be a burn to the palm of her hand. We've cleaned it and administered some antiseptic cream, but it doesn't need bandaging.'

Christopher glanced at her hand before enveloping us tightly in his arms. Our little family of three back together again.

'Mamamama,' Eden babbled, sinking her gums into my shoulder. I was overwhelmed, so full of love I could have burst. Almost as though I'd never known true happiness until that moment. Eden was home.

58

JIMMY PEARSON

The Hounslow side street I'd left my car in was grotty and seemed to have been overlooked by the council collection services. Bins overflowed and cans of Super Tenants littered the gutter. My dad's car looked out of place, despite its age, by the fact it had all its wheels. However, it was the first place I'd found that didn't have double yellow lines or permits required to park.

The residents of the small terraced houses had gone all out for Halloween, with most windows adorned with orange and black bunting, some already with flashing pumpkins, despite it being broad daylight. At the far end of the street, a couple of boys kicked a football against a graffitied wall, but they paid me little attention. I wasn't convinced the Mondeo would be safe, but it didn't matter. I wouldn't be back to collect it any time soon.

My Audi was still sitting outside my flat, where all my belongings were. It was a shame to leave it all behind, but I had little choice. It was only stuff, things, nothing worth my freedom. I'd have to buy it all again wherever I ended up. Perhaps in a few months I could pay someone to pack my belongings and put them in storage, in case I ever returned.

Not wanting to hang around any longer than I had to, I ordered an Uber to take me to the airport before clearing out the car. Shoving everything I didn't need into the boot so it wasn't on display and putting anything that could identify me in the holdall. It was half empty since Eden's stuff had been binned and I'd swap it at the airport for a bag the right size for hand luggage. The car seat I'd put by the large rubbish dumpster at the entrance of the close, sure someone would take it. It was practically brand new.

With the car empty, I leant on the bonnet, pulling my cap down as far as it would go in case anyone was looking out of their window, wondering who I was. Thankfully I didn't have long to wait. My Uber driver arrived in less than ten minutes and we drove to Terminal Three.

He didn't try to make conversation en route, and I was grateful. I tried my best to relax, to listen to the radio, but I was skittish. My nerves were already shot to pieces and I hadn't even got to the airport yet. The closer I got to making my escape, the more stressed I felt. The journey was quick and with legs like lead I made my way inside the terminal and towards the Virgin Atlantic customer service desk to see if I could change my ticket.

The airport was bustling, and I almost got run over by a man marching towards the British Airways desk wheeling an enormous suitcase. I swore in his direction, gritted my teeth and ploughed on. The lady behind the Virgin Atlantic desk, wearing a bright red uniform and matching lipstick, was so smiley, her jaw must have ached. She checked the ticket I had for tomorrow and tapped her keyboard.

'There's a flight to Sydney leaving in a little over an hour, stopping to refuel in Singapore. However, I'm afraid there's only business class seats available,' she said in her sing-song voice. *Of course, there was.*

'How much?' I asked out of habit; it didn't matter, whatever it was, my inheritance was going to pay for it.

'It's an extra three thousand, two hundred and sixty-four pounds.' She smiled at me, her eyes wide and expectant like she'd had a few empty cans of Monster underneath that desk.

'Five grand for a one-way ticket!' I said incredulous. But still, I slid my credit card over to her, aware of my chest tightening as she picked it up with blood-red nails. *Please let it work. Please let it not be cancelled.* I'd used my dad's card as opposed to my own, hoping it wouldn't be flagged on any system.

Despite that, I had visions of a call coming through as soon as the card was used, the check-in assistant pressing an alarm button under the counter and a rush of security guards bowling me over. Sweat scratched at my hairline and I smiled awkwardly, my ease with the opposite sex, my smooth lines had evaporated. I hoped she thought I was shy, and not a terrorist or a criminal on the run.

'Could you enter your pin for me please, sir,' she asked, her voice like velvet.

My fingers trembled as I keyed in the pin, but less than a minute later she handed me back my passport and a new ticket.

'You'll need to check in now, at the counter over there.' She pointed behind me, across the concourse to the row of desks with the walkways marked out by the belt barriers.

'Thanks for your help,' I said, not meeting her eye, already scanning for the nearest shop where I could purchase a bag.

Ten minutes later, I'd bought a smart blue short-sleeved shirt to change into and a suitable rucksack I could use for hand luggage. Taking a minute to kneel on the floor of the airport, transferring my clothes over. I barely had anything, some clothes and a few toiletries. It made me nervous, travelling so light. I'd draw out some Australian dollars at the bureau de change, so I could use cash when I got there.

The check-in desk was empty, and I was seen straight away, but this time I made no attempt to engage the assistant in conversation, my T-shirt was damp, and I was aware I was smelling a little funky. Dried sweat mixed with fresh. I held the brand-new shirt in my free hand and the assistant nodded towards it.

'You can use the Virgin Clubhouse if you want to get changed. Although they will be boarding soon.'

I thanked her and headed in the direction she'd pointed, allowed into the lounge once I'd shown my boarding pass. Inside, I found showers to use and was able to dump my T-shirt and put on the new shirt. I looked smarter, even with the jeans – smart enough for business class anyway.

Wishing I could spend longer in the luxury of the lounge, I knew time wasn't on my side and I made my way to security. Standing in another queue round to the X-ray machines. When I got to the front, I put my phone and backpack in the plastic tray to go through the machine. I'd switched off the phone after I'd requested the Uber, taken out the SIM card and tossed it down a drain. I had no time to buy another one to call Eric and let him know I was coming. I guessed it would be one hell of a surprise when I turned up.

With the hair on the back of my neck standing to attention, I stepped forwards, it was my turn to go through.

'Remove your cap please, sir.' The burly security guard frowned at me, his gloved hands beckoning me forward from the other side of the walk-through metal detector.

My heart thundered in my chest and a sheen of sweat glistered on my bare arms, making my skin itch. Trying to steady my breathing, I removed my cap, wiping my shaved head with the palm of my hand. It was slick with sweat despite the shower I'd had. I smiled tightly, jaw clenching rhythmically, and stepped through. The shrill alarm sounded, and I felt a visceral jolt in my gut as I looked up in panic.

'Your belt, sir.' He indicated, pointing to my middle, eyes narrowing further.

I removed it quickly and stepped back around, moving through the doorway again. Did I look suspicious? Man, I had to stop sweating, but I couldn't help it. My stomach churned audibly, concerned I might vomit.

'May I see your passport, sir?'

Already in my hand, I held my passport and boarding pass out, hoping he wouldn't clock the tremor.

He looked first at the passport photo, back at me, then at my boarding pass.

'Would you come with me please.' He gestured to his right, nodding at two more security guards who were waiting by the back wall. They stepped forward, one of them veering off to open a door further down.

I grabbed my backpack from the tray at the bottom of the conveyor belt as people milled around me, collecting their things. Palpitations in my chest juddered through my body as my feet seemed to move of their own accord. As I headed towards the open door, images of Australia and the life I would have had flashed before my eyes in a cruel 'here's what you could have won moment'. It was over. I was going to prison, to spend the next ten or so years behind bars.

'Take a seat please,' the muscle-bound guard said, in the doorway, directing me to the table and chairs inside the stuffy room. With a wide-eyed stare, I dropped my backpack to the floor and sank into the chair, resigned to my fate.

FIVE DAYS LATER

59

JIMMY PEARSON

I'd sat in the side room in Heathrow Airport for fifteen minutes, being questioned by the burly security guard about where I was going and why. Eventually I cottoned on they weren't interested in my name; no alert had been put on me or my passport. It was the fact I was a sweaty mess which had attracted their attention. Clearly, I'd looked nervous and they wanted to know why.

I'd told them I was terrified of flying and hadn't taken my anti-anxiety medication. I had a long flight ahead and was going to buy something from Boots, once I'd passed through security, before I got to the gate. They asked for Eric's details, his address in Sydney, and once they'd searched me and went through my meagre bag item by item, they were happy to let me go on my way.

My life had flashed before my eyes in that room, the revelation I could do some serious jail time. With my face, someone would want to make me their bitch for sure. The thought was more terrifying than anything I could imagine, and I'd sprinted to the gate, relieved to see they were still boarding passengers and I hadn't missed the flight.

I'd been shitting a brick until the plane left the tarmac, expecting blue flashing lights and armed police to descend in action-movie fashion, stopping the plane and hauling me off. It never happened, and as soon as the seat belt light was turned off, I hit the bar on board and ordered myself a few beers. They went straight to my head as I'd barely eaten anything, but I wasn't going to complain.

Whilst there I met a gorgeous posh girl from Staines, called Katharine, who was going backpacking with her best friend. Her dad was loaded as it turned out and the business-class tickets had been an early Christmas present. A bit of luxury before she spent the next six months in hostels with the rest of the peasants.

The three of us chatted, and I told them I was visiting my brother in Sydney. They shared their plans and the countries they were going to visit. We had a bit of banter; Katharine was a good craic, but unfortunately not the type of girl who'd help me join the mile-high club. You couldn't win them all.

Before I headed back to my bed, head swimming from the alcohol, Katharine gave me her number and suggested we could meet on the trail around Cambodia at some point. It took my mind off being a wanted felon for a few hours at least.

On arrival in Sydney, I spent four days with my brother, Eric. To say he was surprised to see me when I rocked up in a taxi was an understatement. He couldn't wipe the grin off his face and kept shaking his head like I was an apparition about to disappear.

I didn't want to risk involving him in anything criminal, so I kept quiet about what had gone on back in the UK, the criminal activity anyway. I wasn't about to make my little brother an accessory. I told him I'd broken up with Eden's mum, after it turned out the child wasn't mine. He was shocked, to say the least, but told me I was better off out of it. He had no children of his own so didn't understand the grief I felt, although he tried to be sympathetic. I missed Eden desperately, her innate babbling and the way she chewed on her fingers when she was hungry. I even missed her smell.

I tried to avoid talking about her while I was there. It was a flying visit I'd said, before backpacking around Asia with some friends I was due to meet in Thailand. Because of the break-up, I'd needed a change of scene and had taken a sabbatical from work, that much was true at least. I deliberately kept my plans vague and he didn't challenge me on it; it was easy to lie with my troubles being half the world away.

I scoured the newspapers for any sign the police were looking for me but found nothing. My social media accounts remained dormant, I was too fearful to touch them, of creating any trace to where the police could find me. I knew it wouldn't be long before they knocked on Eric's door.

Even though no news was good news, it didn't stop me looking over my shoulder every ten minutes or flinching every time a phone rang. I knew once I'd sorted out the finances, I needed to get on my way. The only way to stay free was to keep moving, at least until the dust settled. Although not knowing whether Brooke had been caught, or if Eden was back safely with her parents, was eating away at me.

I moved half of Dad's money from his account into Eric's and told him about the properties that were being put on the market and the tenants who had been given their notice. I shared the solicitor's details we were using and the letting agent too, so Eric could oversee the sales while I travelled. I mentioned the empty property at Chapel Close but told him we were keeping it.

I left my half in my dad's business account, knowing at some point mine might be frozen by the police, but I drew out a lot of cash and got Eric to put it in a safety deposit box which I had the key for. If things got hairy, I had access to money, although I only planned on drawing money out from Dad's account whenever I was about to leave a location.

Four days after arriving, I said goodbye to Eric and his girlfriend, and jumped on a plane to Cambodia with the intention of meeting up with Katharine. Even if I didn't, I'd always wanted to see the world and I had plenty of time to kill before I could even think about going home.

At the airport, whilst I was waiting for my flight, curiosity got the better of me and I used one of the free computers to enter my name and Brooke's into Google. Nothing came up. I was relieved an international manhunt hadn't been publicised.

Before I logged off, I typed in Eden's name, the surname Tolfrey seemed alien. A small article popped onto the screen, published the day before on the *Surrey Comet*'s webpage, her smiling face in a waterproof suit feeding the ducks from her buggy. It was like a gut punch to see her, the child I'd grown to love like she was my own.

> Reigate residents, Alison and Christopher Tolfrey, are pleased to report the safe return of their daughter, one-year-old Eden Tolfrey, after she was abducted from Bushy Park more than four days ago. Surrey Police are yet to comment but have told us an arrest has been made.

I could only assume it was Brooke and she'd been caught out in her lie. By now I was sure she would have given my name to the police. I'd be a wanted man, always looking over my shoulder but I'd follow the story from afar, hoping justice would be served. Logging off, I slipped out of the seat and took my backpack around to departures, excited at the prospect of a new adventure.

All the people I'd meet, the experiences I'd have. To hell with settling down. Life was for living and to live you had to keep moving. That would be my life from now on and I fully intended to embrace it. Because they weren't going to catch me. Not now, not ever.

ONE MONTH LATER

60

ALI TOLFREY

Having Eden home again was amazing. We shut our doors to everyone except the police for a few days and spent time together as a family, refusing to let her out of our sight. Cards and gifts arrived for Eden by the bucketload and the press hounded us for an interview, but we were too wrapped up in our own world and wanted to be left alone. Never before had we taken the time to be together with no outside interference.

The bliss only lasted for a week before Christopher had to go back to work at the surgery. I couldn't go out alone, too nervous we'd be accosted in the street, or worse. I was so terrified of losing Eden again it messed with my head.

We had counselling as a family, which DC Benson arranged, and it helped Christopher and I move forward as a couple, to accept what happened. The infidelity wasn't spoken about outside of the sessions and our lives slowly got back on track. Christopher's violent outburst was discussed at length and he'd apologised many times since, mortified at how he'd momentarily lost control. He understood it wasn't acceptable behaviour under any circumstances and agreed to attend anger management therapy with a private counsellor on a one-to-one basis.

It felt like we had a chance to put it behind us. All of us. There was no evidence Eden would have any lingering trauma from the abduction. Her hand healed perfectly although we'd never know what had burned her, the doctor had confirmed it was a minor injury and wouldn't scar. Christopher said it was unlikely she'd remember any of it at all.

Trying to get back to normal was difficult, especially with Christopher at work. I found I had lots of offers to write pieces on the abduction from a number of women's magazines, but it was still too raw, too personal, and our family had had enough exposure. Locally there was plenty of coverage and our names were a constant source of gossip in the supermarket aisle. Another reason to stay in our little bubble.

We thought about moving, to get away from prying eyes, but I loved our home and Christopher had his job at the practice. We'd built a life in Reigate and couldn't imagine living anywhere else. In trying to move on from the trauma, I redecorated Eden's bedroom, getting her to pick the colour – yellow – and we had a new carpet fitted, one that wouldn't make me cringe every time I saw it. Eventually Eden's abduction would be old news and knowing the public scrutiny wouldn't last forever was what drove me on.

Days after Eden came home, DC Benson visited with DCI Greene to let us know Brooke had been arrested. She'd admitted to knowing who had abducted Eden but not that it was going to happen. The betrayal was hard to hear. When we found out she'd told people Eden was her daughter, we were sickened. I pitied the man who'd got caught up in Brooke's web of deceit. We were told his name was Jimmy, but I harboured little resentment towards him, all of it reserved for Brooke. She'd convinced him he was

Eden's father, who'd then become so desperate for access, he'd stolen her away. As soon as he'd discovered the truth, he'd returned her, risking his liberty. I wasn't interested in punishing him. The real criminal had got what she deserved.

Without Brooke and her crazy fantasy, none of this would have happened. She was clearly unstable. As a result, I'd have to live with the guilt knowing I'd brought her into our lives. I'd trusted her to take care of the most precious thing in the world to me. She became part of the family and we welcomed her with open arms.

One day, when I was stronger, I'd ask her why. What had Christopher and I done to deserve what she'd put us through?

In the meantime, we had a life to be getting on with. Eden was nearly walking and babbling more than ever. I was going to make sure I was a better mother to her than mine had been to me. It was just the three of us, and I'd never let her go again.

THREE MONTHS LATER

61

BROOKE SIMMONS

It's been almost three months, but I wouldn't say I've settled into my new home. It's an adjustment to say the least. For a start, it's much smaller than I envisaged. Just a room to fit my things in. A definite lack of furniture too, it's barren chic. Not that I have much to fill it with, the weekly wage for a kitchen porter is less than ten pounds, but it keeps me in biscuits and shampoo.

The upside is, I have a room to myself and the inmates at HMP Downview are mostly all right. It's taken time to come to terms with the fact I'll be spending at least the next six months here, not to mention having a criminal record which will stay with me forever.

Life will be different when I get out. Who knows what the future will hold? I've been lucky enough to finish my foundation certificate in bookkeeping here. Hopefully I'll be able to secure another accounts assistant role, if I can find an employer to take me on with a conviction. Who knows whether I'll ever start my own bookkeeping business; it's very much one day at a time in here, but I've heard they offer other accountancy courses, so perhaps I'll carry on learning? Anything to make my stay at Her Majesty's pleasure worthwhile.

The days are long and boring, but Mum visits every week and, if I'm honest, the time apart has done us the world of good. I'm finally beginning to appreciate her, now I'm not smothered. She's had to stand on her own two feet, emotionally anyway, so it's made both of us stronger. Although she's struggling to accept her only daughter is a convicted criminal.

I thought I'd been so smart. That texting myself from the old Nokia phone would be anonymous. In reality, sending myself the message alerting me to Eden's whereabouts was what identified me. I assumed the police wouldn't be able to trace the messenger as it was a pay-as-you-go SIM. I thought it would be anonymous, but I was wrong. Even with the SIM destroyed, once I was arrested and they confiscated my iPhone, they only had to obtain the number the text originated from. It was easy then to trace the number through the network provider and request the history.

All the calls and the texts between Jimmy and myself, going back months, told them everything they needed to know. They had the text that confirmed my meeting with Jimmy in the park the morning of Eden's disappearance. Another was the suggestion of Mini Mischief as a possible location to return her.

Sitting in that interview, faced with the evidence against me, I told them everything. How angry I was at being ghosted. Mine and Jimmy's chance meeting at the library. How a stupid snap decision to let Jimmy think he was Eden's father spiralled wildly out of control. The detectives, Tunstall and Vincent, tried to get me to confess to being a part of the abduction. They'd assumed I'd planned it with Jimmy, our narrative was to run away together, with him under the illusion Eden was our child, but I'd got cold feet.

Despite the calls and texts there wasn't any evidence to prove

I'd been a part of the plan to abduct Eden and my solicitor said they couldn't get the Crown Prosecution Service to charge me. However, they had more than enough for perverting the course of justice. I'd known Jimmy had Eden all along and could have saved a lot of time and money, not to mention grief for all involved, if I'd come clean at the start. My solicitor advised me to plead guilty in the hope of a lesser sentence and no trial.

Twelve months was more than any of us were expecting, especially as I'd helped arrange the safe return of Eden and the fact I'd pled guilty, but eventually I made my peace with it. My solicitor thought they were making an example of me, especially as Jimmy had disappeared and was yet to be held accountable for the abduction.

The time inside has been slow. I wrote to Ali and Christopher, but they didn't write back. As far as they were concerned, I was toxic, the cause of a nightmare they would prefer to forget. They'd done an interview in the *Daily Mail* just last week. A gorgeous photo of the three of them, Eden beaming into the camera. It's now part of the growing collage of pictures on the wall of my cell. I miss her face, her sticky fingers and slobbery hugs. I miss Ali's friendship too. I'd give anything for them to visit but it's only my mum that comes.

She told me on her last visit, the police still haven't located Jimmy, they know he got to Australia, but he's moved on since then. A few days ago, I got a blank postcard sent to me at Downview, the picture was of a beautiful sunset over a sandy beach in Thailand. Waves crashing on the shore and palm trees swaying in the breeze. It had to be from Jimmy, his way of showing me he'd won. Despite what I'd done, what I'd dragged him into, he was somewhere in the world, living his best life, and I was locked in a grey-walled room for around twenty hours a day. He'd given me the finger from halfway across the world.

At first, I wondered how he'd known where I was, what prison I'd been sent to. Until I remembered Mum telling me Betty next door had let it slip to her neighbour the other side and within the hour it was all over Facebook, I'd been sent to HMP Downview.

I reminded myself on a daily basis, as I scrubbed the saucepans in the kitchen until the skin on my hands cracked, I'd got away lightly. It could have been so much worse, my sentence ten times as long. All because I'd fallen for the wrong man, one who hadn't felt the same way about me. I hadn't been able to let it go. I saw my chance for revenge, and I took it, relished it at first, but soon after it gave me little comfort. By then I couldn't walk away from the money Jimmy was giving me. The maintenance he paid for Eden was my way out. I reasoned it was a fitting punishment for the way he'd treated me.

I often thought about what would have happened if I hadn't bumped into Jimmy that day. I'd probably be considering a diploma in accounting, continuing my studies, and would have certainly still been friends with Ali and Christopher. They talked before about maybe getting Eden christened one day and I hoped if they did, they'd ask me to be her godmother; however, now I knew I'd probably never see her or Ali again.

It was pretty unfair, after all, I'd brought her back to them. Without me convincing Jimmy to return her, she could have ended up God knows where. Yet I was the one who was thrown under the bus.

Still, in the meantime life had to go on. The money remained in a box under my bed, untouched. Mum didn't know anything about it. The flat I'd wanted had gone to someone else. I withdrew my offer, knowing I was likely to serve some prison time but not for how long I'd be away. I'd find another place when I got out of here. Already I'd decided to move out of the area, perhaps down to the coast like I'd told Jimmy. I couldn't go back to Redhill, not where everyone knew me, I'd be vilified.

Moving away I'd be able to truly start afresh, completely anonymous. Free from my mum's apron strings, able to get a new job and make new friends. It didn't matter where I was in the world, I'd still be able to write to Ali. I'd make sure to send birthday and Christmas presents to Eden. When she was old enough she'd be able to make up her own mind if she wanted to see me or not. It wouldn't be so weird for her to keep in touch with the babysitter, would it?

ACKNOWLEDGMENTS

Thanks very much to the former police officers who assisted with my continuous questions whilst writing this book, in particular Peter Wright and Kay Mcnamara.

I would like to thank the Gangland Governors Facebook page and their many members for all their support. You really are a fantastic forum and the positivity and community spirit amongst the authors and readers is second to none.

A massive thanks to my mum as always and the lovely Denise Miller, who are my initial readers, accepting chapters sent bit by bit and always eager for more. I really appreciate your continuing enthusiasm.

Thanks to my amazing publishers Boldwood Books. I still pinch myself, four books down the line, with how lucky I am to see my ideas in print. Caroline Ridding, THE best editor in town, thank you for letting me wing it! Thanks again to the brilliant Jade Craddock, you're a superstar.

To the fabulous Mary Tolfrey, Boldwood's competition winner to name a character in the book. I do hope your husband, Chris, enjoys the read.

Lastly, thank you to Dean and the girls for keeping me sane during lockdown. I don't know what I'd do without you.

MORE FROM GEMMA ROGERS

We hope you enjoyed reading *The Babysitter*. If you did, please leave a review.

If you'd like to gift a copy, this book is also available as an ebook, digital audio download and audiobook CD.

Sign up to the Gemma Rogers mailing list for news, competitions and updates on future books:

http://bit.ly/GemmaRogersNewsletter

Explore more gritty thrillers from Gemma Rogers.

ABOUT THE AUTHOR

Gemma Rogers was inspired to write gritty thrillers by a traumatic event in her own life nearly twenty years ago. *Stalker* was her debut novel and marked the beginning of a new writing career. Gemma lives in West Sussex with her husband, two daughters and bulldog Buster.

Visit Gemma's website: www.gemmarogersauthor.co.uk

Follow Gemma on social media:

- facebook.com/GemmaRogersAuthor
- twitter.com/GemmaRogers79
- instagram.com/gemmarogersauthor
- bookbub.com/authors/gemma-rogers

ABOUT BOLDWOOD BOOKS

Boldwood Books is a fiction publishing company seeking out the best stories from around the world.

Find out more at www.boldwoodbooks.com

Sign up to the Book and Tonic newsletter for news, offers and competitions from Boldwood Books!

http://www.bit.ly/bookandtonic

We'd love to hear from you, follow us on social media:

        facebook.com/BookandTonic
        twitter.com/BoldwoodBooks
        instagram.com/BookandTonic